Ratoons

By the Author

The Sea hath Bounds, 1946
A Grove of Fever Trees, 1951
Mittee, 1951
Wizard's Country, 1957
A Lover for Estelle, 1961
The Greyling, 1962
Diamond Jo, 1965

Daphne Rooke

Ratoons

WITH AN AFTERWORD BY

R.W. Johnson

Text copyright © 2008 Daphne Rooke
All rights reserved.
Printed in the United States of America.
No part of this book may be reproduced, or stored in a retrieval
system, or transmitted in any form or by any means, electronic,
mechanical, photocopying, recording, or otherwise, without
express written permission of the publisher.

Published by AmazonEncore
P.O. Box 400818
Las Vegas, NV 89140

ISBN-13: 9781935597810
ISBN-10: 1935597817

*Dedicated to
Irvin Rooke*

Introduction

R*atoons* takes its name from the new growth springing out of the sugarcane roots after cutting or burning: the symbol of renewal. I lived for some years at Longacres, a sugar-farm in Natal. Rereading the book brings those years vividly before me. We were only an hour's run by train from Durban, yet once you were at Longacres, you were cut off from the ordinary world. My mother, my sister Rosemary and I lived there very happily. We had no motor-car and transport was provided by an elderly horse called Snowhite; or we walked. It was an isolated sort of life.

There are some beautiful memories of Longacres. They have to do with the gratitude the Indians showed for kindness; my mother helped many women in childbirth. They had not much money for buying presents so they used to come to the house on Fridays, laden with flowers with which they decorated every room; and they brought a chicken too and a banana leaf with a dollop of curry on it…they cooked the chicken on our stove.

It was at Longacres that I first used my imagination creatively… my sister and I were walking home from the village. She was in front of me and was held up by a black mamba. It towered over her, swaying in the rhythm that meant it was going to strike. She was saved by a young mounted policeman who was riding by on patrol, fell madly in love with him and only recovered when she saw him in the blue serge suit he wore off-duty.

In my story she became the golden-haired princess, the mamba a dragon and the policeman a knight. He appears in *Ratoons* as Chris van der Westhuizen. Before I wrote that story my imagination had conjured up ghosts and giants: I spent my childhood in terror. I had learned to use experiences as material for fiction: all my work is based on images of reality.

My best friend was Amoya, a beautiful Indian child; with silver rings on her toes. She was part of *Ratoons*. I taught her to read and write, she taught me something of her language and religion. We were twelve years old and she was already married but not yet living with her husband. That changed within a year and by the time she was fifteen she had a son. Her husband was a brutal man…poor Amoya.

Our friendship continued. I believe such a friendship would not have been possible between two boys. There would have been resentment and shame because of racial inequalities, whereas Amoya's predicament was due to the customs of her own people. Amoya's aunts told her to warn me that I would get brain fever from too much study, or lose my looks… She began to embroider a petticoat towards my trousseau. It is nearly sixty years ago but I still think of her; in her soft draperies, a ruby in her nostril and a hibiscus flower in her hair, working on my petticoat while we talked of books and ideas, despite the dangers. She died young, at seventeen, released to another incarnation.

Daphne Rooke
Fingal Bay, New South Wales, 1990

Chapter one

When Aunt Lucy died she left me her Durban house and thirty thousand pounds in gold shares. I converted the house into a hospital for the training of Hindu nurses. This was for Amoya's sake. She was one of the first Indian girls in Natal to become a nurse. Natal Indians have discarded the caste laws, but they still have some prejudice against allowing their, gentle daughters to leave home and we turn out only a few girls a year, never more than six. The real value of the hospital lies, I suppose, in its usefulness to the bigger hospital across the road.

Since I married I take no active part, but sometimes I have to go there. The doctor's office used to be Aunt Lucy's bedroom and I never go in there to attend meetings without the feeling that I might be confronted by the big four-poster in which Aunt Lucy slept for fifty years; by the chest of drawers and the wardrobe, stuffed to bursting with elegant, unused clothing.

Recently I met Dr. Naidoo for the first time. She was dressed in a crackling white coat, but I noticed the tiny holes in her nostrils and ear-lobes and I imagine that sometimes she wears a sari and jewels. While we talked I wondered about her, this granddaughter of

Leela's who speaks such good English. Does she believe that she will live again according to her karma? Does she believe in the malice of demons and ghosts, as Amoya did?

She is considered our greatest achievement, but the credit for her education must go to her father, Sowa. He gave her up as a penance, though at the same time he took the precaution of marrying her off to an old man who died before she knew him; for Sowa, that shrewd man of business, grows more devout with the years.

He is rich today, but he was a starveling three-year-old when his parents brought him to our farm at Westongate at the beginning of the year 1899. Famine had driven his people from their holdings farther inland and they were glad enough to return to the canefields to work for rice and a few shillings a month.

My father and I watched them file across the narrow bridge near the Awetuli Falls. Zetke the induna stood near us, his arms folded, and already he was picking out in the strangers traits by which he could nickname them. First came the agent, a fat little man dressed in a serge suit as shiny as his brown face. He carried a suitcase of varnished wood on which his name and address had been printed in bold white letters: Mr. Bannerjee, Westongate, via Durban, Natal, South Africa. This always gave people the impression that he was either planning a trip overseas or had just returned. We knew him well, for he was willing to execute all sorts of commissions. He had recruited these Indians and persuaded my father to take them because they were cheap. There had been no difficulty in naming him; Zetke naturally called him The Fat One.

"They are like goats following him," Zetke murmured experimentally.

Twenty men followed Mr. Bannerjee, most of them wearing only loin-cloths, but some, the younger ones, in trousers and shirts. Last came the women, shading their faces with their tattered saris, their languid children on their hips or holding to their skirts. Here and there a golden bracelet glittered astonishingly on an emaciated arm.

"What a crowd of scarecrows," said my father. "Mr. Bannerjee and his talk. I'll be lucky to get a day's work out of the lot. Hey,

Bannerjee." Mr. Bannerjee waited politely for him to catch up and the whole troop came to a stop.

Zetke shouted triumphantly, "Skeletons. All coolies are thin, but you are skeletons." His Zulu arrogance seemed to touch none of the Indians except one tall woman with a child on her hip. When Mr. Bannerjee waved them on again she spat out a long stream of betel-nut juice that fell like blood on Zetke's toes. Zetke dug his foot into the earth and before she could pass him, snatched her child from her. He ran back with the boy to the bridge and held him playfully over the ravine. The other women screamed, but the mother was too frightened to utter a sound. I took the child from Zetke and gave him back to her.

"He was only having a game with you," I said.

Leela never believed that. From that day she looked on Zetke as an enemy and on me as her benefactor.

She hurried to join the others, who were streaming into the barracks. Mr. Bannerjee, having cajoled John again with specious arguments about the cheapness of this labour, was directing the families to their rooms. He was smiling now. His mouth was an Aladdin's cave, for each tooth was crowned with gold and smack between his two front teeth was a diamond chip; but this he seldom showed because he was afraid he might tempt a thief. He had mastered a flat-lipped smile that made of his mouth a rectangular opening in the disc of his face and it was only to the rich that he showed the full glory of his teeth.

The Indians took root at once. We heard their chanting and the bleating of a goat when they sacrificed at the new moon, we watched the smoke rise from a funeral pyre by the river, we saw them at a wedding-feast; and smiled at the bridegroom garlanded with marigolds. These were their flowers loved for their sacred colour. We did not grow marigolds in our gardens, for their very scent belongs to the Indians. At times they took the Awetuli River for their own and made of it another Ganges. Afterwards we were to remember how softly they came amongst us.

My mother, who was ill at that time, gave Leela to me as a companion and each afternoon we would go for a walk as far as the falls. She was sixteen, the same age as I was, and nearly as tall, She would do anything for us, for she had been with her mother-in-law since she was ten and she was tired of the old woman's nagging.

I like to remember those slow walks through the cane. There you have in your ears the sound of sighing cane and surf. In September when the rains come you see the green on the newly-planted fields. At first it is only a tinge of green, but as the stools of cane take shape they look like a silken cover on the lands. When the year is out and the cane has been harvested the hillsides are brown beneath their burden of trash; and you wait again for the rains. Beneath the soil there takes place a wonder of regrowth as the ratoons spring from the cane-roots to make the fields green once more. It is then that the red flowers fall from the kaffirboom and leaves like hearts grow from the thorny branches.

If Leela knew anything of the beauty of those early summer afternoons she never spoke of it; this was for her the time of the festival of fecundity. Piety was in her and of her, an unseen force, joyous and ghastly.

Her grandparents were in the first boatload of Indians indentured in 1860. When their five years' contract on the canefields was up they were given a small holding near Rushtown instead of their return passage to India, for they were required to spend yet another five years in Natal. They died before their time was up, lamenting for their motherland, but their sons were prosperous and happy until the droughts ruined them. Then they could not make enough money to buy rice and without rice they starved. Nothing was left except a few hoarded bracelets, and the family was scattered. Leela's father and uncles worked in Durban, for not even Mr. Bannerjee would have dared to bring them to the farm, they were so thin and old.

Mr. Bannerjee had got into enough trouble for bringing her husband Perian. Though he was young he was worn out and John grudged him rice. He had been born in India. His father had come to Natal alone, thinking he would soon return; but Perian was close to sixteen before the money came for the journey, ten pounds for the mother and five children. Another year and the Government would not have allowed Perian into Natal, said Leela, and that might have been a good thing for her because he liked drinking cane-spirit which upset his stomach. When he was drunk she kicked him, provided always that she was out of sight of her mother-in-law. Sometimes she grew nervous of this treatment of her husband and then she would make an offering to the hungry goddess in the shrine near the river.

When I grew tired of her broken English I would take her hand and race down the break with her. Afterwards we would lie on the bridge near Awetuli, each with a piece of sugar-cane to chew. She did not look at the startling pattern that the green bush formed with the waterfall and the shining black rocks, for like the Zulus she thought this place was haunted and that a demon might rise from the pool beneath the falls. To guard against this she fingered a lucky charm.

Often she pulled the strings of the tobacco bag in which she kept her money and counted over the farthings and pennies that she had hidden from her relations.

"Cane is a temptation to a lazy man," my father used to say. "Look at Farrell. He'll sit on his backside and watch the stuff ratoon three or four times before he'll think of ploughing it in. And then he wonders why he is broke all the time."

John made every acre of his land pay, though he would never admit that he was doing well. He was so secretive about the returns from the mill that he collected the post himself and when he did his accounts he locked his office door, for he believed that we should become extravagant if we knew he was making money. He was not mean with his land. To the end of his life he experimented with cane, trying to find an indigenous variety that would stand up to anything that Natal could offer in the way of disease, but he had no luck, out of tens of thousands of seedlings. I used to help him tie the carefully selected male arrows to the female, and with the gathering of the seed. When the seedlings came up, slender as blades of grass, how carefully we nursed them until they were transferred from the pots to the fields. Other planters laughed at him, but there was always this leaven in him and he taught me to love the land.

I know the very texture of the soil thereabouts for I caught from him the habit of picking up a handful of earth and running it through my fingers. The soil on the hillsides is red and sandy, just the stuff for sugar-cane, but on the flats it is clayey, richer but more difficult to work. John often cursed the black loam of his low-lying land. Often he put his greedy fingers into the Drews' sandy soil.

That should have been his land. In the early days Nicholas Angus, his father, owned thousands of acres along the South Coast, but he gambled away most of it in gold speculation. The land was cut up into smaller farms and sold. Our farm was entailed and for this reason John felt the lack of a son as bitterly as an Indian would have done. When his father died John inherited nothing but the homestead and eight hundred acres of land; and a tin trunk full of gold shares which were worthless at that time. These he divided amongst his brothers and sisters and then wouldn't forgive them because the shares soared later. I knew none of his brothers and sisters except Aunt Lucy, who was unmarried. She had been left well-off, for she had not only the gold shares but the house in Durban and her mother's money; and the tin trunk in which the shares had been stored. I resembled Aunt Lucy, and my parents hoped that she would leave her money to me. This resemblance carried a barb in it, for they were afraid that I would turn out like her and they were strict with me. In his happier moods John said the likeness was only skin-deep, and we should all thank God that it was a good skin.

On summer mornings when I was a little girl I would sit with him beneath the flamboyant while he drank his tea. Now and again he leaned forward to give me a sip from his cup. The tea was strong and bitter, but I dared not pull a face, for I never knew when he would lose his temper with me. In that morning air we could see clear down the valley to the ocean and I used to imagine that I could see the lighthouse on the Bluff at Durban, but John said that was impossible with Durban fifty miles away.

An iron rail hung in the flamboyant and when he had finished his tea, John hit the rail with a hammer to summon the labour. The rail had hung there ever since I could remember and it was used too as a firebell. Sometimes, if time were short, John would fire the cane, but he preferred to strip the tops before harvesting. Rain might ruin the crop after it was burnt, nor could it stand longer than a week without cutting. With labour plentiful the safe way was the sure way, he said, and fires had been known to get away. There was always a watch kept for fire from lightning or from the match or cigarette of some careless fool who did not live by cane.

From our vantage point I saw year by year the changes that took place in the surrounding countryside. My first memory is of our cane, bright against the sombre bush of uncleared land. At that time there were no houses in sight except the Lamberts' bungalow, a big box sitting on the hill opposite; but now sugarcane covered the low hills for mile upon mile, a green wave spilling along the South Coast northwards into Zululand. Even the Farrells had planted cane. Drew's Pride had been built.

It was John who gave the big house its name and the Drews good-humouredly accepted it, though they always had printed on their stationery the name Broadacres. My grandfather had cleared the site, meaning to build there when his fortunes were at their peak. He had planted the oak-trees that grow there now; and the plans for the house were in the trunk with Aunt Lucy's gold shares. Jonn did not grudge the Drews their house as much as he grudged them their land. He used the house as an answer to anybody who dared to question the future of sugar-cane. "Look at Drew's place," he would shout. "That man hasn't got a penny invested in any other industry except sugar. He's got plenty of money, hasn't he?" He would say to me half-jokingly, "Helen, you ought to set your cap at Richard Drew. He's the eldest and he'll inherit the place for sure. Wouldn't you like to live in that big house?"

The people of Westongate looked up at the house from their bungalows; Indians and Zulus alike regarded it as an honour to work there. Even strangers, passing through Westongate in the train, would lean out of the window to ask who lived in the big house on the hill.

It was at Drew's Pride that I first heard Chris Van der Westhuizen's voice. I was happy that afternoon because my mother had allowed me to wear my shoes instead of the boots that she believed would prevent my ankles from thickening. Mrs. Drew played the piano and I wished that I could get up and dance through the beautiful room in my new black shoes. When the tea was brought in Mrs. Drew asked me to play.

"Just play the one piece, Helen, and by that time Mr. Drew and the boys ought to be here." She smiled at me when I had finished playing. "You're getting on nicely. I wonder where Walter and the boys are. They'll come trooping in at five o'clock ravenously hungry and put everything at sixes and sevens in the kitchen." As she poured the tea the reflection of a white-shirted figure showed in the pane of the french window.

"There's somebody out there now, Mrs. Drew."

She went to the window. "It's Chris. Where are the others, dear?"

Then I heard his voice, as deep as Zetke's. "They went up to the Farrells', I think."

"Well, come in and have tea."

"I don't want any, thank you."

"But you can't just sit out here alone."

"I'll watch the peacocks." There was restrained laughter in his voice now.

"Oh, Chris, do come in."

I tried to look through the window, but Mother plucked at my skirt to remind me of my manners. "Why won't he come in? Is he shy?" she asked.

"Chris? No, he's not shy. It's just that… Well, if he doesn't want to do a thing he doesn't do it. A difficult boy…." She lowered her voice. "He's half-Dutch you know, my sister's son. She wants to get him away from the Dutch influence, that's why she sent him here. They're so rabid, aren't they? It's a pity she married this Van der Westhuizen. The chances she had…. Chris was supposed to go to Richard's school for a year, but they couldn't do anything with him there, he only lasted a term. He has such funny ways…. He's not uncouth…. People like him. I'd like you to meet him. Chris…" She called again, but there was no answer.

She played to us after tea, and my mother listened politely, leaning back with her eyes closed. I slipped out of the room on to the terrace. There was no sign of the boy. I ran to the other side of the house. The peacocks squawked, flapping into a shrub on the lawn, there was a movement behind the hibiscus hedge.

"Chris," I called. I stood still, waiting for him to come out of his hiding-place.

"Where are you, Helen?" my mother cried.

On the way home she scolded me for going out of the room while Mrs. Drew was playing.

"I wanted to see what this boy Chris looks like."

"You shouldn't do things like that. John would be angry if he knew about it." She was tired after the visit and she allowed me to drive the cart. I forgot Chris then.

I saw him on the bridge when I was walking with Leela. He was older than I had expected, perhaps eighteen. He turned to look up at us standing on the steps, and there was in him a submerged power that showed even in this slight movement. I would have gone down on to the bridge, but Leela, who was usually so polite, jabbed my back and then pulled me into the break. The next day he was there again, and this time I withstood Leela's prodding and went on to the bridge.

"You're Chris Van der... I can't remember."

"Van der Westhuizen," he said sullenly. "If you can't remember it call me Van as they did at that school."

I waited for him to ask my name, but he stared at me in silence. "My name is Helen Angus."

"You visited my aunt the other day."

"Why wouldn't you come in to tea?"

"Because I get sick of my aunt's tea-parties. I'm sick of this place." He spoke slowly with a rounding of the vowels. "I saw you outside. You were running in time to the music, just as if you were dancing."

"I called out to you, but you didn't answer."

Leela said anxiously, "Coming along. Your mama waiting." She tugged at my dress.

"I'll come here tomorrow afternoon," Chris said as we went up the steps.

Leela was almost running. "Him looking at you that boy." She rapped her delicate breasts. "Bimeby him grabbing you."

"You're evil-minded," I said. For the rest of the way home I had to explain to her what that meant; but she did take me to the Yogi across the river to have my horoscope cast.

I picked a bougainvillea flower and with this as a pointer he scanned his leaflets industriously. He was expensive, half-a-crown a reading, but he found the omens propitious and the money was well-spent, for Leela did not tell my mother that Chris walked with us each afternoon from the bridge to the Halfway Tree that marked the boundary between Drew's farm and ours.

This tree was a part of our family. Aunt Lucy had been thrown by a horse there and she might have bled to death if my grandfather had not decided that day to fell the tree. After the accident, instead of cutting down the tree he put a railing round it and sent a boy to water it every day so that it would be a monument of his love for her. It was not stunted like the other kaffirboom, but tall and spreading, as big as these trees grow in India, so Mr. Bannerjee said. Whenever John quarrelled with Aunt Lucy he threatened to cut the tree down, for she was superstitious about it.

One afternoon I eluded Leela. I gave her a sixpence to buy some sweets, promising to wait under the Halfway Tree for her. She was suspicious, but she liked sweets and she was too mean to buy any for herself out of her pocket-money. She went off at a run to the store in Westongate and as soon as she was out of sight I hurried to the bridge. I was breathless when I reached it and Chris went down into the ravine to fill his hat with water from the pool so that I could bathe my face. Then when I had rested for a while we walked back to the Halfway Tree and, leaning against it, waited for Leela. I had never known such happiness.

"I stayed here because of you. I was homesick for the Transvaal...."

His cousins rode by. When they saw us Eric and George whistled and shouted, but Richard, the eldest, did not turn his head. They were soon gone and we were alone again in the splendid circle of the cane.

Chris said fiercely, "Richard seems to think that you're his girl. I told him that you loved me. It's true, isn't it? Helen?"

"Yes."

I wound a stalk of grass on my finger. The sap oozed pleasantly from it and I became preoccupied, watching the ridges turn red from constriction.

"That's not the idea." Chris twisted some grass into a ring. "There. With this ring…"

"Don't, it's unlucky…"

We had forgotten Leela and she caught us kissing. She screamed and covered her face. She would not look at me as we walked home.

"What you doing?" she mumbled, thrusting the packet of sweets into my hand. "I telling your mama this."

"Don't tell her, Leela, and I'll give you all the sweets."

She took the packet and in return she hung a trinket round my neck that she said would ward off trouble. The next afternoon I ran away from her as soon as we turned the bend in the break. Her plaintive voice followed me, but by the time I reached the bridge I could no longer hear her. Chris was waiting there for me. He had robbed a beehive, and when I sat next to him he gave me a comb of honey. The honey was dark as the stout Aunt Lucy drank with her meals. We were sticky and we went down into the ravine to wash our hands in the pool beneath the falls. It was hot here in spite of the water and the shade, for vapour fell on the crowns of the big trees and on the undergrowth to rise steaming to the pale sky. Chris had been swimming in the pool and his hair was still wet. I put my hand into his hair to brush away the water. His eyes were soft as an animal's now.

"Promise me you'll never marry anybody else but me," he said.

"I promise."

Leela was on the bridge, imploring me to come with her, but we laughed at her. "We'll hide from her," said Chris.

"Don't worry, she'll never come down here," I said. "She thinks this place is haunted. John comes down here to shoot the monkeys when they become a pest and she thinks that's unlucky. She believes in all sorts of ghosts." I showed him the charm she had given me.

"You shouldn't wear that. My aunt says that a coolie can cast a spell over you."

Leela had plucked up enough courage to start the descent into the ravine. She was lost to sight in the thick bush, but we could hear her chattering to frighten the ghosts.

"I know a way out of here; she'll never find us," Chris said.

He led me along a narrow path that he had made. All the while he showed me the tracks of wild creatures on the soft sand; the spoor of a likkewaan making for the water, the curving mark of a snake, the droppings of a hare. Leela's voice grew fainter behind us and was lost.

"I can take you right down to the sea," said Chris. "But some of the way is rough. Are you frightened?"

"No. I've never been so deep into Awetuli. It's beautiful."

There was a tribe of monkeys in the trees and we clapped our hands to frighten them. We saw a python sunning himself against a log and we frightened him too, and all the birds. The river was hidden beneath reeds and water-lilies, but we heard it all the way down to the sea.

There the glassy waves were curling over one at a time, unvarying. The tide was going out. Pools of water formed on the sand, but they disappeared quickly like a mirage. All the beach was empty except for the black-capped seagulls. They ran a little way before us and then rose to settle farther on. No wind blew and the sand was smooth, marked only by the prongs of the seagulls' claws.

It was Mr. Bannerjee who found us. Chris had fallen asleep. I slid from under his heavy arm and went back with Mr. Bannerjee.

"It is late, Miss Angus. Leela is nearly off her head. She will lose her job now, I suppose."

"How did you know where to find me?"

"I walked for miles and in fear and terror of my life. I was coming back from seeing your father on a matter of business when I found Leela crying on the bridge. I decided to urge you to return and I found the path to the beach. It was a most uncomfortable walk."

Mr. Bannerjee was short of breath and we went the rest of the way in silence; along the sands to the good-luck cairn and across the road, not through Awetuli. Sweat shone on his face and ran into the bulges of his neck, mixing with the coconut oil that seeped from his hair. He had taken off his coat and he carried it on his arm so that he had the appearance of a man on holiday.

Forlorn Leela drooped on the bridge. She roused herself to point at my dress. Now I became tearful and went down to the pool to wash out the purplish stain. Mr. Bannerjee had walked on into the cane-break.

When he saw my tears he said briskly, "Remember that the fruit of rashness is repentance. But now you must keep your wits about you and listen carefully. Your father is bound to be angry at the lateness of your return." He pointed at the evening star. "If you say you have been on a visit to one of your friends he will find out that this is not the truth. Therefore tell him that you went to the Yogi to have your fortune told and he was in a trance. You waited at his hut until he was able to speak to you. There are times when a lie serves the purpose of truth and in this way you will save Leela and escape punishment yourself." The diamond and the gold showed fleetingly. "I will leave you now, trusting that there will be no trouble."

Leela looked up fearfully at the evening star and keeping close behind me followed me up the hill. We met my mother at the Half-way Tree.

She said, "Come home quickly. You can go to bed and I'll lock the door until he cools down. He has gone to the Farrells to look for you; he has already been to Drew's Pride…." It was not until she had me safely in my room that she questioned me.

"Where have you been? I was frantic with worry."

"I went to the Yogi to have my fortune told again, and he was in a trance. I had to wait…"

She pretended to believe me, but she watched me carefully and I saw Chris only three times after that when he came to the farm late at night. Leela was put to work in the kitchen, and for a shilling she would carry a note, although she was angry with me for losing her her good job.

Chapter two

If Drew's pride was a source of comfort to John, the Farrells' house was a dire warning. It stood up defiantly in a clearing that might have been cut out of the cane with a pair of scissors, and tents were grouped under the trees to accommodate the children and Mrs. Farrell's relations who came in a constant stream from the Rand to spend their holidays on the coast. John could have torn down the house and the tents with his bare hands. He didn't care what sort of a shack a coolie or a native put up across the river, but a farmer, he said, should have had the decency to build a respectable house.

The Farrells came to Westongate when the last touches were being put to Drew's Pride. Miss Pimm, taken in by Henry Farrell's appearance, whispered that he was a remittance man; he was related to the peerage and he intended to build a double-storied house of his own design. She was the postmistress and everybody believed her, but after he had built the house and installed his wife in it and the four girls in the tents, Miss Pimm made the discovery that the remittances he received were payments of an insurance against phthisis. The man had been born and bred on the Rand, and he had worked in the mines. Mrs. Drew, who had been nervous about the eclipse of

Drew's Pride, was sufficiently relieved to befriend Mrs. Farrell and so Westongate forgave them their history and even their poverty.

John would not give way. He made it plain to them that they had no right on the canefields. Their lands were unkempt and their fences so bad that the donkeys were forever breaking out and trampling our young cane. One night he shot a donkey. Zetke buried it secretly in the cane and even Mother did not remonstrate, for the donkey had torn one of our foals to pieces.

It wasn't long before Mrs. Farrell came inquiring for her donkey. She drove up in a little cart to the north field where John was re-planting.

"The Buffalo tosses his head and snorts," said Zetke.

This description of John was so apt that I burst out laughing and Zetke repeated himself many times over.

"Henry is short of a donkey for the ploughing, Mr. Angus," Mrs. Farrell said. "You haven't by any chance seen Neddy, have you?"

"Neddy?"

"He's a big grey jack with a dark cross…"

"Oh that. He tore one of our foals to shreds."

"I don't believe it. Our Neddy wouldn't do a thing like that."

"Well, he did. But I don't think he'll do it again."

"What do you mean? What have you done to him?"

"I might have shot him." John took off his helmet, wiped his forehead and slammed the helmet on again.

"He was a pet," wailed Mrs. Farrell. "We could do anything we liked with him. You wait, I'll summons you for this."

"Summons away."

"Helen, you're a witness, you heard him say he shot our donkey."

"I only said I might have shot him. Besides, you'd have to produce the corpse."

He laughed and Mrs. Farrell lifted the whip to make a feint at his helmet. Now the Indians were laughing and John turned on them with nasty threats. He seized the donkeys' bridle and led them down the break. He must have jabbed them when he got them out of sight, for the cart went rocking down the hill and we could hear Mrs. Farrell's complaints long afterwards.

It was a mild day in October, late for planting, but the ratoons on this field had been eaten by rats. The trash had been ploughed in and the ground harrowed and harrowed again so that the top-soil lay light and airy. This land is hilly, the best of our fields, but in constant need of nourishment, and there was the carrion stench of bonemeal on the air.

The men had settled down to work again. John stood with his legs astride, his head slightly lowered, massive and arrogant, an insult to the puny Indians.

"Sometimes I'm sorry I took this lot of coolies on, although they're cheap," he confided to me. "I've done without coolies for years, I'd rather put up with Zulus any day. In the long run this crowd will be expensive. They're skin and bone, I can't see them standing up to the work. Look at that old daddy-long-legs there."

Perian's body had no depth to it, as though life had been breathed into a shadow. As he swung his hoe to scoop a hole I saw the outline of his ribs and when he bent to place the cutting and kick soil over it, his backbone started up like a knotted rope beneath his dull skin.

"I know him. His name is Perian. His wife Leela works in the kitchen."

"About all he's got strength for too. He's got some sort of damn dysentery. He can't plant a row without nicking off into the cane to do his business. Disgusting." At that moment Perian, always unfortu-nate, threw aside his hoe and made off across the field. "Hey, where the hell do you think you're going?" John shouted.

Perian disappeared into the cane. Zetke thought it the most exquisite joke when John strode after little Perian. I sat down next to him prepared to be friendly, but he ignored me. He had been cool to me since I gave his mother away to the police.

She had been my nurse and when I was a child I loved her as much as my parents. Every afternoon we would cross the bridge and sit with her relations in their dim, smoky hut. She was a story-teller, for she knew the old way of living before the laws were changed. She had seen a smelling-out. It was to her own uncle that the witch-doctor had traced evil spells that caused the cattle to die. He was a man of deep laughter, this uncle, so kind that nobody had suspected him of witchcraft; and he was strong and would not die willingly. She had seen girls go mad and coo like pigeons for the Tigoloshi, the little monster that lies in wait for the women in the reeds. Their offspring were strangled at birth. Once in Awetuli there grew a Death Tree, she told us. Her sister sat beneath the Death Tree and the leaves began to sing: Boo-boo-boo. The branches shook and enfolded her and she bleated like a goat when she died.

By the time we started for home, the ravine would be deep in shadow and we went over the big bridge, the long way round, for nobody but a fool would go near Awetuli Falls except in broad daylight. We spat on a small stone and placed it on the good-luck cairn near the kraal; but this did not keep the evil eye from poor old Hlele.

When he saw that she had leprosy, Zetke's father hid her in a hut on the hill, but she used to grow lonely there and she often wandered down to the kraal. She would steal one of her grandchildren for company. I saw her one day. The children were afraid of this ancient thing that had no fingers and they ran from her, but she carried off a fat toddler. I told John about her. The police made Zetke's father burn down his huts after they had taken Hlele away, and we were all kept in quarantine for six weeks.

Zetke was inclined to blame me for the whole affair. I spoke to him several times before he answered me.

"What do you think you are doing? The coolies do all the work while you sit here on your haunches."

He was a tall Zulu, then about eighteen years old, with a soft, good-looking face that he could contort into a frightful mask. He rolled his eyes and gnashed his teeth now, but I laughed at him.

"Why don't you do some work? Must these frail coolies do all the work?"

"I am their master. I examine each cutting so that they may have no excuse if the cane does not come up."

"What if there is a drought?" I countered.

"That could easily happen. They have already bewitched the canefields. There are rats everywhere. See, even the cuttings have been gnawed." He set aside a spoiled cutting. "Of course there will be a drought, for there is this coolie witch-doctor, an old one full of cunning spells." He spat a long stream of tobacco juice into a paraffin tin that stood beside him. "I have caught ten rats in that tin," he boasted and he made of the Zulu words a song of triumph. "Even now there is one swimming about in there, but he will drown soon, if the tobacco juice has not killed him."

I looked into the tin. Zetke, with a proprietary air, looked too. A cane-rat was swimming soundlessly, with no hope of getting out, for the water was too far from the top of the tin. Zetke beckoned to John, who had come out of the cane, followed by the downcast Perian.

"What is it?"

"A rat. I kill them by the dozen," said Zetke.

We all stared into the tin. The rat was not afraid of us. His eyes met mine. Without thinking of what I was doing, I leaned over and snatched him out of the water by the tail, flinging him as far as I could. Perian allowed him to run unharmed over his foot. Zetke, yelling curses, gave chase, but the rat got away.

John raised his hand as though to hit me and I felt ashamed, for the Indians were watching us avidly. I ducked the blow and ran down the break. All the way I could hear his feet pounding after me, but when I reached the gate he turned back, for Mother was in the garden.

She held me off at arm's length. "Whatever is the matter, Helen?"

"John was chasing me. I pulled a rat out of a tin and let it go. He's furious...."

"I should think so. Why on earth did you do a thing like that?"

We sat on the garden seat and I leaned my head against her shoulder. The very smell of her was comforting, a wholesome smell of starched print and lavender.

"The rat seemed to ask me. It looked straight into my eyes."

"Nonsense." She pushed me away gently. "You let your imagination run away with you. The rats have cost us hundreds of pounds, they spoil acres and acres of cane…. Go and get your work-box and do some work on that necklace; you've been at it for months now." She had a cheerful, commanding voice that pushed you along before it so that you were glad to do what she told you.

Her voice was the only robust part of her, a constant surprise coming from that fragile body. John should have married a woman as strong as himself, but he chose her, a poor thing who had nine miscarriages one after the other. She was forty-eight and in her seventh month again. She was ashamed of this late pregnancy and now for the first time she spoke to me about it.

"You must try and keep on the right side of him, Helen. You'll be alone with him when I go into the hospital in a few weeks' time."

I tried to sound surprised. "Hospital, Mother. What for?"

"You know as well as I do. I'm going to have a baby and this time I don't want to fall into Mrs. Lambert's hands."

I was making a necklace of syringa berries and I bent my head over it so that she should not see me smile. A berry, six glass beads, a berry, six glass beads…. I stole a look at her. The sunlight showed every wrinkle in her clean, rose-tinted skin. Her hair was already brushed over with white so that her fertility seemed an astonishing thing.

"Leela says that the omens are good for anybody having babies between now and December."

She smiled, easier now that she had overcome her reserve. "That's because she's expecting a baby herself. I want to teach you to make a few simple dishes, because I know what is going to happen—she will serve curry every night and your father will finish by throwing it at her. I really should have shown you a long time ago. But I'm always so tired…."

"What about this afternoon?"

"I'm afraid not. Look who are coming to visit. Oh dear, they're all in the cart: Miss Pimm, Mrs. Lambert, Mrs. Drew. Now what on earth…. It's not my visiting-day…. They can't be coming for tea, it's past five.

"We've come to tell you the news," cried Mrs. Drew and then there was a chorus, "War has broken out in the Transvaal. The Boers are marching on Durban." They tumbled out of the cart, tripping over their skirts in their hurry.

"We had to come and tell you, stuck out here miles away in the cane," said Miss Pimm. "Why, it might be a week before you knew."

"Thank you," Mother murmured. "I'll tell the girl to bring some tea."

Miss Pimm giggled. "Well, to tell the truth, we had something a little stronger to drink before we left Drew's Pride. Mr. Drew opened a bottle of wine, white of course.... Aggie wouldn't have any, she never touches anything strong." Miss Pimm beamed on Mrs. Lambert.

"Walter always believes in marking an occasion," said Mrs. Drew indulgently. "He's gone off now to see what Colonel Edington thinks of the situation. After all, he was at Majuba...."

"I have some apricot brandy," said Mother. "If you would like a little of that...."

Everybody looked at Mrs. Drew. "Just a sip then," she said. "As Walter says, this is history."

"And you need something to buck you up," Miss Pimm added tactlessly. "There's your sister in the Transvaal amongst all the Boers."

Mrs. Drew sighed. "Yes. Won't she feel out of things? I'm glad I've got Chris here; at least he won't be forced to fight against his own mother's people. Walter has taken him to Colonel Edington's...."

"He seemed glum," said Miss Pimm. "Quite angry, I thought."

Mrs. Drew cried into the apricot brandy. "Don't cry," said Mother. "After all, it's only natural that he should feel glum."

"Natural?" said Miss Pimm.

"Yes, it's natural," I said loudly.

Mrs. Lambert stared at me over her glass of water. "Helen." Her voice was always sweet and low, an excellent thing in a woman. Aunt Lucy said that Mrs. Lambert disliked me because I resembled her; and Lambert had been so madly in love with her that he had hanged himself from the highest branch of the Halfway Tree, but had been cut down before he died. That was why he had gone to the Transvaal, where he had married Mrs. Lambert and begotten a daughter.

She was a short, square-hipped woman whose features were overshadowed by a bulbous, cherry-coloured nose that should have been the heritage of a drunkard, but there Nature had played a prank, for she was a proven teetotaller. The Lamberts had owned land on the South Coast as long as the Anguses had, but Lambert would never return after his attempted suicide. He allowed his farm to go to rack and ruin while he worked a claim on the diamond diggings. As soon as he died, Mrs. Lambert descended on Westongate with her daughter Nancy. She had the land cleared and planted with cane. She should have been doing well, but she spent a great deal of money on Nancy and to make ends meet she went out nursing. It was a common sight to see her driving through the breaks, with her luggage, a cretonne bag and a hatbox, in the charge of an umfaan. Leela and I had often speculated about the contents of the hatbox. Nancy knew, but she made a great mystery of it, hinting that it contained a secret instrument for midwifery.

John was coming through the gate and the chorus broke out again, "The Boers are marching on Durban." It seemed now that they would all stay to supper, for Colonel Edington and Mr. Drew had arrived with a bottle of brandy. When I saw that Chris was not with them I kept out of sight, for Colonel Edington would be at his worst with all this excitement and probably pinch me. I had seen something tied in a corner of Leela's sari when she came out with the tray and now I had the chance to ask her if it was a note from Chris.

"You paying me," she said.

"He's already paid you," I whispered, but I gave her a penny and she was satisfied with that.

Chris had written that he would come to the farm that night when the lights were out. It would be late before our lights went out that night, I thought, as I listened to the chatter of the visitors.

There was the calf to feed. He was a tiny red-and-white creature whose mother had an abscess. He lay in the fowl-pen and the moment he saw me with the bottle he staggered to his feet, wobbling towards me; but when he heard his mother bellowing for him he rebelled against the bottle. He stood with his nose pressed against the wire-netting and when I coaxed him away I had to let him pump my leg and suck my fingers before he would drink.

As the rhythm of his drinking grew stronger, the bottle moved in my hand and a feeling of power and serenity came to me. Leela said that you could be sure when you had missed three times. When I saw Chris that night I would tell him and then we would brave my parents....

The brilliance of the sunset had passed, leaving the golden hills as soft as breasts against the sky. The cane, gold too in that light, lifted beneath the wind as though it breathed. Nearby a smug hen chuckled as her chicks settled beneath her. The ducks chased midges, with a sweet sound like water going secretly between rocks and rushes. A big Muscovy drake made a half-hearted attempt to pursue the ducks and then stood waiting patiently until they quietened down. His benign and sensuous expression reminded me of Colonel Edington, who liked to flirt with young girls but always said he meant no harm.

"Helen," said Mrs. Lambert sharply, "I've called you twice and you sit there day-dreaming. Twice, I called you."

I was embarrassed. "Did you really? I didn't hear you. I was just thinking about that old drake over there, he reminds me of somebody. I won't name names."

"A case of speak of the devil, is that it?" she said grimly.

I looked at her in dismay. "Oh, I didn't mean you," I cried, but she was not convinced, for she caressed her nose anxiously.

She took swift revenge on me. "That calf has a touch of ophthalmia. You shouldn't be near it, not only for your own sake but everybody's. I'll speak to your father about it."

"Don't tell him. He'll destroy it."

"That sort of thing is catching. It's my duty to tell your father and I have never failed in my duty yet, my dear." She bent over the calf, holding her skirts away from him. "It has got ophthalmia. You'd better come out of here at once. Besides, supper is ready, we're waiting for you."

I sat by the calf until Zetke came to take it away. He grinned at me.

"This thing could cause much sickness, therefore I have orders to kill it."

"Hide it in the grass, Zetke...."

He put the calf across his shoulders. "My wife and I will eat this calf and out of the skin I will make a covering for my little brother."

"I will pay you money if you hide it. Otherwise I will tell the police that you smoke dagga."

"First I will take two stones...."

I ran to the house to beg John to shoot the calf, but by the time I had made myself heard Zetke had gone.

"He'll probably keep it and let it grow up, you know what Zulus are about cattle," my mother comforted me.

I knew Zetke better. He would remember his mother. When he was an umfaan he used to bring monkeys to me crucified on sticks and I paid my pocket-money for their freedom, for he told me of the ways he knew of killing them.

The visitors left at last, but still the household remained wakeful. Basket, the calf's mother, broke out of the kraal and hung about the fowl-pen, keeping everybody awake with her bellowing. John got up three times and drove her into the kraal, but she broke out again each time. He muzzled her, but still we could hear her; and Mother said her full-throated bellow was preferable to that repressed moaning. John decided to tie Basket up. I shone the lantern in her eyes while he got a rope round her horns and dragged her to the kraal, where he tied her by the head to a tree. She looked uncomfortable there, poor thing, but at least the place was quiet.

I waited at my window for Chris. The moon came up, rousing the dogs to a fury of barking. They stopped only long enough to listen to the answers from the neighbours' dogs. John shouted at them and I went out to catch them. They took to the cane as soon as I called them, but at last I had them all in the shed, locked away so that they should not bark at Chris when he came down the break. Now and again there came a muffled crash and I wondered what the dogs had knocked over in their hunt for rats. The Drews' dogs were still barking, a far-off sound that merged with the muted song of cane and surf. The moon stood high, so bright that I could see the leaves of the flamboyant and the shape of the hills beyond. I heard Mother speak. There was a rattle of curtain rings and I knew with a sinking heart that she, too, was looking over the quiet hills.

Chris had come to the gate. He looked towards the house, but now I dared not move, for Mother was on the veranda.

She called out, "What do you want here?"

His voice was like the whisper of the wind. "Helen…"

"Go away," she said. "There will be trouble. Go away at once."

"Linda…" John was calling to her and moving across their room.

"I'm here, John, on the veranda."

"I thought you were speaking to somebody."

"Only to a dog. I'll sit in Helen's room, you go back to bed. I'm restless tonight."

Swiftly I crawled beneath the bedclothes. She came into the room and with a fierce gesture pulled the curtains across the window.

"Are you awake, Helen?"

I did not answer and she sat down on the chair beside the bed, her hand on my hair. She was still there when I awoke at dawn.

It was Mr. Bannerjee who told me that Chris had run away that night to join the Boers.

Chapter three

Aunt Lucy always spent a month with us during the winter and for the rest of the year she lived in her big, ugly house on the Berea. She chose the cool weather for her visit because she had a horror of snakes. Once she had trodden on a puff-adder that lay beneath a newspaper. I was a baby when this happened but I know by heart what her feelings were when she put her bare foot on that paper.

She had already paid us the visit, but she arrived unexpectedly towards the end of October, announcing that she had heard from somebody high up in the Army that the Boers would be in Durban within a week. She had brought all her clothes and there were two packing-cases on rail. These we had to send back afterwards at great inconvenience.

Mother and I spent our time now sitting in the garden with her listening to her stories, or worse, playing cribbage with her. Since her youth had faded, the present had lost its meaning for her and she spoke only of those happy days when she had been the toast of the Light Horse. Even John said she had been beautiful, but now everything about her was sharp; the apexes of her elbows, her knees pressing through her silk dress, her knuckles as she leaned on her stick. She tried always to fatten herself and drank stout with her meals, and a tonic wine that sometimes made her tipsy. John said that she hadn't married because she was so busy getting his mother to leave her the Durban property that she never had time to catch a husband; but when they had a serious quarrel he varied this by saying that nobody would have her because she was a loose woman. This did not make her as angry as one would have expected.

"It's such a nuisance having her here again," Mother complained to me one morning. She spoke in a whisper, for Aunt Lucy had a way of popping round the corner when you least expected her. "I'm really not up to being polite to her, Helen."

"If she tells us that story again about the time they drank champagne out of her slipper, I'm going to say I've heard it before."

"You'd be cut out of her will and John would never forgive you."

"Careful. Here she comes." I could hear her stick tapping on the cement path alongside the house. Lately she had had trouble with her feet and John said this was gout brought on by all the wine she drank.

She sat down opposite to me and looked at my feet. It was one of her beliefs that if she stared like that long enough she embarrassed you. I put a cushion over my feet and went on with my necklace. She tried looking at Mother's feet, but Mother knitted placidly at a jacket for her baby.

Aunt Lucy's nose, cleaving the air, pointed directly at me. "Did Mrs. Farrell find your father?"

"Surely she's not still looking for her donkey!" Mother exclaimed.

"She was and I could hardly look her in the face because John told me that he said to her: 'You'll have to find the corpse before you summons me, Mrs. Farrell.' " Aunt Lucy laughed on a note like an Indian mynah's. "I felt like saying, 'My dear lady…' As if she expected the donkey to be alive after what it had done. Not if I know John. Mind you, I will say he is calming down. At least he didn't attack the donkey with brute force; he shot it so he tells me. Why, I remember when he was a boy… This donkey had annoyed him and he simply picked up a cane-knife and nearly sliced its head off."

"Don't," said Mother. "Surely we can find another topic of conversation, Lucy."

"Of course. I keep forgetting about your condition. One doesn't expect it in a woman of your age. Goodness knows I don't want to harp on any subject, let alone John carving up a donkey, more or less as if it were a chicken." She sat quiet for a few minutes and then began, "Did I ever tell you about the time I won first prize at the Arts Ball? I went as a mealie cob. Such an original idea, don't you think? It was all done in green-and-white satin…."

She rocked her chair backwards and forwards with a maddening rhythm, pleased with Mother's hypocritical smile.

"You look sleepy, Helen," she said at the end of the story. "I suppose it's the heat. Isn't it getting hot? Oh dear, the snakes will be coming out…. I think I'd sooner face the Boers. It might be a good idea if I hired that umfaan to keep watch. He could sit at my feet." She pointed to the boy working in the garden.

"The snakes were here in droves last year," I said. "John notched sticks to keep a tally and he used up three sticks."

Aunt Lucy shuddered. "Oh dear. I can never forget that time I trod on the puff-adder. I was nervous before that of course, but it didn't use to haunt me. It was before you were born, Helen, or was it? No, you were a baby in arms." I opened my mouth to tell her that I knew all about the puff-adder, but Mother achieved an expression between a smile and a frown that boded no good for me if I offended Aunt Lucy. "Yes, there I was lying in bed reading the paper one Sunday. You know the habit I have of throwing the advertisement columns on the floor, it does annoy John so…. The others had all gone to church, but I didn't feel well…."

"It was on Helen's christening day," said Mother.

"That's right, I gave her the most beautiful little hand-worked robe, it cost over thirty pounds. It was beautiful. Have you kept it, Linda?"

"Yes."

"Well, get it and show it to Helen."

"I've seen it."

"Oh yes, of course you would have. Don't we become forgetful as we grow older?"

"You're only sixty, Lucy, that's not old," Mother said.

"Fifty-eight. Five years older than John...."

Something stirred in the grass at her feet. At first I couldn't believe what I saw; a puff-adder, brilliantly marked. It must have crawled from an overgrown rockery nearby where the umfaan was moving stones and digging out weeds. As Aunt Lucy rocked forwards the tip of her long narrow shoe just missed it. A convulsion of laughter shook me. At that moment she saw the snake. She was out of the chair and up the veranda steps, her stick thrown aside and her pains forgotten.

The umfaan ran across the lawn and killed the puff-adder with a blow from the discarded stick. Now the dogs rushed on it and began a game, but the umfaan pushed them away. He sat down on a stone and with his penknife slit open the snake to extract medicine from it. I borrowed the penknife to make a notch in Aunt Lucy's stick.

"Look at the notch, Aunt Lucy, you can always show it to people when you are telling the story," I said, carrying the stick to her.

"You heartless girl...." She was sobbing and drinking her tonic wine.

Nothing would induce her to stay. When John came home from the fields she was sitting on the veranda with her luggage at her feet as though she were on a railway station. The tin trunk was right next to her, for it contained her gold shares. John could never convince her that they would be safe with a broker. The shares had lain in the trunk since her father's day, she said, and no harm had come to them.

She forced John to drive her to the station. In silence she climbed on the cart. We waved to her, but she did not respond. She had her hand over the back of the seat holding on to the tin trunk with the evident intention of not relinquishing it until she reached home. I couldn't help thinking what a nuisance she was going to make of herself in the train.

Mother laughed as soon as the cart was out of sight. "Well, it's an ill wind that blows nobody any good. At least we shan't have to play cribbage every night or listen to her tiresome stories." In the middle of her laughter she frowned and her body jerked ominously with pain, but her voice was still lively. "I think I'd better lie down for a while. I did too much, packing all that stuff for Lucy. Don't go away, Helen."

"Are you all right? Shall I go and fetch Mrs. Lambert?"

"No...." But now her voice was less sure.

I began to work on my necklace again. Chris. He was far away, perhaps even dead on the veld. I'd have to tell Mother, she would think of something... some way of hiding me from John. Terror rippled through me. When he lost his temper he was like a wild animal. There were times when not even Mother could manage him and then you couldn't think of him as the man who took you on his knee and petted you. I went to Mother's room. I couldn't tell her yet, she might get ill, but I wanted the comfort of her presence.

A hullabaloo of Hindustani had burst from the Indian barracks and I went to the window to see what was going on. The women were bargaining with a merchant. He was a bearded man with an imposing turban and he sat aloof from the haggling, except that now and then he thundered out a price above the uproar.

"The man with the silks is here."

"Well, go and have a look. If he's got a pretty green I'll make it up for you later on."

I ran down the hill to join in the bargaining. The Drew boys when they were younger used to chase the Indian women, yelling, "Coolie Mary yama karya purya". But I never teased them like that, although it was fun to have a flood of Hindustani let loose at you and to see the passive women grow angry.

I snatched a piece of silk from Leela. A sparkle came into her eyes as I wound the silk about me like a sari and swayed stiffly, singing through my nose. The other women laughed, but Leela grasped the silk and tugged until I gave it up to her while the merchant spluttered to see his goods handled like this.

Leela's body was distorted by pregnancy, but her face and hands and feet were as fine as ever. I think she was aware of her loveliness, though she shrugged her shoulders when I spoke of it. She carried herself proudly and often I saw her cleaning her teeth with charcoal. In those days she always wore a flower in her hair. That afternoon she was wearing a frangipanni above the bun coiled into the nape of her neck. The flower fell to the ground while she was struggling for possession of the silk and Mr. Bannerjee picked it up. Leela would not take it from him, not with her mother-in-law watching them. Everybody knew that Mr. Bannerjee was in love with her; and now she had left him standing there like a fool with the frangipanni. This would have been an awkward moment for anybody else, but Mr. Bannerjee used his wits. He went back to the chair where he had been sitting and began to make notes in a little book, studying the flower. The women, reminded that he could read and write, looked at him with respect again. I peeped over his shoulder. There were some numbers on the page and now he was writing: Waxy petals, gold shading in centre, sweet....

"Are you studying botany now, Mr. Bannerjee?"

He closed the book on the flower. "There is no subject in which I have not some interest, Miss Angus. When I was studying in London I was noted for the diversity of my interests." He looked at me keenly. "Did you know that I went to the university in London?"

"Yes."

"I did two years there." He began to smile, but catching the merchant's eyes on him shut his mouth firmly so that no glint of the diamond should incite robbery. He wrote in his book again, this time working out figures with the air of a banker.

"Your father owes me money, Miss Angus, and he refuses to interview me. I am going to sit here until he pays me, even if it is for six months."

"Well, if you eat his rice all that time, you'll be paid, won't you, Mr. Bannerjee, and then you could give him a receipt, paid in full."

Mr. Bannerjee laughed into his hand. "I would post the receipt to him, of course; it would be as well in such a case to put some distance between the Buffalo and myself."

I laughed too and bent down to pick up Sowa, who had been sitting happily at his mother's feet. He made no noise when I swung him round, but his grandmother shrieked at me.

"You make him sick," said Leela sourly.

I plumped the child down and squatted opposite him. His body was still blighted by hunger but he was pretty, with fine eyes and a light-brown skin. I took a sweet from my pocket and gave it to him. Now Leela smiled on me. I put my finger on the caste mark between his eyes. Emotion came tardily into that secretive little face. He began to cry and Leela swooped on him, scolding me rapidly. All the other women added their voices to hers and I burst out laughing. They moved away. Now I could look through the bale in peace. Leela had thriftily decided against buying that day and I chose the piece of silk that she had wanted.

The merchant lit a cheroot, cupping his hand to capture the smoke. I said, "You're not supposed to smoke in the canefields. My father would run you off if he saw you."

He smiled at me, but he kept on smoking. Mr. Bannerjee paused in his calculations and coughed delicately, with the pencil in front of his mouth. The merchant, reminded of his presence, handed him a cheroot. Mr. Bannerjee blew smoke rings, one after the other, and soon there was a crowd of children round him and the women, too, watched him, smiling. Long ash grew on the cheroot of the fascinated merchant. He pulled himself together at last and carefully extinguished his cheroot.

"You take that piece?" he asked briskly.

Still the women would not approach him while I was there and I went home with the feeling that somehow I had been defeated by them and by Mr. Bannerjee's smoke rings. I had only just left the clearing when the bargaining broke out again.

The house was quiet. I called out cautiously for Mother. There was such a long silence that I thought she must have fallen asleep, but when I tiptoed to her room I found her staring at the lock, in an attitude of waiting.

"Do you like this shade?" I put the silk beneath her hand.

"It's pretty. Is your father anywhere in sight yet, Helen?"

"He would hardly have had time to get to Westongate."

"Yes, of course. I think you had better go for Mrs. Lambert then. You run there yourself. And send Zetke with a note to your father; he can get the doctor."

I left Leela with her and ran to the top of the hill where the Indians were planting. There was no sign of Zetke. The men were loafing in the shade and they made a rush for their hoes when they saw me. I sent the strongest man with a message to John.

Mrs. Lambert was dozing over a recipe book. She was still in her dressing-gown and she was annoyed because she had not seen me coming down the cane-break. Usually she missed nothing, for she kept a sharp lookout over the countryside.

"It's Mother, Mrs. Lambert. She's ill. The baby...."

She put the book aside on a small cane table, "gracious. She's hardly seven months. Has your father sent for Doctor?"

"Dad's not at home. He took Aunt Lucy to the station. There's nobody with Mother except Leela."

"Mercy. Let me get my luggage. I've been taking things quietly today. Touch of heart." She stood up and the gown fell open. I saw that she had nothing on underneath except a pair of bloomers. Her breasts hung in defeat to her stomach, her legs in front were knotted by varicose veins, royally purple. She pulled the gown about her peevishly.

"Did you know that Nancy got invited to East Griqualand by the Marstons?"

"Yes," I said sulkily.

"They are keeping her there for three months. Such nice people. They play polo. And it's just as well she went away, she is so sensitive nowadays if I go out on a case. Now you run around and lock up,

Helen, and then tell the umfaan to inspan." She went into the bedroom and began stuffing clothes into the cretonne bag.

I had locked up and shouted to the umfaan to bring the horse and cart, but still she wasn't ready. She stood fumbling with her corsets.

"I'll lace you, Mrs. Lambert, I'm quick at it, I always do it for Mother."

She gasped when I had finished. "You'll have to undo it, Helen. It's too tight. No wonder your mother is so delicate if she pinches herself in like that. Quickly, I might faint." Her nose and lips had turned blue, I tugged fiercely at the corset strings. "Looser, my dear, much looser than that," she kept saying, but at last I had her laced to her satisfaction. Then I had to help her to pull her dress over the solid mass of her bust, now victoriously hoisted above her corsets. She picked up the cretonne bag and the hatbox.

"Have you locked up? Oh, the cat. Put him out. There he goes. Catch him."

I dashed after the cat that had taken refuge under the sideboard. When I seized him by the tail, he whipped round with a yowl and clawed at my arms. I held on, shrieking for help. Mrs. Lambert bent down stiffly and smacked the animal.

"You nasty thing. Now we'll have to put iodine on those scratches."

She carried the cat out and flung him over the veranda ledge. She was in a hurry now and while she daubed my arms with iodine, she called for the umfaan in such a loud voice that my head sang. The umfaan came to the door.

"The horse is in the pound."

"You'll have to pay to get it out then, you little…" She looked at me helplessly. "Well, how on earth are we going to get there, Helen?"

"We'll have to walk."

"Walk? Those hills. Still, I have to do my duty…."

She gave her luggage to the umfaan and we set off, the umfaan struggling behind us all the way and lost to sight at the first bend in the break. While we were walking downhill Mrs. Lambert had breath for conversation.

"Why did your aunt go home so suddenly?"

"She nearly trod on another snake. It was right underneath her foot while we were sitting in the garden."

Mrs. Lambert brightened. "Fancy that. She's like my cousin Angelica. My cousin Angelica had a charm for snakes. Wherever Angelica went she saw a snake and she got bitten by a mamba in Rhodesia, three times in the back it got her. At least that is the story her husband told the police and there was a dead mamba hanging in a tree to prove it. But when he got back to Johannesburg he tried to make love to his own mother-in-law and told her that he had killed his wife for her."

I said respectfully, "And did the mother-in-law hand him over to the police?"

"Of course. There was a scandal about it. But he was white-washed. He told the police his mother-in-law was too fond of the bottle and that she had made up the story. She did drink, of course."

We were beginning to climb the hill and as she sweated so her temper worsened. "You should have come in the cart for me, Helen. I'm not used to walking. In fact, I refuse to walk. In the very poorest household they provide transport for the nurse and your father is a rich man."

"It all happened so suddenly."

"Well, my heart is likely to give out with all this climbing up hill and down dale. If I faint, undo my corsets and pull my garters down and then put my head between my knees."

On the ascent of the last hill, although I pushed her part of the way, she gave up completely and sat down on the bank of the cane-break. Her breath came between her pursed lips in an invisible bubble of sound, the colour in her nose seeped into her cheeks.

"My heart feels queer," she said.

I fanned her face with my hat. "Do try, Mrs. Lambert. I'll make you a cup of tea as soon as we get there."

"I may never get there. Break off a piece of sugar-cane for me, Helen, the moisture might put new life into me."

She stripped the cane methodically and crunched into it. I lost all patience.

"You don't seem to be worrying about Mother...."

"My dear child, if I can't go on, I can't go on. I'm doing my best. Besides, I know your mother, she'll be hours yet. Just give me a few minutes to get my breath back."

"Well, don't talk so much."

"How dare you !"

"If you don't hurry up, I'll have to leave you here and go on by myself."

"Oh, will you?" She spat out some pith and took another bite of sugar-cane. "And pray what good will it do you when you get there? When I've had a rest, we'll go on."

"Take off your corsets, that might help."

"I suppose I could do that. Mind you, why I should put myself out like this when you've been so rude to me..." She disappeared into the cane, but at that moment I heard the clip-clop of hooves.

"Wait a minute, Mrs. Lambert, there's somebody coming along. We might get a lift."

She peered out of the foliage. "Who is it?"

A donkey came round the bend, with Zetke majestically astride. He kicked the donkey into a gallop when he saw us.

"You could ride it," I breathed.

"Never," said Mrs. Lambert. "My dear child, what if I fell off? Where would you all be then?"

"I know this donkey, it's a good riding donkey. I've often been on it."

"Well..."

"Get off your donkey and let the chieftainess ride it, Zetke."

He began a long palaver about the urgency of his business, but I took hold of the donkey's bottom lip and held on until at last he dismounted. The next thing was to get Mrs. Lambert on the donkey.

"I've ridden all over the Transvaal on horseback," she assured me, "but I'm not getting any younger and that's a fact. Besides, it's difficult in corsets." She took out her handkerchief and fastidiously wiped the donkey's back so that her sweat should not mingle with

Zetke's. I held my hands for her to mount from while Zetke stood at the donkey's head to stop him from bolting. There was no danger of that. He stood still on three legs and settled down into a placid doze, enjoying the shade of a little tree that grew at right angles to the bank. Zetke got him to move by prodding him in the behind with a stick and he galloped off, but as soon as he was out of range he found another patch of shade where he drowsed until Zetke sent him flying again, this time with a shrewder thrust. So at last we arrived home.

A group of Indian women stood outside the house and Mrs. Lambert waved them away as she swung herself off the donkey. " Shoo, scat, noisy things," she said as though she spoke to trouble-some fowls.

Leela murmured to them and they went away sulkily, but she came towards us smiling. "Baby. She so." She separated her hands a few inches.

"A girl?" Mrs. Lambert drew down the corners of her mouth. "Oh, won't they both be disappointed."

"Boy chile."

"Well, don't call it she, that's ridiculous," said Mrs. Lambert, hurrying into the house. "A boy is he and a girl is she. You'd think you would have learned that by now." She was put out at having arrived too late and her face coloured passionately when she was confronted at Mother's door by the old midwife who had delivered the baby.

"Now off you go," she cried. "And you too, Helen, I don't want anybody getting in the way. Go off somewhere by yourself and take this old Mary out of the way, I can't stand their jabbering."

I took the old woman by the arm. She sat down opposite me on the veranda, staring into space with clouded eyes. She was a white-haired woman, dressed in a dirty, faded sari and I was deceived by her shrivelled face and trembling hands into thinking that she was about eighty years old, but Leela told me afterwards that she was little over thirty.

"Pay," she said. She seemed to know only this one English word and she repeated it over and over again.

"You must wait until the master comes home. I haven't got any money to give you."

She took two pennies from the little bag at her waist and holding them out to me pointed to herself. I thought she wanted to give the pennies to me as a token, but when I reached out for them she returned them hastily to the bag. "Pay," she said again.

She went through the pantomime of the pennies so often that in desperation I tried to find some money in John's office to give to her. There was no money in any of the unlocked drawers and I stood at the window for a while hoping that she would go. She caught sight of me and held up the pennies. I turned my back on her.

The office was a bright, square room, the best in the house. Big windows facing east made a frame for the canefields and the sea and the sky. John needed only to lean out to see the weather-vane on top of the flagpole; and through his binoculars he could watch the labour on the farthest hill. The walls were covered with his trophies from hunting trips in Zululand. There was a fine zebra skin on the floor, brayed by the Trappists at Mariannhill. His guns were in the corner, and the snake-stick that he had notched three times last summer. There were photographs of all his family, the one of Aunt Lucy blurred behind splintered glass. He had smashed it to the floor one day when they quarrelled. Everything that made up his life was there; charts marked to make a report on new varieties of cane, his neat ledger, notes for a letter to the Association.

The old midwife shuffled into the room. I turned on her angrily but she held up the two pennies again. The only way to get rid of her was to pay her and frantically I hunted on the desk for some money. I found a florin underneath the ink-well and I gave that to her. She understood money well enough, for she nodded her head and held up five fingers. I thumbed my nose at her. She seemed to understand that too, for she scuttled off, complaining in a loud voice.

Mrs. Lambert rushed into the passage. "Oh, she has gone. Making a noise like that. Thank goodness you got rid of her. Proper old death's head. You can come in and see your mother, but just for a second and no talking, Helen."

Mother lay so still that I thought she was asleep. Her hands, always thin, were curved like claws on the counterpane. A fierce loneliness sprang up in me and I touched her hands, trying to straighten the fingers.

She opened her eyes. "Helen." Her voices was as strong as ever. "A boy. Won't your father be pleased? I only hope he doesn't kill himself celebrating. I wish he'd come home."

I whispered, "We're not supposed to talk. John has probably gone after the doctor. Mrs. Lambert had to ride Zetke's donkey, she couldn't get up the last hill."

"That old coolie woman, Helen. I'll never forget it."

Mrs. Lambert came into the room. "Go out of here at once, Helen. I do believe that you've been talking, Linda, you're a naughty girl."

I found the baby in the kitchen. He was lying in a crib next to the paraffin stove, but I could see nothing of him except his nose and eyes and mouth, for he was encased in cotton-wool. It didn't seem possible that he was as small as he looked and I unwrapped him gently. His face was no bigger than a monkey's and his legs and arms were as thick as my finger; but he was a boy all right. Zetke came in with some firewood and stared at him in amazement.

"Look at him, Zetke," I said. "Isn't he small?"

"Aau. My father, did you ever see a person so small? He looks like a monkey."

"How dare you say my little brother looks like a monkey?"

"There is no argument, he looks like a monkey."

It was true, the baby did look like a monkey. I gazed at him mournfully and began to wrap him up in the cotton-wool. Mrs. Lambert caught me.

"You wicked girl, how could you do a thing like that? What do you think I put the hot-water bottles round him for? He's got to be kept warm. Why, he's so weak that he will have to be fed with a dropper. No baths, he'll have to be oiled. It's even dangerous to breathe on him."

She chased me out of the kitchen, but as soon as her back was turned, I had another look at him. This time I put my hands over my mouth so that my breath would not hurt him. There was a knock on the door. Mrs. Lambert's umfaan had arrived at last, and he held out the hatbox and the cretonne bag. Here was my chance to see what was in the hatbox. I lifted the lid, and the umfaan leaned forward to look. Inside was a china chamber, white figured with gold.

"Beautiful," murmured the umfaan.

Leela came to see what I was laughing at. She reached out to steady the box, jostling me. There was a crash as the chamber fell and broke. The umfaan howled and ran away, Leela strolled into the yard, but there was no escape for me. Mrs. Lambert raced into the kitchen.

"Quiet," she hissed. "You gave your mother a fright. And look what you've done." Tears came into her eyes. "Oh, you dreadful, dreadful girl. That's been out with me on every case for the last twenty years. You can't always rely on the conveniences on farms…."

"I'll replace it."

"You can never replace it. I've had it for over twenty years. In Rhodesia, in the Transvaal. And I always take it with me, because every time I've left it behind, there's trouble. I'm not superstitious, but I can only hope and pray that this isn't an omen…."

Leela collected the pieces of china and put them in the rubbish-bin. Her face was alight with laughter and I got away from her quickly, terrified that I might get the giggles.

I said, "Come with me to the shed, Mrs. Lambert, there are some of my grandmother's things there and you can pick out another one for yourself."

She shook her head hopelessly, but she followed me. "My word, it's a proper storehouse," she exclaimed.

There hadn't been room for my grandmother's furniture and ornaments, but John stacked them in somehow rather than allow Aunt Lucy to keep them all. I found a fine gold-and-green-and-black creation on a shelf above the cane knives. I presented this to Mrs. Lambert after I had blown the dust off it.

"It's really quite valuable because it's so old," I said.

"Well, it's certainly nice, Helen, but of course I couldn't take it without speaking to your mother…. My, it's pretty."

"Mother won't mind, she doesn't like any of these things, but John made Aunt Lucy share because that was the way the will was worded."

"Well, if you're sure your mother would be agreeable...." She carried the chamber into the light to examine it. "Not that I would need it here, mind you, I only brought mine for luck so to speak. But you should see some of the places. Death-traps. Snakes and spiders and seats so wobbly you could fall and break your leg; I knew a girl who did. The Farrells'... Well, the less said the better and I'm very fond of her." She took a breath. "Helen, there's somebody driving down the break. Speak of angels and you hear the flutter of their wings, it's Susie Farrell herself. She's come to offer help. I know her, a heart of gold. You go and greet her while I tidy myself up."

She hurried to the house, the chamber discreetly hidden by a fold of her skirt. There were in fact three vehicles converging on the farm; and each was the outward sign of its occupant's importance. Mrs. Farrell rode in a lowly Scotch cart drawn by two grey donkeys, her own property. Miss Pimm sat behind a handsome bay mare, but she did not own the mare or the gay little dog-cart. Mrs. Drew had the smartest turnout of all; she drove two-in-hand and she was the owner, what is more. In the bearing of each there was some self-consciousness. Mrs. Farrell was bluff, as though to imply that it didn't matter how she got about, she arrived at her destination as surely as those with flashy horses. Miss Pimm was fierce, daring anybody to remark that she had borrowed Colonel Edington's outfit. But Mrs. Drew. She was the spirit of the big house on the hill, of fat returns from the sugar-mill. Durban shopkeepers fell over themselves to give her credit and in Westongate she was treated with the same deference as the Vicar; although most people thought she was a little daft because of the peacocks in the grounds at Drew's Pride.

Today Miss Pimm was able for once to thrust herself before Mrs. Drew. She was the bearer of news. "John Angus asked me to bring a message. He has borrowed that fast horse of Colonel Edington's, the one whose mother was a racehorse, you know, and ridden off to Illovo to find the doctor. Quite exciting; there was some man in history did it if I remember."

"They were always doing it in history," said Mrs. Drew with the professorial air of the rich.

Then they all said together, "How is your mother, Helen?"

"Speak very softly," warned Mrs. Lambert as she led them to the garden seats. "We mustn't go into the house, as she is not to be disturbed. She's having a little sleep now. Helen, would you run along and ask the Mary to bring out some tea for the ladies ?"

"Oh, we wouldn't dream of it," they cried.

They began to croon like doves over Mother's illness. Miss Pimm's voice isolated itself challengingly, "There ought to be a law against a man like John Angus making a pig of himself at his time of life."

I looked back at her to show that I had heard but she repeated obdurately, "Pig," and might have said it again if a flutter of words from the others had not screened her voice. I went quietly into Mother's room. She was straight and still, as though she hoarded her breath.

"They've arrived," I whispered.

"Fill them up with tea, they'll soon go. I hope she told them that I couldn't see anybody."

"Miss Pimm came with the news that John has ridden to Illovo for the doctor. You should have heard what she said about him."

"You should hear what he says about her." Mother smiled at the recollection. I buried my face against her to stifle my laughter. John once said of Miss Pimm, "The trouble with Pimm is that she has guarded her virginity like a registered packet, but so far nobody has called to sign for it."

"What are you laughing at? How do you know what he said?" Mother asked suspiciously.

"He's always saying funny things about Miss Pimm."

"Well, don't repeat them. Sometimes your father can be rather coarse. Did Mrs. Lambert tell you I might have to go to hospital? It all depends on what the doctor says."

"All she has done is boss me. I found out what she had in the hatbox…"

"Listen. They're in the kitchen having a look at the baby. You'd better go, she said I wasn't to talk."

Leela had the tea ready and the visitors, pretending not to notice her, stared at the baby devoutly. Mrs. Lambert stood by like a conjurer who has performed a baffling trick. When she saw me she whinnied with exasperation.

"You mustn't make things difficult, Helen. You're forever going in there. You could cause serious harm to your mother, you could even cause her to pass away."

"Dhai bringing baby!" said Leela suddenly.

That floored Mrs. Lambert. I realised joyfully that she hadn't told the visitors the whole story and a look at Leela's face told me that she knew she had scored a point.

"Speak when you're spoken to," Mrs. Lambert snapped and whisked Mrs. Drew into the garden. The other two followed, looking back at Leela, the baby and me as though we had all done something faintly disgraceful.

"She silly ahss that one," said Leela. "She saying Die, Die alla time. Me I don't eating for three day and I giving cakes, that helping your mama. You giving me flower to take. Dhai…." She laughed." Dhai thinking you praying that god," and she pointed to the weathercock on top of the flagpole.

Still laughing, she carried the loaded tray outside. This brought forth exclamations of reproach. They had come to help, not to drink tea and make a nuisance of themselves, declared Mrs. Drew; and she reluctantly drank two cups of tea and ate four little rock cakes. There was an air of festivity, decently restrained, over the group and Mrs. Lambert relaxed sufficiently to ask how the latest Westongate courtship was developing.

"She refused him." Miss Pimm shot the information at her before anybody else had a chance to answer.

"How do you know he even asked her?"

There was of course no reason for Miss Pimm to flush unless she had been reading somebody's correspondence. "It's an open secret."

"She has a fast look," reflected Mrs, Drew. The conversation at once became more lively.

Mrs. Lambert poured a cup of tea out so hastily that she slopped some into the saucer. "Take this to your mother, Helen, but don't stand there chattering to her." She raised her eyebrows to warn the others not to say too much in front of me. Mrs. Lambert was the real power in Westongate. Through her nursing she knew the innermost secrets of nearly every household and she had never been known to give away one of these secrets, so that everybody was polite to her thinking of the havoc she could bring about if she did talk: when she listened to gossip it was always with the air that she could explain everything if she wanted to.

Mother had fallen asleep and so I walked down the break to see if John was coming. On the other side of the fence, the visitors' voices rose and fell in a pattern of scandal. They were talking now about a woman who was living with Jenkins, the hotel proprietor, while her husband was fighting in the Transvaal. "Somebody ought to write to him about it…." But Miss Pimm wanted to talk about John and she interjected constantly, "As I always say, John Angus is…" but nobody took much notice of her, for John's sins were stale. "There's another man in the picture, I believe…."

Miss Pimm tried again. "It must be John Angus. All that family is the same. Remember Lucy,"

"They say she was as pretty as a picture," said Mrs. Lambert.

"Fast. This Helen has the same look. She'll take some watching. And think of old Nicholas Angus. He was a by-word. Coolie Marys, intombis …"

"Enid…" That was Mrs. Drew feebly remonstrating.

"It's perfectly true. My father wouldn't have him in the house. And his son is no better. I could tell you a few things…."

"I'd believe anything of a man who would deliberately massacre an innocent donkey," said Mrs. Farrell. "If it wasn't for Linda, I wouldn't set foot on this property."

"I'll tell you something about John Angus," said Miss Pimm.

I coughed loudly and there was a silence behind the hedge.

"Is anybody there?" Mrs. Lambert called.

They left soon after that, a little meeker. "There's one thing about Westongate people," Mrs. Lambert said, looking after them affectionately, "they're staunch when you're in trouble. You couldn't call your mother sociable, she'd go six months without calling on a soul, but the minute they hear she is sick, they rally round."

"I wish my father and Aunt Lucy could have heard what Miss Pimm was saying about them."

She didn't know what to answer to that and she went inside, mumbling, "I daresay, I daresay…." The one to tell was Aunt Lucy. She loved quarrelling and she probably knew a great deal about the Pimms….

There at last was John driving down the break. I put my hands to my mouth and yelled, "It's a boy." He sent the horse into a gallop. Mrs. Lambert's umfaan, loitering nearby, hid himself in the cane, for above the sound of the horse's hooves John's voice rose in a Zulu war-cry. Mrs. Lambert soon sobered him. She was at the gate as he pulled the horse to a stop.

"Now, don't you come charging in here, John. Your wife is very poorly. Where's the doctor?"

"Right behind me. Pimm stopped us and told us the news." He was shouting with excitement. "A boy, hey? How is he?"

"Puny. Don't build up any hopes."

She was haughty with John, but she fawned on Dr. Stewart as she led him to Mother's bedroom. I beckoned John.

"Come and look," I whispered. We tiptoed to the crib. "Isn't it small? Nobody is allowed to touch it. She says it will have to be fed with a dropper and wiped with oil."

"God," said John, looking helplessly from his big hands to the baby. "Good God, a man is almost ashamed to own it."

"Zetke says it looks like a monkey."

"That boy needs knocking down, he's getting too damn cheeky."

Mrs. Lambert came to the door. "Doctor would like to speak to you," she said patronisingly. She caught my arm as I followed John. "Not you, Helen. You'd better go outside while he has a chat with the doctor."

Mother seemed stronger the next day and even Mrs. Lambert was optimistic when she seated herself at the tea-table in the afternoon.

"Well, we've had a peaceful day so far, touch wood," she said. "Our patient seems a little better today, but Dr. Stewart is still advising care. It probably means an operation, John. I suppose he mentioned it to you?" She looked at him with disapproval.

John stared her out. "How's the boy?"

"I'd have the minister out to christen him if I were you."

"What for?"

"What for? Well, if anything happened to him, which God forbid…."

"All I asked was, how is my son?"

"And I told you in the most tactful way I could, John. I'd have the minister out after the service on Sunday."

"Why? Does he know anything about rearing babies?" John asked obstinately.

"No. It's not for that at all, quite the reverse in fact."

She helped herself to a cake. I avoided John's eyes, for she had taken one of Leela's butter cakes. She had eaten half of it before she got the taste and then she put it on her plate, staring at it with loathing.

John said, "Have a biscuit, Mrs. Lambert, they're out of a packet. Now what were we talking about? Oh, the christening."

"What do you think of calling him?"

"Nicholas. After my father."

"I like that. My uncle, on my mother's side…" She paused, listening suspiciously. A Zulu girl was singing in the cane-break, her voice high and sweet. Other voices, deeper and stronger, moulded the melody into a plaint. "What's that? Surely they're not coming here?"

John said placatingly, "I've got to pay them, they've waited two days for their money already. They're the day girls, there are only about ten of them and I've told them to keep quiet."

"Well, see that they do. We can't have noise." She bustled off to Mother's room and John shook his fist in that direction.

49

"I can't stand much more of her."

"Let's ask Aunt Lucy to come and help. Tell the old devil to go home."

"Lucy! She wouldn't stir a step to help anybody, the selfish swine." He moved impatiently and, taking the cards and money, set himself up at the table beneath the flamboyant tree, in readiness to pay the girls who were lining up. It was strange to see them standing there so quietly, for this is the time for jokes and shrieks and laughter. I sat at the dining-room window trying to concentrate on my necklace, but my eyes were heavy. The beads jumped and blurred and I dozed with my head against the window-sill.

When I awoke, John was paying Tandazele. She was the last girl in the line and I could hear the voices of the others in the break as they started homewards. She was young, a tall girl with skin glittering from dried soap. The shape of her head was drawn against the clear sky; the short straight nose, the well-turned lips, the hair in a hundred little plaits threaded with beads. She wore only a piece of bright green silk knotted under her armpit.

It was taking John a long time to pay her. The very way he sat made me angry; with his legs wide outspread so that his trousers stretched unwrinkled across his thighs. His helmet was pushed back and his hair lay in clusters of curls, like a boy's. He marked the card and then he jabbed Tandazele low in the belly with the pencil. Arrogantly she pushed his hand away.

"Very beautiful," he said in Zulu.

She held out her hand for her money. He dropped coin after coin on her palm and as she looked down at the money he walked round the table and put his hand on the back of her neck, pressing her head down. So they stood motionless.

I leaned far out of the window and yelled at the top of my voice. The girl sprang away and ran into the cane, but he turned on me, swearing vilely. It was only when Mrs. Lambert came to the door that I realised how shocking the noise must have been in that quiet house. John became silent as though a hand had been clapped over his mouth. Mrs. Lambert hurried back to Mother's bedroom. Leela was clearing away the teacups and when she saw that I was crying she touched my head gently.

"You not crying. Please you not crying. Your mama getting all right. Bimeby we giving goat, hey?" She stared into space in a holy and withdrawn mood.

John was walking up the steps. In a few seconds he would be in the room with me. I became as still as Leela.

"Take those things out, you lazy devil," he said to her, swinging the bag of coins as though he meant to hit her with it. Leela, calm still, took the tray out of the room and John dumped the bag of silver on the table. He shuffled the cards, glaring at me. I tried to string my necklace and, though it went wrong, I kept myself busy on it so that I should not have to look at him.

Mrs. Lambert came into the room quietly. She said, "Linda passed away a few minutes ago, John. You must get Dr. Stewart. She sat up when she heard you and Helen quarrelling and tried to get out of bed. She wasn't supposed to move at all, I kept telling her that." She stared at each of us in turn. "These things happen. She was a nice person, a lady…."

Her words were feeble against our silence and presently she went out of the room.

"It was your fault, you bitch," he whispered.

Chapter four

Before Mrs. Lambert handled the baby she put on her spectacles as though he would slip through her fingers if she were not careful. She oiled him quickly, for he turned blue with cold as soon as he was taken out of his crib, although the kitchen was so hot that we sweated. I was there to fetch and carry, but it was hard to follow her instructions, for she always put a safety pin in her mouth, too busy to set it aside on the table. With her frenzied gestures she made it plain that I was the biggest fool she had ever had to do with.

One afternoon I had the temerity to murmur, "It's close in here," and Mrs. Lambert said something that sounded like 'Oh, for Christ's sake,' but it couldn't have been that, for she had never been known to blaspheme.

"What you saying, ma?" Leela asked. Perhaps she imagined the same as I had.

Clasping the baby under the shoulder, Mrs. Lambert at last removed the safety pin from her mouth. "I didn't say anything."

"You speaking," said Leela.

"How many times have I told you I don't want you in here when I'm bathing Baby?" She waited until the door closed on Leela.

"I ought to send her packing, but I couldn't be bothered training another girl. Anyway, we'll have to make new arrangements very soon. I can't stay on here when Nancy comes back from East Griqualand. Perhaps your aunt will come and stay with you."

"She doesn't know anything about babies. Besides she wouldn't come here in the summer."

"Well, what's to stop you from going to Durban? You could get a trained nurse in there. This child needs proper care, I wouldn't be surprised if he hasn't got anaemia."

"He's very thin, isn't he? Zetke says he looks like a monkey. I wish he'd put on a bit of condition."

"Rome wasn't built in a day. It's a lucky thing that he is alive, never mind fattening up, Helen."

"Mrs. Farrell says he should have a wet nurse."

"Pardon? Did you say a wet nurse? Whom did she think of getting?"

I was abashed. "Well, I suppose one of the natives or Indians...."

"I don't hold with it. Babies suck their habits in with the mother's milk. You wouldn't want him growing up like a Zulu or bowing down to false gods like the coolies."

"I never thought of that. Mrs. Drew says that donkey's milk is good."

"It's a pity they don't take the whole case over. It would save me a lot of trouble." She pointed imperiously to the stove where the bottle was warming in a pan of water. She took the bottle from me and sucked heartily to test the temperature before she fed the baby. "You may open the windows, Helen."

Leela must have been listening at the door, for she took this as a signal to come in to prepare the dinner. In one hand she carried a long-necked chicken and in the other some curry-paste on a banana leaf. It was pretty, the golden paste on the shiny leaf, but the smell of it made me sick, for she cooked curry for us every day.

"Not curry again, Mary," protested Mrs. Lambert. "We can't have curry again tonight."

Leela held up the chicken like a trophy and I caught the

affronted look in its eyes. "Me I making new curry tonight, very nice. My mama showing me." She put the chicken and the curry-paste on the table and ranged beside them onions and garlic and smooth purple bringals.

"The very sight of that stuff is enough to put me off for good and all. I refuse to eat curry again tonight," declared Mrs. Lambert, "I simply couldn't eat it if the King of India himself curried it. Helen, why don't you try your hand at a bit of cooking?"

I retreated to the door. "I have never cooked a meal in my life. I can only make milk puddings."

"Can't you make even a simple little stew? There's nothing more becoming in a young girl than the ability to cook. When I was your age, my dear, I could run a house for twenty-five people and so economically. Look at Nancy. She can serve up the daintiest meals. Surely your mother showed you how to do a little plain cooking, Helen?"

"She was going to…."

Mrs. Lambert gasped as I began to cry. "There, there, I didn't mean to upset you. I thought you would be over it by now, more or less. My dear child…" She tried to put her arms about me, but I escaped her and ran into the garden.

It was three months since Mother died. Leela's child had been born. The cane was taller by a foot now and the syringa trees were dropping their berries in the grass, but time was of no accounting in my desperate need of her. There is a shrub that still reminds me of her. It is called Yesterday-Today-and-Tomorrow, for yesterday the flowers were white and today they are mauve and tomorrow they will be purple. They are flowers for the garden only, for they die as you touch them. She had planted a bush by the tank and it was blooming now.

What was the use of crying? I went to the gate and stood there until the tears dried on my face. Before me the canefields swept over the low hills to the ocean. There were Zulu girls resting in the field near the house. Tandazele had gone away, but I saw her image in every one of them. Had he forgotten? Had he already forgotten when he took me in his arms and cried through the night because Mother was dead?

I could see the broad band of the river, golden-brown, and on the other side of it the road, almost the same colour as the river; beyond, a virgin hill mysterious and dark. In my grandfather's day it was the stamping-ground of game, but now the white tick-birds perched on the backs of the cattle. Zetke could still go in and bring down a wild pig or a polecat. Natives hid there from the police, but Zetke said they were fools, for they could be hunted out in time. "If the police were after me I would not hide on the hill," he used to say, "I would go boldly through Durban and on to Zululand, across the Lebombo to Tongaland, for there I know of a man who is a powerful witch-doctor, a trainer of hyenas, and he would hide me." They were prophetic words. It was to Tongaland that he was exiled after the fire, far away from his family and the countryside he knew.

The road skirts the hill, leading to Westongate. To this day there are no more than fifty bungalows strung out along the beach front. They seem to have been erected hastily out of wood and iron or asbestos as though the tenants had not meant to stay long; yet some of them have been there for a lifetime. I could count the windows of Drew's Pride, sparkling like a fairy castle on its green hill across the valley. If I went up there for afternoon tea, I would be out of Mrs. Lambert's way for a few hours. There would be music, perhaps some news of Chris....

The land lay tamed beneath the sun. Only in the grass was there a slight movement as a stalk bent under the weight of a grasshopper. The canetops hung limp and unstirring and the palm-trees were stiff as cardboard against the sky. Then at the Farrells' homestead I saw natives moving about, their busyness an offence in that quietude.

Mrs. Lambert came outside and put her arm fondly about me. "I'm cooking Maryland chicken," she said. "What a nice change it will be. Will you like that, Helen?"

"Yes." I was pleased that she should be trying to make amends, but I moved away from her quickly for I could not bear those prying fingers on my body.

"There's one thing about you, Helen, you never let yourself get slovenly, although you take so little interest in things. Always nicely corseted. I'm afraid I'm inclined to let myself go...." Her sharp eyes had spotted the movement about the Farrells' homestead. "Good Heavens, what on earth is going on there?" She stared across the valley as though she wished she could stride over in one step to find out what was happening. "Get your father's binoculars, Helen."

She snatched the glasses from me, but she soon gave them up, for she could not focus them properly. From what I could make out the natives were moving the house.

"That can't be," said Mrs. Lambert. "Why don't you go and find out what is happening, Helen? It will pass the afternoon for you. I can't for the life of me think what they might be doing. A walk will do you good, you're getting plump from all the sitting around… and Leela's cooking." She laughed and squeezed my waist to show her goodwill.

"I was thinking of going up to Drew's Pride for tea."

"If they've noticed anything, they've probably gone over to the Farrells' to see for themselves what is happening," she said persuasively.

"Oh, all right then, I'll go. But I'm not walking, I'll go in the cart."

I shouted to Zetke to inspan. He had been whitewashing the shed and he was only too glad to lay aside his brush. Without waiting for an invitation he climbed into the back of the cart.

The Farrells were moving their house. When he saw this Zetke let out a wild yell of enthusiasm, but our arrival passed unnoticed in that activity. Natives ran backwards and forwards, manoeuvring the house on rollers behind a team of oxen. Mr. Drew and his three sons were there, all enjoying the diversion. Mr. Farrell alone was in deadly earnest. He had hold of a boy by the throat.

"For God's sake don't waste time throttling the labour," shouted Mr. Drew. "We'll need every one of them by the time we get this thing into position."

Mr. Farrell flung the boy aside and worked off his excitement by lashing the oxen. The natives chanted as they worked, led by a small, thin boy whom Zetke instantly pushed amongst the workers so that he himself could take over the job of chanter.

Mrs. Farrell was wheeling a pram savagely in an attempt to

get her baby to sleep. When she saw me she gave up and sat down on a tree-stump.

"It's a day for callers," she said, "You've just missed Mrs. Drew. The dust was too much for her."

I sat down next to her. "Mrs. Lambert sent me over to inquire how you are."

"We're feeling the heat, that's why we're moving the house. It's too much for Peter." She whisked off the net from the pram and I stared at the baby. He was pale, but his cheeks were rounded and there were dimples on his hands. Now for the first time I realised how ill our baby was, and I understood the look that Mrs. Lambert sometimes gave him, as though she estimated how much longer his life would last.

"We're moving the house to those fig-trees on the edge of the clearing," said Mrs. Farrell. "I said to Henry this morning, if you don't move the house today I'm leaving you and taking the children with me. So he sent a note over to the Drews to ask them to lend us some labour and their oxen. You could have knocked me over with a feather when they all came to help, and in such good spirits, you'd think it was a picnic. She took the girls back to Drew's Pride so that they would be out of the way, so good-natured." She drew her breath in sharply as the house swayed. "I thought for a moment it was going over."

The house had only two rooms, one built over the other in a separate storey. To attain the upper room, which was the bedroom, the Farrells ascended an iron ladder placed against the wall; four rungs from the top they swung themselves through the window into the bedroom. Not so long ago I had thought this a fascinating arrangement and part of the entertainment in visiting there had been a journey to the bedroom. Mr. Farrell was always talking about the staircase he was going to put in, but to the last that ladder remained against the roof. Whenever it rained the Farrells quarrelled bitterly and stories got about that Mrs. Farrell, who was stronger than her husband, beat him until he promised to build her another house. But she forgave him when the sun shone and the only change he ever made was to add a veranda, like a frill round the lower room, and this was used as sleeping-quarters when Mrs. Farrell's family came to visit. The girls did not achieve a bedroom until they married, but a sort of box was fixed up for Peter at the end of the veranda.

For all the sweating and chanting the house still stood about fifty yards from the trees and only five yards from its original position. It was destined to get no farther. There must have been a nest of puff-adders underneath it, for a boy caught one crawling up the side of the excavation and he had no sooner killed it than Mr. Drew saw another. He took a lunge at it with a stick, missed his footing and stepped on its tail. He howled in agony as it struck. The boys packed on to the snake and killed it.

Zetke emerged from the confusion. Mr. Drew allowed him to cut the wound and suck out the poison, but when he tried to use his medicine he was pushed away. It was then decided to put him in our cart and drive him to the doctor. In a matter of seconds the Drews had vanished from sight.

The dust remained suspended in the air for a while and then slowly settled so that the house perched on its rollers had a forlorn look of permanence. Most of the labour had melted away and Mr. Farrell was pessimistically measuring the distance to the trees.

"It's no good, we'll never get it there before nightfall," he reported to his wife. "I think the best plan would be to return it to the old place and try again tomorrow...."

There was nothing in the story that Mrs. Farrell laid about him with a stick, for all she did on receiving this news was to burst into tears. Even this comfort was denied her. The pig had got out of its sty and everybody had to help get him back again, for he was young and fast.

"He'll get out again," said Mr. Farrell with morose pride. "He's a jumper. I've built that fence up twice. It wouldn't surprise me if he could clear six feet."

Zetke was lurking in the break well out of sight, for it was obvious that nothing but hard work remained for those foolish enough to stay.

"Witchcraft," he said. "We come here in a cart, we are singing and even taking a puff or two from a dagga cigarette to get more strength and in a moment everything is gone." He must have had more than a puff at the dagga, for he leapt and sang all the way home. Instead of walking through the gate he sprang over it and Mrs. Lambert looked at him in astonishment.

"Is he drunk?"

"No, only excited. Mr. Drew got bitten by a puff-adder."

"My dear. I've been on tenterhooks waiting here. And where on earth is the cart?"

"Richard drove his father to Westongate in it because Mrs. Drew had already gone home in theirs. She couldn't stand the dust, they were moving their house to a cooler spot...."

"Moving their house? What next?"

Mrs. Lambert, overjoyed, made me tell her the story three times, but still she wasn't satisfied. If there had been a cart available she would have set off at once to hear everything again from Mrs. Farrell and then driven on to Drew's Pride. As it was she had to tear herself away from me to attend to the baby.

A flash of red showed on the hill. That would be the Drews' cart. I followed its passage through the cane, picking it out on the hills and losing it again as it disappeared into the low-lying cane. An old native was driving the cart. He gave me a note for Mrs. Lambert.

"Good grief," she said as she glanced through it, "what a calamity. Mrs. Drew does nothing but faint, she says. Look at the handwriting all up and down, she must be terribly upset. She says she would have sent Richard or George for me, but at a time like this she must have all her sons with her. She'll send the cart back in the morning, the horse is dead-beat and is that all right. I told your father I would be needed suddenly and now it's happened. I said to him only last night, 'John I don't mind a straightforward case for a few days and besides I've got my duty to Nancy.' But he said, 'You're the only one I can trust, Aggie.' After a bereavement like that how could I refuse?" She read the letter again. "I'll go up for a few hours. I don't like to do it, a child of sixteen. And so dreamy. Do you think you could feed him, Helen? If I could get Susie Farrell, but she'll have her hands full moving the house and they have their own baby when all is said and done...."

She sat thinking for such a long time that I said, "Shall I tell the Drews' boy to go?"

"No, don't do that. I'll have to go up, perhaps I'll even have to stay overnight. Nancy will be home from East Griqualand in a day or so. I was going to ask Mrs. Drew to have her for a few weeks and I might as well take this opportunity. It's too lonely here for Nancy. I'll go, Helen, and I'll be back first thing in the morning. Now write this down and remember everything depends on you. A feed every hour. Three teaspoonfuls of condensed milk in half-a-pint of boiled water and the merest dash of butter. Have you got that? Now don't give him too much at once, only a quarter of it and then heat it up again for the next feeds." She came close to me. "You've got to realise this, Helen, the little boy is very, very weak. I think it's one of the most depressing cases I've ever been on. Sometimes I think I'm going mad here, you know, you're so quiet, never a joke or a smile…. Now remember, if the baby shows the slightest sign of growing weaker during the night, send somebody for me straight away. But don't grow alarmed if he goes a little blue round the lips, that's only wind. Do you think you can manage for tonight, Helen?"

"I'll try."

She talked on and on, but at last she climbed on to the cart and sat up with the hatbox safely on her knees, one hand clasping her skirts so that they should not brush against the driver. Just as he started up the horse she looked down at the hatbox and was reminded of my clumsiness.

"Now, Helen, remember this. If you drop your little brother, you can't replace him, nor will you ever forgive yourself. If he lived he would grow up hump-backed or an imbecile or both. So be very, very careful."

After this warning, I didn't feel like picking up the baby, but Leela had no qualms. She put her own baby on the kitchen table and with careless confidence snuggled our baby against her breast.

"Him wanting drink. Him smelling my tits."

"You vulgar devil, put that baby down at once."

She put him into the crib and patted her breasts complacently, but she looked at me with respect as I studied the paper on which

I had written Mrs. Lambert's instructions. While I fed the baby she suckled her own child, the little Chanjaldi, in unspoken rivalry. Sowa came and nuzzled his sister away and she hung head downwards from Leela's lap while Sowa nursed. With her free hand, Leela felt in the pockets of Sowa's trousers and brought out a penny. Sowa tried to take it back from her, but she dropped it into her money bag, smiling at him all the time.

"Give him back his penny, Leela," I protested.

"I putting away. Bimeby him getting rich. Perian giving him penny when him drunk."

Sowa wandered off, his hands exploring his empty pockets. "You should have let him keep his penny. I'm sure he wanted to cry."

"Sowa not crying."

She put her baby on the kitchen table and went to the stove to prod the chicken that Mrs. Lambert had left frying in the pan. Both babies slept now and the kitchen was quiet except for the spatter of the fat.

"Bimeby your baby borning," said Leela, turning to face me.

"Be quiet, you bloody fool...."

"Can talking nice now, alla time old mama she shouting Leela..." She moved the pan to the side of the stove and sat at my feet. "Plenty time me giving flowers."

She did not touch me or look into my face, but remained quiet, entranced by prayer. Serenity spread outwards from her and poured over me, stilling the child within me. With a whisper of sound the little barefooted Sowa came into the room. He fumbled with his mother's blouse.

A door slammed and John rushed up the steps as though driven before a mighty wind. "Where's Mrs. L.? What's happened here?"

"She's gone to Drew's Pride for the night. They were moving the Farrells' house and Mr. Drew got bitten by a puff-adder. She had to go and give a hand."

"Old bitch. I'll sue her if anything happens to the baby. Of all the heartless things to do, to leave a little motherless baby...."

"I have everything written down. I know what to do."

"What's the stuff in the bottle?"

"Condensed milk and water and butter."

"No wonder the child is such a runt. Condensed milk and water. Why don't you give him cow's milk?"

"It's too strong for him, Mrs. Lambert says."

"He isn't getting on the way he should. Look, even Leela's kid has got more meat on it and they're not a fat race." He pinched poor little Chanjaldi's legs and gave Leela a predatory look. "You feed another one?"

"She's already feeding two. And besides, Mrs. Lambert says they grow up with funny ideas."

"Rot. If he drank from a goat would he bleat like a goat? If he drank from a cow would he grow horns?" Zetke had brought in some firewood and now John pounced on him. "I want a foster-mother for my child."

"There are no babies in our kraal. There is a terrible bewitch-ment and if the police would mind their own business we would have a smelling-out."… He had smoked more dagga and he was brave and bright-eyed. "I could get you a she-monkey out of the trees."

He fled, but he must have remembered what John had threat-ened to do to him, for the next day he sent a message by his father to say that he would be detained at his kraal for a few weeks to help with the cattle. It was nearly a year before we saw poor Zetke. The police found four dagga-plants in his mealie lands and he was sent to prison.

When Mrs. Lambert returned the next day she did not bring the hatbox and the cretonne bag with her and we knew at once that she did not mean to stay. She examined the baby, drank a cup of tea and promised to call in twice a week to see how he was getting on. I begged John to allow me to take the baby to Durban, but he was casting around for a strapping Zulu girl to act as wet-nurse and he put me off from day to day.

Sometimes I dreamed that he knew my secret and I would get out of bed in the middle of the night to corset myself. One night I saw that nothing would disguise the thickening of my body now, and I knew that I would have to go to Aunt Lucy at once.

The next morning, as soon as John had gone out on the lands, I told the umfaan to inspan the cart and I set off for the station. Leela sat beside me with the baby. The umfaan who had done the harnessing was unaccustomed to the job and he had bungled it. I had to keep getting down to straighten and tighten the straps. Just before we reached the bridge a strap gave way and I got down to put it right. There was the sound of galloping hooves behind us in the cane-break and John rode up.

"What the hell do you think you're doing?"

"I'm going to Aunt Lucy...."

"You're not taking him away. I've got a girl at the house now, waiting to feed him."

"John, I have to go to Durban."

It happened that this was one of the days that Mrs. Lambert came to visit the baby and we saw her driving down the break now. She caught sight of us and turned the horse. "So you're taking my advice, John," she said. "I can tell you it's a relief to me to know that he will be in good hands. I worry about him all the time." She lingered for a few minutes to tell me about Nancy's latest dress and before she drove away she gave me a thrust that left me speechless. "Mind you, I've been expecting for a long time to hear that you'd left Westongate, Helen. The number of girls I've known who have had to make a hurried visit to their aunts in the city...." Her eyes were malicious, but she was smiling at me and the effect was so horrible that Leela touched a lucky charm that her mother had given her to ward off the evil eye.

"What did the old bitch mean by that?" John asked.

Leela had begun to cry and suddenly he knew. I might have pitied him if I had not been so frightened.

He said, "Sometimes lately I've thought... But I couldn't bring myself to believe it...." He raised his riding-crop and cut me once across the face. He flung the crop far into the cane. "Turn round and go home."

I climbed on the cart. Leela, awkward with the baby in her

arms, wiped the blood from my face with a corner of her sari. John rode next to me and I saw that his hands were shaking and that he leaned from his horse to retch.

"Whose child is it?"

"I don't want to tell you."

"Whose child is it?"

"Chris Van der Westhuizen's."

For a moment he didn't recall the name and then he turned in the saddle to look up at Drew's Pride. "When? When do you think it will be born?"

"Two months…."

As he dismounted he kicked a dog from under his feet clean across the break into the cane. The Zulu girl who had been waiting at the gate sprang to her feet and when she saw my face she cried out and ran away. John shouted after her, but she disappeared into the cane.

He locked me in my room. I heard him throwing things about in his office, but afterwards he began to groan as though he were badly hurt. In the evening he unlocked my door.

He stood on the threshold with his face averted. "You're not going to Lucy. I'm not having her gloat over me for the rest of my life. I'll think of something. You stay in there until your face heals. I know a woman in Durban who might take you in."

It was quiet on the farm at this time of the year. The Indians' contracts were up and the barracks stood empty, waiting for the cutters. Only the despised Perian was not paid off. John kept him on because Leela knew about me. Those were long weeks of waiting. A scab formed over the cut on my face and hung there obstinately. When it peeled off John told me he would take me to Durban; we would catch the train at a siding ten miles down so that nobody should see me. But Leela and I had miscalculated and three weeks too soon on an April evening my pains began.

When he heard my murmuring he opened the door and pushed Leela into the room. She gave me a pill to chew. It must have been opium, for when I awoke my mind was still confused with dreams and I thought Mrs. Lambert was in the room with me. Her face dissolved and only Leela remained, her shadow big in the lamplight. I did not let her know that I was awake, for I was afraid of her. I knew of her loathing of childbirth and of the dhai who had blinded a woman with pepper. Tear a child from the living mother, fearful are the ghosts of those who die with the child unborn…. I was thirsty, but I knew she would not give me water.

She was coming towards me. I pushed her away, but I could not watch her all the time, for the pains were strong now and growing faster and faster. She bent over me again with a knife in her hand. I raised my legs and kicked her across the room. A few seconds later my son was born.

I knew now why she held the knife and I whispered, "I'm sorry, Leela."

She was chattering praises as she wiped the baby's eyes. "Plenty strong like mans. Plenty strong your baby." He roared so hard that I could scarcely hear what she said.

I slept and when I awoke John was sitting in the chair by the window.

"Give me a drink of water, John. She wouldn't give me water."

He held the cup for me while I drank. "Well, it's over, Helen. It's something to be forgotten."

"Where is my baby?"

"Lie still. Helen, you'll do yourself an injury."

"Where is my baby?"

"It's best for you not to see him. I'm going to write to this friend of mine to see if she can get him adopted. That's what Lucy did."

"I want to see him."

"No. I'll tell you what…. Lucy used to nurse a doll, it made her feel better and after a while she got over it completely. I'll bring your little brother to you. You can hold him."

"I want my own baby."

"Helen, you can start again. I'll forget about this and we'll be just the same as we always were. Nobody knows. You can make a good marriage, you're young and so pretty; you can easily get over this. The coolie woman will hold her tongue, I've paid her well. She wanted money for this and for that, purification and all sorts of tommy-rot, but I paid up and she is satisfied now."

"I must see him, John."

"No. You lie there and get well. Then forget it and start again."

"As Aunt Lucy did?"

"She was a fool. Lucy never had brains. She went wild after we got rid of Lambert. He was no good, as bad as this Dutchman of yours. I hope he's dead, shot through his..." He brought his son to me. "Here, nurse your little brother...."

I sat up and took the baby from him. "Bring my own baby to me."

"Helen, don't look like that, don't hurt him."

"You've killed my baby."

He moved towards me swiftly and I saw his fist coming down on my face.

Sunlight fell on the lace cloth on the dressing-table. It was a cloth worked in a design of whorls within squares and I remembered it from childhood. Mother had transferred it from a tea-cloth to this one. My mind seized on it and on the familiar room; the faded pink curtains and the marble clock that Aunt Lucy had given me.

I went on to the veranda. There was nobody in the house, but down at the barracks I heard a child screaming. It was Sowa, lying on his back and drumming the ground with his heels because his mother was feeding a White child. It was strange to me, a strong child who pulled like a calf at Leela's nipple. She smiled at me, but at the sight of him so close to her I felt a stirring of jealousy and went out of her room. I saw John walking down from the shed and I tried to hide myself in the cane, but he followed me.

He said, "You'd better get inside. Look at your nightdress. Get inside."

I shivered, for the trash underfoot was damp. The wind spilled big drops of dew from the canetops down my neck.

"Tell me...."

"He came round again, but he died during the night. Nobody knows, only that coolie woman and she thinks he died of weakness. I buried him with your mother; it's all right, I said a prayer over him. Now go inside and don't make a fool of yourself in front of the Mary. It wasn't your fault, don't mind so much. It was an accident. If anybody is to blame it's me. I got frightened of you, I thought you were going to hurt him. I know women are funny at a time like that. He fell beneath you, I wasn't quick enough. I was going to send for the doctor, but when she saw he was finished, the coolie woman said, 'Take the strong child, master.' I saw then how easy it would be."

I waited for him in my room and presently he brought the baby to me. "Nicholas Angus," he said, and when I shook my head, "It's the only chance for you now, Helen, and for me too." The child smelt of Leela.

Gradually my jealousy of Leela supplanted the remorse and terror I had felt at first. I used to spray eau-de-cologne on Nicky's blankets and pretend to Leela that I did not know she nursed him. I had nothing for him, I was as dry as old Basket.

I complained to John, but he said, "I'm paying her sixpence a time. You don't have to feel badly about it."

"He smells like a coolie. He'll never get rid of the smell."

"What about it? Bonemeal smells, but you're not too proud to eat sugar and to live on sugar-cane."

The yellow bag in which Leela carried her money was full of sixpences and sometimes she took them out to count them in front of me. As soon as I was strong enough I weaned him by taking him to Durban.

Chapter five

When Nicky was six months old we came back to Weston-gate and it seemed impossible that anybody would know that he was not John's son, for he was an Angus, a big hearty child. I took him with me to Mrs. Drew's birthday party. I put him into a beautiful little dress that Aunt Lucy had given him and I was careful of the flounces as Leela lifted him up to me. She climbed in at the back of the trap, for she was to watch him that evening.

The horse was going well and John was in a good humour. "You look your old self tonight, Helen." When I did not answer he put his arm across my shoulders. "Never mind. There was blame on both sides, and I acted for the best. You've made Nicky look grand, a bit fluffed up for a boy, but the ladies will like that."

"Aunt Lucy gave him the dress."

"That selfish old…. She should be here looking after the baby, give you a chance to become young again."

"She's frightened of the snakes."

"Snakes, my foot."

We were approaching Drew's Pride. The house loses its enchant-ment when you come close to it, for you are astounded by the effrontery of its architecture. Walter Drew was a sensible man and when he built the house he meant to escape the worst of the summers on wide verandas, but his wife was not content with sensible things. John never got over his scorn of the georgettes and laces with which she tricked herself out, and of the peacocks wandering about the garden. "Just like a coolie who has come into a bit of money," he said. But the peacocks were there through no fault of hers. Mr. Drew took them from Mr. Bannerjee in payment of a debt. He was a man of compromise.

He compromised with his wife over the house and the result was a structure of red brick with turrets and balconies on the upper floor. Downstairs there are spacious verandas that throw the house out of all balance; yet in spite of its pretentiousness it is comfortable. On summer nights, with the wide windows open, the rooms take to themselves the cooling sea-breezes, the scent of frangipanni and all the little sounds of night. But when the great winds beat in from the sea, the house stands warm behind its closed shutters, answering the storm with groans and sighs and sometimes with a shriek as a slate hurtles from the roof.

Richard Drew was on the terrace. We caught him throwing a pebble at one of the peacocks. The scream it gave brought Mrs. Lambert to its defence.

"Shame on you, Richard," she cried archly. "Fancy throwing stones at birds, a grown-up young man."

"Was he tormenting the peacocks again?" said Mrs. Drew. "You're to leave them alone, Richard." She came forward in a great fluster to greet us. "Oh, how glad I am that you could come. I often feel so guilty, I never seem to be able to call on you as often as I would like...."

Somewhere in the garden Nancy was laughing. Mrs. Lambert tried to take Nicky from me. "Why, the little darling. I'm glad I came tonight, just for the opportunity of seeing him again. I'm afraid I'm neglecting my duty. I should be with my patient, but her mother kindly consented to sit with her tonight. Let me see my little boy. What strides he has made to be sure. A few months ago he was a bag of bones and look at him now. I always say there's nothing like condensed milk and water, but you must have that touch of butter, it makes all the difference." I felt a sudden glow of affection for her, she had noticed nothing; but still I kept the baby in my arms.

"How are the puff-adders, Walter?" John was roaring at Mr. Drew.

"Come inside, come inside," said Mrs. Drew. She seized a huge cane fan as we followed her into the sitting-room and the draught from it lifted the down on Nicky's head. "What a terrible time we had, John. Show them your leg, Walter."

Mr. Drew pulled up his trouser leg to show us the puce marks left from the snake-bite. "It's nothing now," he said apologetically.

"But you should have seen it," countered Mrs. Lambert. "Swollen up like a bag of blue jelly. And Mrs. Drew, she fell down in a faint every time the word snake was mentioned."

"I've a perfect horror of them," murmured Mrs. Drew.

"Like Aunt Lucy." I sat down on the sofa and arranged Nicky's dress to the best advantage, but nobody commented on it.

"My cousin Angelica was the same," said Mrs. Lambert. "She had a horror of snakes and it was just like a premonition…."

Mrs. Drew must have heard about Cousin Angelica before. She hid behind the cane fan while she whispered to me.

"Give the baby to your Mary and go and look for Nancy and the boys. They're somewhere in the garden."

"I'll wait until he goes to sleep. He's used to me, he might start crying."

"Nobody will hear him upstairs. Ah, here comes Nancy now. You two must play a duet."

Nancy stood in the doorway, making the most of her dimples. She wore such a pretty dress that Mrs. Lambert abandoned her Cousin Angelica to draw my attention to it.

"Come in and let Helen see the dress, Nancy. Do you like it, Helen?"

"Yes. Yes, it's pretty. I'll take Nicky upstairs now."

"Here, give him to me, Helen," said Mrs. Lambert. "You can stay down here with the young people."

The tawny sunset light filled her eyes and softened her face above the rigid black silk that she always wore. She stood with her arms outstretched. The evening breeze brawling into the room caught up the edges of her skirt and whisked her hair about so that for a moment she had the appearance of a dancer. Sheets of music from the top of the piano fluttered to the floor.

"Goodness, wasn't that sudden?" exclaimed Mrs. Drew.

Mrs. Lambert dropped her hands to her sides. "You're just as dreamy as ever, Helen. Sitting there, simply staring at a person. I asked you to let me hold the baby."

"I'll take him upstairs. He has become so used to me...."

Leela padded behind us when we went upstairs. Mrs. Lambert arranged a nest of pillows for Nicky on the bed and almost snatched him from my arms, staring at him for a long time before she put him down. She waited in the room while I patted him to sleep.

"I see you've still got that Mary," she said as we went down stairs again. "I don't trust Indians. I've heard some queer tales about them in my time. They'll cast a spell over you. I always burn any hair I cut off and all my nail clippings. Let them get hold of those and there's no knowing what they'll do. You should see the old man they've got here, sits on his crossed legs all day and not a stroke of work out of him. Casting spells, no doubt. The others must be frightened of him. They do all his work and feed him." She pushed me before her into the sitting-room. "I've just been telling Helen about this old fellow you've got here, Stella, this Indian."

"Oh, the Yogi."

"Leela told me all about him," I said. "She says that he goes to India every night and walks about the streets of Madras and then the next morning he can tell them everything that's been going on...."

"Good Heavens," said Mrs. Lambert.

"He's a holy man. Leela says that if he wants to he can raise himself up and float above the ground."

"It doesn't sound healthy to me," said Mrs. Lambert. "To tell you the truth, I never trust any of them. My late husband always used to say they'd steal the eyebrows off your head if you didn't watch them." She seemed even more anxious to talk than usual and her face was alive with an intelligence that frightened me. Her eyes were on me all the time, probing me, telling me that she knew.

Richard crossed the room to me. The place was full of people now and I could hear John's voice as he bellowed at Mr. Farrell.

"I'm sure my father is going to start an argument," I said.

"And I'm sure Nancy is going to play 'The Blue Danube'. She has been practising for weeks. Tum-tum-tum-tum. It's so long since I saw you that it's almost as good as talking to a strange girl." His cool, fair skin shone in the light as he smiled at me.

He was twenty, an uneasy imitation of his father. Both George and Eric, his younger brothers, in turn copied him so that the whole family was stamped with the same manner; a mixture of poise and boisterousness. They were never bored by the parties, the picnics and the teas over which their mother presided.

I said, "I have to look after the baby…."

"We've been having some fun. We tied a string to a dead mamba's tail and pulled it across the break when Farrell was passing and do you know he ran for his life."

"How could you? Grown-up young men." I mimicked Mrs. Lambert.

"That's not all. You know old Ramsammy. He lives on the Farrells' place now and he reported Eric to the police for shooting across his gardens, so we took his scarecrow down and made him stand in the garden for an hour. There wasn't much difference between him and the scarecrow."

"He's very old, one of the Indians my grandfather indentured in 1860."

"You'd have laughed all right if you'd been there."

"Was Nancy there?"

"Heavens, no. Mama never lets her out of her sight."

"Everybody thinks she has grown very pretty."

"She has too. I want you for my partner tonight. Give me your programme."

"I shouldn't dance, I'm still in mourning. Everybody would be horrified."

"No, they wouldn't. Before you came everybody agreed that you should dance, that it was a shame that you had had your youth stolen from you…."

Nancy skipped up to me and held her hands out. "We're to play our duet. You don't mind if I take her from you Dickie?" She pulled me to my feet.

"I haven't practised for ages."

"Oh, how could you ever forget 'Beautiful Isle of the Sea'? We'll play that. Everybody has heard it only a thousand times."

I sat down at the piano with her. We began to play, Mrs. Drew beating time with the fan.

"You're going too slowly," said Nancy out of the side of her mouth, "Two, three, four…"

"You'd better slow down."

"This is awful. As long as we finish together." She giggled and we broke down. The second time we got through the piece so successfully that Nancy was all for playing another duet; but Leela was at the door, beckoning me.

"You play 'The Blue Danube', Nancy. I'll see what the girl wants."

"Who told you about 'The Blue Danube'? I was saving it as a surprise for later on, but I might as well play it now."

I followed Leela into the hall. "I can't making Nicky sleeping," she said.

I tried to nurse Nicky to sleep, but he screamed the louder. Peter's nurse carried her charge out of the room, grumbling because he had been woken up. Nancy had finished playing "The Blue Danube" and now Mr. Farrell was singing "When the fields are white with daisies I'll return…." I put Nicky on the bed and he screamed as though he was in a fit.

Richard came to the door. "They're going to start dancing in a few minutes as soon as they can shut Farrell up."

"The baby won't stop crying."

"What's the girl for?"

"She can't make him stop either."

"Well hurry, or I'll have to ask Nancy; she hasn't filled her programme yet and my mother is dropping hints."

Leela and I searched Nicky for pins and for bites. There was not a mark on him. He had already drunk every drop of the milk in his bottle and even the calm Leela began to look wild-eyed. Having achieved this, he snuggled into my arms and went to sleep.

I heard Mrs. Lambert coming up the stairs, marking each tread with a sighing grunt. I put Nicky on the bed and tiptoed to the door, but she was there before me.

"Richard asked me to come up and take charge of the baby. I see it isn't necessary."

"He has only just gone off."

She said softly, "My dear, I haven't made a mistake, have I?" Her voice was breathy with excitement. "I looked after your mother's baby for three months, remember. I can recall his every feature. You'd better tell me about it, Helen. She knows something about it." She pointed at Leela, who cried out sharply and hid her face in her sari. "I knew it in a flash, while you were sitting downstairs on that sofa with him. I thought, she looks like a proud young mother. I almost said it aloud. What happened, Helen? You, what happened to the master's baby?" We would not answer her. "I won't say I blame you, Helen, or your father, this is a bitter world for a girl who goes wrong. There, sit down, you've gone as pale as a ghost. You'd better not come downstairs for a while. I'll tell them you don't feel well, shall I?" She tore up my programme and rustled the pieces in her hands. "I knew all along your little brother couldn't live, I knew it the minute he was born. He was too weak…."

The dancing had started downstairs. I whispered, "Go away now. Please go away."

Chapter six

We had two good seasons after Nicky was born. The cane was free of disease, there were few rats and no high winds. The returns from the mill were the best we had ever had, even John admitted that. Soaking rains fell throughout the summer and long before the harvest the cane stood fourteen feet high, so dazzling that I often longed to see the cutters in, for I was tired of the endless green. John, too, found something to grumble about. The weeds kept pace with the cane and he had six gangs of girls hoeing every day.

The smell of guavas was everywhere that second summer. They rotted beneath the trees, no matter how fast we picked them. We had guavas with every meal and I made dozens of bottles of jam. Indians selling vegetables in Westongate gave away avocado pears and paw-paws with each order, glad to be rid of them. The amatingulus ripened early and the hedges on the banks of the ravine were red with fruit long before the cool weather came. The kaffirboom were thick with leaves and beneath them there was a perpetual rain from the spitting-bugs that infested them.

When Nicky was bathed and put under his mosquito net, I would sit beneath the flamboyant tree watching the break for Richard

Drew. He had been away on active service for more than a year and now he was home on leave. Every afternoon he rode out of his way to pass our gate and to avoid Nicky I met him there. The moment Nicky heard our voices in the garden, he trotted out and climbed on my knee. He persecuted Richard.

I remember one lovely afternoon that March. The break was in shadow, but the hills were still glowing as we walked slowly hand-in-hand, stopping to allow the horse to crop the grass growing between the ruts.

We stood at the bottom of the hill and looked up at Drew's Pride. "I wish we could live up there all alone," said Richard. "You could have a jade-green couch in your sitting-room and lie there looking across the sea. I'd make a bright red harness for your little brother and tie him up in the hall when he came to visit...." He became suddenly serious. "Helen, I've been wanting to tell you something ever since I came back. I saw Chris. Don't look at me as if I were speaking about somebody dead.... Haven't you forgotten him yet?"

"Yes. I never think of him from one month's end to the other."

"Then why are you crying?"

I told him the truth. "Because when you spoke about him, I remembered the way I used to feel. I've changed so much."

"He was wounded and taken prisoner. They're shipping him off to Ceylon...."

"I'm sorry."

"I was sorry too when I saw him."

"Was he badly hurt?"

"No. But he's considered quite a dangerous customer.... Does this make any difference to you?"

"No."

We walked back and the horse pulled against him all the way, put out at having been turned from its stable. The tiny burrs of blackjacks stuck to the hem of my skirt and Richard bent to pick them off one by one. "Helen, tomorrow at the picnic you must try and shake off your confounded little brother. I'll get rid of Eric and George...."

"And Nancy?"

"Even Nancy."

"We can pick some amatingulus and I'll make some jelly. Zetke says he saw a buck's spoor on the hill and John is going to lend him the rifle. We'll have amatingulu jelly with the venison and you may come to supper."

It was not until I tucked Nicky up that I wept for Chris. There was no moon that night and Drew's Pride was a jewel on the hill. Often John stripped a piece of cane to show me the red stripe at the core; from the outside the cane seemed healthy. I knew as I looked at the lights across the valley that there was in me too an inward decay.

The next morning I wore my new dress, although it was too smart for a picnic. John laughed when I came in to breakfast.

"Good God, why are you done up like a coolie Christmas at this time of the day?"

"We're going for a picnic." I tried Nicky with a spoonful of paw-paw, but he shut his lips firmly and when I forced the spoon between his teeth, two big tears like glycerine rolled down his cheeks.

"A picnic, hey? Old Mother Lambert tried to drag me into it, but I made short work of her. Guavas." He picked up the dish of fruit from the centre of the table. "Take these away, Mary."

Serya ran into the dining-room. She had taken Leela's place, but she had none of Leela's calm. She was fat and she panted while she waited on John, for she lived in terror of him. Leela owned a market garden now on the other side of the river and never a day passed that she didn't try to sell something to me before going the rounds of Westongate. At this hour we always heard the squeaking of her baskets as she came up the pathway.

"Hell, look who's here," John said now.

Leela swung her baskets from her shoulders and sat on the step. "Cabbage, ma."

"Go away, Leela," said John, "We don't want anything today."

"Cauliflower, ma."

"Will you go away?"

"Beans, ma."

"No," shouted John.

"Pineapple, ma."

"Leela, we don't want anything today."

"Turnips, ma." This time John was silent. "Carrots, ma."

"She has gone through everything in the basket," said John. "If she doesn't go away now, I'll kick her off the place."

Leela started from the beginning. "Cabbage, ma." Now Nicky climbed down from his chair and ran to her. He put his hands through her greasy hair, he tried to pull the jewels from her nostrils. "You liking banana, Nicky?" she asked affectionately. She peeled a banana and he gobbled it up before I could stop him.

"Give me a cauliflower, Leela." I gave the money to her and she put the coin complacently into her bag. She took up her yoke again and trotted down the pathway with swinging baskets.

"You shouldn't give in like that." John poured vinegar over an avocado pear. "They know if they keep at you long enough they'll get something out of you."

I wiped Nicky's hands and face before I put him back in his chair. "They're having a hard time of it with this glut. They can just about scrape enough money together to buy rice."

"Serves them right. They should have stayed here. They're too independent, that crowd. They got plenty of rice when they were working here, and they weren't worth it."

I tried to get Nicky to eat a piece of bread and butter, but he wouldn't touch it. "He doesn't seem to fancy anything this morning."

"You're making a real namby-pamby out of him. Even, the way you dress him. Little Lord Fauntleroy." He reached for another avocado.

I said tartly, "I read the other day that one avocado is equal to a pound of steak. At that rate, you've had three pounds of steak already."

"And I haven't started yet." He raised his voice. "Serya, bacon and eggs."

He gave a piece of bacon to Nicky, but I took it away. "I wouldn't let him eat a thing that woman cooked. She's so filthy even the Indians look down on her. She's the dirtiest thing I ever saw and I've given her notice. Guess what I caught her doing the other day?"

John ate more slowly. "What?"

"It was when Mrs. Drew came to tea. I went into the kitchen and there was Serya with a tin of condensed milk, blowing down one hole to make the milk come faster out of the other. Think of the betel-nut she chews. That's why I had black tea."

"You might have told me."

"It would have looked funny with Mrs. Drew here. She knows you always take milk."

"Oh, I see. You didn't want your future mother-in-law to know what a bad housekeeper you are, no fresh milk in the house." He was feeding Nicky and the perverse child ate everything he offered. "I've reared Nicky," he exulted.

"Well, why don't you look after him today? I'd much rather go to the picnic by myself."

"I know what you're thinking about. Now you mind your p's and q's, young lady. You don't want to go lolling around with boys this weather, not with your nature." He added hastily, "Don't think I'm up against Richard. Nothing would please me more.... But you don't want to be too free and easy." He looked through the window, contemplating the Drews' shining acres with satisfaction. "Hasn't he given you any..." He had almost said hope, but he caught himself in time. ".... any idea of what his plans are yet?"

Serya ran into the room, puffing with excitement. "Those peoples coming."

The cart was already at the gate. Mrs. Lambert was on the front seat with Mrs. Drew and Eric. Nancy sat between Richard and George at the back. Her bosom rose with the promise of the majestic fat that has since encompassed her, and it was impossible to trace the skeleton beneath her gleaming skin, for where there should have been the outlines of bones at her jaws and wrists and ankles there were creases and dimples. Even when she frowned dimples shot into her forehead. She frowned now because I wore my new dress. -

"Surely you're not wearing your best dress on a picnic, Helen?"

"It's not my best dress."

"I thought it was."

Richard made a place for me next to him. Had Zetke seen John then he would surely have named him Ox for his mildness.

"Take the Mary with you, Helen; she can keep an eye on Nicky."

Eric had let the horse go. He took his time about pulling it up, for it is not often that one sees a fat Indian woman running at top speed. Serya's ankles were so thin that it was a wonder they didn't snap off with her weight. John waved to us almost as though he blessed us. The dreadful howling of the dogs followed us. We had lost one from snake-bite that year and we were keeping them on the chain until the weather cooled.

"Always reminds me of a death when I hear dogs howl," said Mrs. Lambert, "I remember a case I was on once. There was this lonely farm…"

"To be well-dressed is to be suitably dressed," said Nancy.

I leaned against Richard and smoothed my skirt over my knee. There had been rain during the night and I could smell it in the earth warming beneath the sun. A cloud of blue finches flew up beneath the horse's hooves and settled on the canetops.

Nancy forgot my silk dress.

"Faster, faster," she cried, clapping her hands.

Snake-lilies were blooming along the river bank, massed yellow and red. Their beauty is evil and I told Serya to keep Nicky away from them and from the kaffirboom.

"You are an old hen," said Nancy.

"Helen is right," said Mrs. Lambert gloomily. "One drop of moisture from a spitting-bug is enough to blind you and the pollen from those snake-lilies gives you sore eyes. If I were you, Helen, I wouldn't let him out of my sight."

Richard called out to me. "Come on, we're going to play cricket. You can be on my side, Helen."

The Farrells had arrived and Mrs. Farrell was already bowling to her husband. He fell on the stumps, but he was given another chance, for it was discovered that Mrs. Farrell had no right to be bowling—she was on his side. There was no languor in us despite the heat. It had become a matter of life and death to get Mr. Farrell out, for he was hitting the ball so far that we spent most of the time looking for it. Nicky tried to join in the game, but he was knocked over and after that he sat on a little wooden box to which he had taken a fancy. Serya, to amuse him, made a wreath of yellow and purple daisies, but I wore it.

We waited until Nicky had fallen asleep before we began picking amatingulus. I didn't want him to go near the hedges because we were likely to come across a mamba at that time of the year. The fruit had been spoiled by birds and some of us decided to walk to Awetuli and try our luck there. We cut through the cane to avoid scrambling over the brush alongside the river. The heat was at its fiercest in the break and Nancy and I lagged far behind the boys. We rested on a hilltop where the cane was not high enough to shut off the breeze from the sea. Below us lay the Indians' huts, little places of tin thatched with banana leaves or grass, some of them so far out of plumb that they looked as though they had been dealt a blow; yet the market gardens surrounding them were laid out with precision. Leela came out of her hut. Her voice sounded clearly through the stillness, "Ba, ba." A few fowls rushed for the handful of mealies she flung to them and she drove them into their coop.

"It must be getting late," I said. "We'll have to hurry, Nancy."

Leela, with a lethargic movement, unknotted the corner of her sari and took a letter out. She tore it across and across. The wind pounced on the fragments and carried them to the water's edge.

I smartened my pace. The trash beneath the cane rustled with the movements of surreptitious creatures and we came upon a cane-snake so drowsy from the sunshine that it remained festooned on the bank in spite of our approach. I would have passed it, but Nancy threw a clod of earth to make it move. She missed by yards.

"Oh, leave it," I said impatiently. "They're harmless. Look, I could touch it." I put out my hand. The snake lifted its head and for a second I saw its quiet eyes. Then swifter than a lizard it flashed into the cane.

"Let's go back," said Nancy.

"We've come so far, we might as well go on."

"I'm not going on, I won't...." She began to cry.

"Wait here then and I'll go and tell the others."

I lifted my skirts and ran down the break, shouting for the boys. They were near the ravine before I caught up with them.

"Nancy wants to go back, she's crying...."

The boys grinned. Eric punched Richard in the chest. "You couldn't plan a thing like this. We'll go back with her. Helen, you and Richard can get the amatingulus. Do you think you can carry the baskets back?"

George considered this so funny that he subsided on to the bank, covering his head clownishly with a basket; but Eric was already away, yelling like a Zulu. Richard took the basket from his brother's head and propelled him down the break.

"Nancy will sulk," I said. "I should have gone back with her."

He looked at me, smiling. "Nancy won't sulk with me."

"She's in love with you."

He was holding the baskets, one in each hand, as though they were laden. "Chris is still in love with you."

"I don't care," I shouted.

He laughed. "No need to yell about it. Come on, let's hurry and get the amatingulus, or your reputation will be ruined."

We passed through mature cane, the tops teasing our faces. Rats and lizards scurried before the sound of our feet and I began to sing, to frighten any lazy snake that might lie in our path. The cane grows thick here in greasy unmanageable soil. Richard broke off a stick and gave half to me. It was firm, and sparkling with juice, I remember, too sweet for his taste. He threw away the section that he had stripped.

I followed him down the steep steps cut into the side of the ravine and waited on the narrow bridge while he gathered the amatingulus on the slopes. He filled only one basket.

"The stuff is not worth picking," he said. "It's too early in the season." He stretched himself beside me on the bridge. "Have you ever been down there, Helen? It's beautiful. Come down with me now. We could have a swim in the pool." I spat out the last of the pith from my sugar-cane and watched it float lightly on the air before it settled into the intricate whorls of the pool. "Helen, come down for a swim with me."

"And die of bilharzia."

"Nancy would."

"Damn Nancy."

I sprang up, but he pulled me down on the boards beside him, wrestling with me. The empty basket went spinning into the ravine. With sudden exuberance I matched my strength against his.

"Richard, we'll roll off the bridge."

He clung to me in an ecstasy of laughter. The sky brightened with sunset and we saw the tick-birds flying to roost, but we stayed on the bridge. Awetuli was in shadow. Frogs beneath the bridge were singing with little notes that rolled and turned and jumped.

"I'm going now, Richard, it's so late."

"Stay a little while longer, Helen. I wish we could stay here forever."

The pins had come out of my hair. I searched distractedly on the boards for them. "I'm so untidy. Mrs. Lambert will notice. And only one basket ..."

"I'll go down and get the other one."

"It's too dark down there, you'll never find it. We'll have to make up a story as we go along."

"It doesn't matter. Nobody will say anything...." He hesitated. "Nobody will say anything when we tell them we're going to be married." He turned to me with astonished tenderness. "Here ... on this bridge.... I wasn't sure before, Helen, but you've forgotten Chris. You've forgotten him, haven't you?"

I answered him sadly, "Yes, I've forgotten him."

Chapter seven

Nicky's little wooden box lay forlornly in the middle of the field, kicked over by some careless foot. I could see only Serya in the clearing, walking about as though she were looking for a pocket-handkerchief. She got down on her hands and knees to peer behind some bushes and then stood on tiptoe to look into the trees.

"What's she doing?" I said. "It looks as though Nicky has hidden away from her."

"And it looks as if everybody else has gone home. Old Lambert must have got annoyed."

There was no anxiety in me and I walked sedately beside Richard, giving him a hand with the basket. I had eaten some of the amatingulus and my lips were sticky from the milk. Richard rubbed the grey flecks off my mouth with his handkerchief, and smoothed my hair. Serya was watching us now. As we walked down the slope towards her she retreated, pulling her sari across her face.

"Where is Nicky?"

She answered me in Hindustani. Richard, with leisurely movements, put the basket on the cart.

I said, "I think Nicky is lost," but there was no conviction in my voice.

Alertness subtly tensed his body, but his voice was still casual. "He won't be far off. Where are the others?"

"Looking for him, I think."

"Here comes Zetke," said Richard, and the alertness pervaded his voice now.

"I have run to the house, but he is not there," said Zetke.

He had command of his breath, but there was the sheen of sweat on his body and a faint tremor in his muscles that told of a mighty effort. "This is the one who knows where he is." He raised his stick and advanced on Serya. "What have you done with the boy?"

I waited for the stick to come down on her head, but Richard caught Zetke's arm. "Stop that. Come along with me and we'll look along the breaks."

"He couldn't have gone towards Awetuli, we would have seen him," I said, "and the only other break leads to the house."

"He was in the break. Look, here is his footprint." Zetke carefully traced for us the shadowy imprint that Nicky had made; but still I didn't believe that he had gone that way. I began to look about aimlessly as Serya had done.

Cattle bound for the kraal grazed with the horses along the river-bank. They raised their heads to stare at the bush bordering the river and I ran forward, ready to scold and shake Nicky for giving us such a fright.

Mrs. Drew came quietly out of the bush. When she saw me she began to cry. "I can't find him anywhere, Helen. I called and called him...."

"Where are the others? Perhaps they've found him."

"No. Mrs. Lambert and Nancy went home more than an hour ago. She was furious with you. George has gone further down the river to look for Nicky and Eric is at the coolie huts.... Here he comes back now."

Eric splashed across the drift. "They haven't seen him," he shouted.

"Come on," said Richard, "We'd better find him before it gets really dark." He waited for George, who was running up from the river-bank. "See anything?"

"Not a sign."

Mrs. Drew and I were left together in the clearing. Serya had sneaked away and she was already crossing the drift, holding her skirts above her plump knees, for the water was high.

"Let her go," said Mrs. Drew. "She's useless. She won't even talk English. It's all her fault. She fell asleep…. He kept asking where you had gone, Helen."

I looked towards the canefields. The threat of night lay in their purple hollows and in the fading sky. It would be better if he had gone that way and not towards the river.

"He was sitting on his little box," said Mrs. Drew rapidly. "I tied his bottle of milk to his belt so that he could have a drink whenever he wanted it and then I told him to sit there until you came back. We all went for a walk to the beach to gather shells. I couldn't very well take him with me, could I ?" She began to cry again. "I kept turning round to wave to him. The Mary was sitting near him then, making another garland. When I came back she was lying asleep under a bush and he was nowhere to be seen. Everybody began to pack up and go. It was some time before we realised he was lost. He wanted you, Helen."

"He couldn't have followed me, we should have seen him."

"I don't know. Mrs. Lambert kept showing him the direction you had gone in. I remember her saying, 'Naughty Helen went along there, she's run away from poor Nicky….'"

"Why didn't you tell us this before?" I said savagely.

I ran back along the break to Awetuli, expecting to see him at each turn; but there was nothing there except a likkewaan, scuttling for the river. I stood on the bridge at Awetuli and called his name. My voice frightened the birds settling down for the night and they rose up out of the trees to be lost in the gloom almost as I saw them. I heard a distant shout and I began to climb down into the ravine, but Richard and George came on to the bridge before I had gone halfway down.

"There's somebody down here," I called, "Come down quickly."

They joined me and we stood there shouting, but now there was no answer. "You must have imagined it," said Richard, "or perhaps you heard one of us calling in the break. There isn't a sign of him except that one footprint. We'd better get back to the house for lanterns." He pulled me up the steps to the cart waiting in the break.

We drove home silently. There was still a flicker of hope in me, but it went when I saw John standing alone at the gate. I sprang down from the cart and faced him.

"Nicky is lost."

He came for me head down, like a dagga-mad native. Richard and George and Zetke pulled him from me. Mrs. Drew fainted. Richard carried her into the house and when she revived he sent her home with Eric.

"You'd better go with her, Helen. Eric can organise a party there and get word to the police. I'm taking a party from here and working up the river. George has gone over to the Farrels and they can work down from there to meet us. Your father is going to Awetuli."

"I'll stay here, he might still come home."

The fire-bell was clanging. Indians and natives jostled each other in the yard, Zetke was lighting a row of lanterns.

John came towards us. "We're going to look for him now. You're to stay here and if he is found, give three clangs on the bell, a pause and another three clangs. I'm leaving three coolies to ring the bell. See they don't stop. It's possible that he will make for the noise."

They went away. I searched the house and the shed, thinking he might have hidden away and fallen asleep as Peter Farrell had once done. The fire-bells on the other farms were answering ours. He would hear the noise and come towards it. He would surely come towards the noise.

Light. I lit every lamp in the house and hung lanterns in the trees. At each corner of the garden I buried a pot in the ground and put a lighted candle into it. The candle threw up a glow that could be seen from a long distance. Would he make for the lights? Hope was strong in me at first and every minute I looked down the break for the lights that would mean he was found; but by midnight nobody had returned from the search. The Indians waiting to take their turn at the bell had played cards at first, but now they were asleep. The man on duty leaned languidly against the trunk of the flamboyant as he struck the iron. Ours was the only bell ringing now.

There were mambas and pythons and puff-adders in the cane, the river was deep…. The fire-bell stopped ringing. My whole body flushed with hope. They had seen him, he was at the gate. I snatched up a lantern and ran into the garden. The Indian had fallen asleep against the tree-trunk. I seized him by the hair and he awoke with a scream. I took up the hammer and beat at the iron until I could no longer stand. None of the Indians slept after that, for they were afraid of me.

The night was almost gone and still he had not been found. I plunged into the cane, shrieking for him. I smashed the sticks and trampled them and then for a long time I lay still. A snake crawled over my legs and I hoped that it would bite me and that I should die, but it rustled into the trash.

In the dawn I went back to the house. Perhaps he had come home while I was away. He might have climbed into his bed; but his bed was empty. I searched the rooms again, moving all the furniture away from the walls. I went through the shed and through every room in the barracks.

"Have you hidden him?" I cried. "Have you bewitched him?" The women cowered away from me while I shook out their bed-clothes and looked into their boxes. I set out for Drew's Pride to search the barracks there and then I meant to go to the huts across the river, for I thought that the Zulus or Indians had taken him for a sacrifice; but I turned back, thinking that even yet he might hear the bell, and coming home, find me gone. Again I shrieked his name across the canefields. The Indians were silent, but the Zulu women sent up a cry of terror.

Even Leela did not go out with her baskets that day. She stayed with me until John came home at dusk. He stood in the doorway of the dining-room, looking at me dully.

"We've finished searching this side of the river. We dragged the pool beneath the falls. Nothing. I've put the cutters in, starting from the river, I'm sacrificing the lot. Drew and Farrell are doing the same."

"Richard says that he would walk in a circle."

"Zetke thinks that he has gone across the river, but you can't trust what he says. He had the bones thrown by the witchdoctor. That's all right for finding cattle, I told him."

"What does Zetke say?"

"It seems far-fetched, but he says he traced him to the spot where he turned in from the break, and to some stepping-stones across the river about five miles down. He says he is on the hill." He rested his head on the table. "Time is so important, Helen, but none of us can go on tonight. Zetke's got fever and I'm finished, I've got to sleep...."

I set the Indians to striking the bell again, I lit the lanterns and candles. Then I went in search of Zetke. I found him in the shed, huddled into a blanket.

"Wake up, Zetke, we must find my son."

He sat up, shivering in his blanket. "I have walked a day and a night. Now I have fever."

"You who are strong. Zetke, come with me to find my little son."

"Where is your father, the Buffalo?"

"He, too, is a weakling. Smoke some of your dagga and that will make you strong."

"No. Do you want me to die?"

"Then give me some for my father."

He gave a little calabash to me. "Tell the police and see what happens to you when I come out of prison. And be careful, this is not snuff. He must mix it with tobacco. There is enough for two men."

I awoke John and made him eat some of the food Leela had cooked. He would have fallen asleep again, but I put the dagga cigarette between his lips.

"Smoke this. It will wake you up and we'll go on the hill and search for Nicky."

"Dagga." He spat into his hand.

"Smoke it. It's doing you good already. Smoke it, John. Hours count now. You've got all the rest of your life to sleep."

He puffed fastidiously at the funnel of paper. The dagga had no effect on him at first, except to make him cough. He put the cigarette down, swearing as he wiped his eyes.

"Filthy stuff." But the drug had begun its work and his body tautened. He smoked avidly now.

We crossed the river and the road and made our way up the hill along a narrow path. I remembered to put a stone on the good-luck cairn when we passed it. We went slowly, for we stopped often to call for Nicky. Our voice cast a spell over the hillside and nothing moved as we listened. The path had been forced through tall trees between which bushes grew in a tangled mass and not even the whisper of the breeze penetrated here.

John said, "Look, the moon is rising, he'll be able to see his way now."

"That's lightning, not the moon."

When we reached the top of the hill we sat down to rest. The dagga had made John sick and he bowed his head. I could see the grey in his hair. An owl floated noiselessly over him, a part of the shadows sprawling before us in the light of the lantern. We were so quiet that we could hear some movement in the undergrowth now, the rustling of a leaf beneath a cautious foot. I put my hand on John's arm and he lifted his head to listen. We heard nothing but the forsaken hooting of the owl. John called out and we heard the step again, nearer this time.

"We were mad to come up here," John whispered. "Every damned criminal for miles around hides in this bush." He raised his voice and spoke in Zulu. "My son is lost. He may be on this hill. If you find him we will give you money and hide you from the police."

A tall bearded man stepped out of the shadows. I did not know him, though our eyes met briefly.

He said, "Helen. You showed them my letter," I knew that deep voice and I would have gone to him, but John gripped my arm.

"I had no letter from you, Chris."

"I have been hiding in Awetuli, but I had to get out last night. I thought you had given me away when I saw the lights and heard the bells ringing. I gave a letter to the coolie woman. I wanted food and clothes and money."

"I would have brought them, Chris."

"Well, it's too late now," John began, but I turned to him eagerly.

"Chris can follow the faintest spoor. Oh, find him, Chris. Zetke thinks he may be on this hill."

"Find him for us and we'll give you whatever you want," said John. He dropped to his knees and traced a map on the ground. "Look here, this is the way my induna boy thinks he went. He says he traced him to the spot where he turned in from the break about half a mile from Awetuli. Something must have frightened him and he went through the cane in a big semicircle that brought him back to the river. There are some stepping-stones about five miles down. If he did cross he wouldn't strike the road, because it swings away here from the river towards Durban, and so he would be in thick bush as soon as he crossed over. It's feasible, nobody uses those stepping-stones now and there are no paths."

"Time is important, Chris. He's been missing for a day and a night, he'll get exhausted…."

"I know where those stepping-stones are," said Chris. "Give me the lantern and I'll go now. If he's on this side, I'll find him. And the food and money and clothes? When will you bring them?"

"I'll go for them now and leave them here in the bush under this tree," said John. "You can see them there before you hand him over to us."

"Good. I'll start now." He picked up the lantern and we followed him down the hill. At the road we left him and went home. I helped John to pack some food and clothes and when he had gone back to the hill with them, I fell asleep at last.

The sun, burning through the window-pane, awakened me. Mrs. Lambert was in the room and somewhere in the house I could hear the voices of Miss Pimm, Mrs. Drew and Mrs. Farrell.

Mrs. Lambert said, "Goodness gracious me, Helen, I didn't think you'd go to pieces like this. When Enid Pimm told me what you looked like yesterday, with your hair hanging about your face and your dress all dirty, I couldn't believe her, but I see it's true. I'd have been here before this, but Nancy has been so upset since the day of the picnic. And then I had Mrs. Drew on my hands. Get up now, I've run a bath for you."

"No news of Nicky yet?"

"Not yet, dear. Now come and have this bath while it's hot. Gracious, look at your frock. Ruined. You haven't changed for days. Mind you, I can understand what you are feeling, more than anybody else." She stood over me while I bathed. "Goodness, Helen, your body is just one big bruise. How did you do that?"

"My father hit me."

"Don't worry, my dear, I won't say a word about it. If anybody has cause to trust me you have." She lowered her voice. "What Enid would give to know half the things I could tell her…. But a nurse learns to hold her tongue."

"Mrs. Drew saw him do it, that's what set her off."

"So that's what she's been hinting at. Well. Nancy has been taking a lot of my time up. You shouldn't tease her with Richard Drew, she's sweet on him and though I know you're only amusing yourself, it's cruel to Nancy."

She sat opposite me while I tried to eat; solid and smug, holding the teapot like a weapon against disaster.

"This tea will put new life into you."

"I brought some papers for you," said Miss Pimm. "And some telegrams from your aunt. She must have spent pounds on wiring you." She opened up the newspapers and showed me the headlines about Nicky's disappearance. "See? Nicky Angus Still Missing. I gave the reporters all the news rather than let them worry you. Luckily I had a photo of the house. And here is a letter in this paper about it. I'll read it to you. 'Sir, I am an Englishwoman by birth, but I may consider myself in some ways a South African. In spite of the climate and illness I have never found it necessary to allow a black hand to touch my children. Surely if more women would look after their own children and not leave them to the tender mercies of the black, then such terrible tragedies need not occur.' There's a lot more, all about natives kissing them and giving them green bananas to eat, this party says there should be a banana tree planted over the grave of every dead child in Durban. She carries things a bit too far. As I always say, you can't be in two places at once and there's no need to be down on anybody in misfortune. Granted, you shouldn't have gone off with Richard like that…. What's troubling me is this. If he's never found, would the minister read a burial service? Sort of consecrate a little spot where you could put flowers…."

I snatched the newspapers from her and tore them up. Mrs. Farrell and Mrs. Drew each took her by an elbow.

"Enid, you may mean well, but I have never heard such a rig-marole in my life," Mrs. Drew chided her. "And I can't say I blame Helen for trying to slap your face. We'll go now, dear. Aggie, you'll stay, I know."

They led Miss Pimm to the cart, and drove off. At least Mrs. Lambert kept silence for a few minutes while we stared across the canefields to the hills where the cutters were working. Their knives flashed with a steady rhythm that was heartening; yet I found my muscles tensing as I waited for the moment they would stop because they had stumbled on Nicky's body.

"This will cost the planters some money, cutting their young cane," said Mrs. Lambert. "It's good of the Drews and the Farrells when you come to think of it. I may have to cut mine…."

"What was that?" She stood up. "I thought I saw something moving in the cane."

"It was the cat chasing a lizard."

"Oh, for a moment I thought…. There's still a bit of hope, the police are still searching. I think I'll go down to the gate and watch from there, Helen. I always feel at a time like this one is so much better moving about. Come with me."

"The sun is pretty hot."

"I know, but I can't rest."

She leaned her arms on the gate. Now and again she stiffened at some imaginary movement in the break and I half-rose from my chair; but each time she relaxed almost immediately. I tried to read. Then I counted to stop myself from thinking about Nicky lying dead in the cane. I had reached a thousand when Mrs. Lambert stood up. This time she turned and came running up the pathway, her nose as bright as a beacon.

"He's found, he's found."

A Zulu girl was in the break and behind her shoulder I saw Nicky's fair head. I put my arms about them both. Somebody was banging the bell to let the countryside know that he was found. Leela put a garland round his neck.

"Take him inside and give him a good hot bath," shrieked Mrs. Lambert, "Oh, the darling little boy. Get away, all of you. I never saw anything like it in my life."

Only the Zulu girl was allowed to come into the kitchen with us while I washed Nicky. I remembered her, the girl Tandazele. She was married now, with clay-built hair and a hide skirt, but there was no mistaking her.

"Where did you find him?"

"Near my kraal, on the far side of the hill. I saw the cattle sniffing at something this morning, their necks out like this and I got a stick and pushed them away. He and a white man were lying there and I knew this was the child they were looking for. At first I thought he was dead, but he was only sleeping, it was the white man who was sick. I took them both to my kraal. The men are away cutting cane and we could not send a message. The white man has gone on the hill again."

"Now who could it have been that found him?" mused Mrs. Lambert. "You'd think he would have come with the girl. We'd have made a hero of him and he would have had his photograph in the paper. We'll give her something nice to eat, anyway, and she must have a present besides." She spread jam thickly on a slice of cake. "I'd better start cutting sandwiches, Helen, and do some baking. People will be in and out, in and out. Well, it will be a change to see this place cheerful. We'd better kill a few chickens too. You don't want to be caught with nothing to eat." She shouted to the umfaan to build up the fire. "My word, that child has kept his condition. You'll have to watch his nerves though, I knew a boy who stuttered through being lost." She smiled at me suddenly, that smile that frightened Leela so much. "There's something I've been wanting to say to you ever since the day of the picnic, Helen. I didn't realise before how friendly you are with Richard…. If anything comes of it you'd have to tell him about Nicky, wouldn't you?"

"What do you mean?"

"Don't be brazen, dear. You and I both know…."

I buttoned Nicky into fresh clothes. "Nothing will come of it. I'll never leave Nicky…." I looked with ear and hatred towards the cane.

The smile spread to her eyes. "He's a beautiful child. It would have been a sad pity if anything had happened to him." He was trying to reach her nose and she knocked his hand down absently. "Don't be bold, child. Some day you will have to tell him, Helen, it's his right to know." She began to beat eggs in a bowl, humming under her breath.

She was still baking cakes when Richard arrived. I had taken Nicky on the veranda and he fell asleep there. Richard bent down and touched his face gently. "He doesn't seem any the worse for wear."

"He remembers only parts of what happened to him. A python frightened him as he was walking along the break looking for me and he hid in the cane. After that he couldn't find the break again. He must have crossed the river early yesterday morning."

"Chris found him. You know that, don't you?"

"Yes."

"Your father turned Chris in this morning." I began to cry softly. "It was the best thing, Helen. Chris was just about at the end of his tether. The war is almost finished anyway." He looked up at me. "You saw him last night. He told my mother; she was allowed to talk to him for a few minutes."

"Yes, I saw him." There was a snapping silence. "I can't marry you, Richard, there's too much in the way, there always was."

"Chris?"

"And Nicky. I'm sorry…."

He got up slowly and went down the steps to his horse without another word to me. John came home soon afterwards. He was in a boisterous mood and gave mealies to the Zulus for beer and a demi-john of cane-spirit to the Indians. He invited everybody who called to stay to supper. I was glad of the noise that night. I didn't want to think of Chris or of that dark hill haunted by the owl. Nicky had only a vague memory of him; but he always remembered Tandazele and loved the sound of her name.

I found it easy to forgive Leela. She had torn up the letter Chris gave her because she said he brought only trouble to me. Soon I would live at Drew's Pride…. But she had gone back to her hut for rice and given him fruit too when he waylaid her on the bridge.

We went to Durban that week, for John said it would do us all good to get away from the sight of the cane.

Aunt Lucy was at the station to meet us.

"We'll have something to drink in the tea-room first," she cried. "It will be quite a treat for you, Helen, after the quiet of the farm." She was wearing a long feather in her hat and she nearly poked Nicky's eye out when she swooped on him to kiss him.

"I'll wait outside and read the paper," John said.

"Oh no you won't, John, you come in with us. It will be a change for you too."

She was talking at the top of her voice to attract attention and John followed her into the tea-room, grumbling that the whole town was laughing at us. The air in the tea-room was rich with the smell of hot pies and toast and coffee, though it seemed impossible that anybody should want such things in that heat. Sure enough, a man at a table nearby was eating his way through two browned pies, over which he poured sauce after every mouthful; he washed it down with steaming coffee. The big fan above his head did no more than stir the beads of sweat bursting from his rebellious pores.

A waitress, blooming in spite of the heavy air, said brightly, "Black coffee, as per usual?"

She had spoken to John, but Aunt Lucy answered. "We'll have ginger-ale."

The waitress lingered by the table while we sipped the ginger-ale. John winked at her and shook his head towards Aunt Lucy. The waitress did not take the hint. She polished the table-top and energetically shook up the sugar in the bowl. Aunt Lucy's eyes were blazing with excitement. The waitress, encountering a look from John, banged the sugar-bowl on the table, gave an irritated flick with her duster, and flounced off.

"One of your fancy girls, John?" Aunt Lucy asked.

"Seen her a couple of times here when I've been in town on business."

Aunt Lucy said something like Monkey Business and he became so sulky that he would not talk to either of us. As a treat for Nicky, Aunt Lucy had decided that we should go by ricksha to her house. She had hired two of the showiest boys in Durban and they pranced up to us as we came out of the station. Great seeds encircled their ankles and knocked out a little tune as they moved; they had swatters of cows' tails at their wrists, their trousers and shirts were snowy, set off by broad bands of beadwork telling of amorous girls waiting for them at home. They had oxhorns and turkey feathers on their heads, and their legs were painted white in an intricate pattern. No wonder Nicky was overjoyed when he saw them.

John refused to get into the ricksha with me. "I think Lucy is going mad in her old age. I'll walk, but you go along or she might be annoyed."

I rode alone, for Aunt Lucy had taken Nicky with her. My ricksha boy was in fine fettle, caracoling so that he drew the eye of the most jaded bystander. He was the only lively thing in the street. Durban had slowed to a crawl. The heat rose up in languid waves, gathering together the smells of the city; from hot tar and sweating bodies, from the sea, from the musk and incense of the Indian silk bazaars.

John was a little way ahead of me, a tall, white-clad figure strolling easily with the crowd. He stopped to look at a Zulu girl who clung to her husband's hand like a child, for she was from the country and dazed by the traffic. She wore her finery and she clinked as she walked, the rhythm set by her brass anklets and bangles. Her face had a withdrawn and innocent look, though her clay-built hair showed that she had been married many years and her beadwork boasted that she had proved fruitful. She was not unlike Tandazele and John watched her until she was out of sight.

An Indian boy sprang forward, imploring him to buy a bunch of flowers. It was Leela's son Sowa and his sudden rush made John step backwards on to a native beggar. John cursed Sowa and dropped a coin into the beggar's hat. The man's leg, swollen with elephantiasis, was thrust out before him in the hope that people would trip over it, then they would be sure to give him something. Zetke's cousin had elephantiasis and he told me about this trick of which nobody could complain because he couldn't bend his leg.

I stopped the ricksha and called Sowa to me. "What are you doing in Durban?"

"I going to school," he told me, happily accepting the sixpence I gave him in exchange for some asters. "My uncle bringing flowers from Westongate and then I selling and buying books. .. ." He was not yet seven, but his face was already as shrewd as an old merchant's. We had persuaded Aunt Lucy to spend Christmas with us and she had engaged Sowa to sit at her feet and watch for snakes. She soon sacked him, for she found him going through her shares in the tin box and bullied by John he had confessed that he expected to find gold after having listened to Aunt Lucy's conversation. Aunt Lucy wasted time explaining to him exactly what gold shares were and he had so easily grasped the principle that he had asked for shares in lieu of wages. Aunt Lucy paid him in cash, but she always respected him for his astuteness.

The ricksha boy rang his bell, impatient to be gone. I looked about for John, but I couldn't see him nor did I catch a glimpse of him all the way up the Berea.

Aunt Lucy was struggling to get Nicky out of the ricksha.

"What a little fiend he is," she said, admiringly. "Angus to the backbone."

We left Nicky riding up and down the street and walked towards the house. It had a bad-tempered, fat face because of the arrangement of the two bow windows downstairs and two narrow dormers close to each other upstairs. Inside there was a peculiar smell, not unpleasant, but sweetish, as of many old scented things cluttered in cupboards; furs and evening-gowns and scarves and artificial flowers that Aunt Lucy hadn't worn for years. The rooms were crammed with ornaments that ranged from tiny china shoes to huge urns. There was a herd of ebony elephants, useful as doorstops. Nicky could sit astride the biggest and it was when we brought this to the gate that he agreed to get out of the ricksha.

"I can't imagine why John didn't come home with you," said Aunt Lucy.

"He thought the ricksha was a bit showy."

"He's up to something, mark my words, or he would have been here by now."

Nicky soon tired of the elephant and we took him into the garden. There were several marble tablets dotted along the walks. I read some of the inscriptions to Nicky. "A garden is a lovesome thing God wot…" and "Who can say why today tomorrow will be yesterday…" but naturally he couldn't make head or tail of them and began to cry for a fat white cherub spewing water into the fish-pond. This cherub and the tablets often led people into the belief that the garden was a cemetery and new patients in the hospital opposite complained that this was a dreary idea.

We could see into the hospital, right down a broad corridor. A Zulu boy was polishing the floor; a strong fellow kneeling in a silly suit of cream and red, and with big white discs in his ears swinging to the time of his movements. His reflection, joined to his knees, polished vigorously beneath him and he stopped work often to admire himself. As he shifted back he left the dark linoleum glittering like oil. All day long the nurses hurried up and down this river of oil. The young probationers skimmed on its surface and caught hold of the door-jamb to steady themselves as they came to firm ground on the threshold, the trained sisters paddled through it with short authoritative steps.

Aunt Lucy spent hours staring at the hospital. She hated it. She said that Appleby, the man who had originally owned the big house, had turned it into a hospital to spite her because she wouldn't marry him; and now the whole tone of the neighbourhood was spoiled.

The clock struck five and still John hadn't come. We had supper without him. As soon as I had put Nicky to bed I walked down to the tram stop, sure that he would be on the next tram. Aunt Lucy sent the house-boy to call me indoors.

"I shouldn't worry if I were you, Helen. He has probably met a friend downtown. But it is too bad of him to go off without a word to anybody. A nervous woman would be ringing up the mortuary, but I know John, he never thinks of anybody but himself." Then she folded her hands over her stick and prepared to enjoy herself. "You're not a child any more, Helen, it's time you learned about life. I've always tried to guide you in such matters and to take the place of your mother. What I want to say now is this. Your father is a man and men like to go off drinking. It's no use mincing words. John is just about due for a spree. In fact it's natural after the disappointment he has had over you." She became deadly serious. "He might even be carrying on with that waitress. You may laugh, Helen, but I think he knows her better than he would admit. As long as he doesn't think of marrying again." With this thrust she brought out the cribbage board and we played until midnight.

I lay awake, wondering where he was. The sounds from the street died away. Only now and then I heard footsteps on the pavement and I sat up eagerly; but they passed on, leaving a silence that intimidated me, for I missed the whispering of the cane and the surf.

Presently I heard a scratching sound and I leaned over the edge of the bed to see what caused it. Creeping across the floor was a big cockroach, dark-brown and secretive. While I watched, another flew in at the window. I ran into Aunt Lucy's room.

"The place is full of cockroaches."

She looked at me with glassy eyes and then she sat up in bed. "You gave me a terrible fright, Helen. Is your father home yet?"

"No, and I can't sleep, my room is full of cockroaches."

"Fancy worrying about cockroaches when you live amongst all those snakes. Cockroaches fly in, you can't do anything about it. I'll give you a drop of tonic wine, that will soon put you to sleep. In the closet there, Helen. You pour it out. What time is it?"

"About two."

"Well, you might as well give him up for the night. I know what he... Never mind about that. But I can just picture him with that waitress." She filled my glass again. "Drink it up. Yes, he'd like her. There's a coarse streak in John, but I will say this for him, he doesn't bring that type of woman into his home. No, I don't think we need worry about him marrying her. John is canny. He'd want a woman with a bit of property. If it hadn't been for Mrs. Lambert's nose he might have married her." She laughed. "How that woman hates me. He led her a terrible life, you know. He used to compare her with me, so I've been told. She was mad about him. Ross Lambert was one of the handsomest men you ever saw. If John hadn't caught us we would have run away and got married. I was terribly upset at the time. And then he married this Aggie Something-or-other, the ugliest girl he could find. I saw them once in a street in Johannesburg. I thought he was going to faint, Helen, he went as white as a sheet and began to shake. I'd got over it long before that, of course. I was with a man who afterwards found a big diamond on his property...." She sighed. "This tonic is a comfort. It doesn't take much of it to settle your nerves."

I stayed with Aunt Lucy for a week. In the daytime we amused Nicky and in the evening we played cribbage and drank the wine. Aunt Lucy began to talk of giving a party so that I could meet some young men. Before this could materialise, Mr. Bannerjee came to fetch me.

I saw him at the gate one afternoon, looking up uncertainly at the house and I went down to meet him, with Nicky and Aunt Lucy at my heels. Mr. Bannerjee bowed.

"Miss Angus, I have wanted to congratulate you and your father and Nicky on his safe return and also Mr. Van der West-huizen on the heroic part he played, but unfortunately that is impossible under the peculiar circumstances." In such a district Mr. Bannerjee could smile fearlessly. He paused now, closing his eyes, for he had memorised his speech. "The love of a father for his son, the love of a sister for her brother, these are beautiful sentiments. There are no finer attachments than these." Aunt Lucy was twirling her sunshade at Nicky, concentrating so that she would not laugh. "We are told that the gods are jealous of those we love and this was the case when your brother was lost. What agonies were endured...." Aunt Lucy had sent the sunshade sailing over to Nicky.

"No, it's too good for him to play with," I said, closing the sunshade firmly. "Now listen to Mr. Bannerjee."

Mr. Bannerjee began again. "The love of a father for his son, the love of a sister for her brother, these are beautiful sentiments. There are no finer attachments than these." Nicky had prised the sunshade from me and he skirmished towards Mr. Bannerjee, who leapt back just in time. "...than these. To have restored to us what we have lost is to make us doubly appreciative. And now, may I wish you everlasting happiness." He had cut his speech short, for Nicky was determined to jab him with the sunshade. He put the gate between him and the little devil. Now he lowered his voice and cupped his hand over his mouth to make his words more secret. "Zetke told me that the girl Tandazele has not yet gone to her kraal and the husband returns soon from the canefields. We should all be happy to see you in Westongate, Miss Angus."

"What he meant was that you should catch the next train to Westongate and stop John from making a fool of himself," said Aunt Lucy as we watched him bouncing down the street. "I'd come with you, Helen, but I couldn't face the snakes."

She did come down to the station with me. "If you want advice, just telegraph me," she said in parting.

Colonel Edington sat opposite me in the train. He didn't once look out of the window, but kept his eyes fixed on me while he stroked his moustache in a calculating way. I gazed steadily at the tawdry streets. We passed the tannery and the Indian temple set in a garden where a yellow-robed priest walked amongst the peacocks. The train stopped at a siding opposite and we stayed long enough to see a group of Indians pushing and pulling a goat towards the temple; but he turned on them and scattered them, making off across the railway line with the mob in pursuit. Nicky and I laughed, but Colonel Edington still stared at me and stroked his moustache.

The houses grew more scattered and then we were out in the open country, passing only isolated bungalows and shanties. When we came to the canefields, Nicky lost interest in the scenery. He swung his legs and shouted to the rhythm of the clicking wheels. Tandazele, Tandazele, Tandazele. I slapped him hard on the leg. He was too much astonished to cry, but the Colonel whistled. The shriek of the engine plucked the sound from his lips. We were approaching Westongate.

"I like a girl with a bit of a temper," he said as he helped me down from the train.

He became less enthusiastic when he found that there was nobody at the station to meet us. Staring at a girl or flirting with her was one thing, but it was another to have to drive her ten miles after a long day. He drank off a brandy while he was waiting for the horse to be inspanned.

I took the precaution of putting Nicky between us. "Naughty girl," he said with tender gaiety and I had to shut my lips tight or the swear-words I had learned from John would have exploded from me.

"A little bird told me that there will soon be an engagement announced between Richard Drew and a certain young lady…."

"You mustn't believe everything the little bird tells you." The old fool.

"Still heartwhole and fancy-free, eh?"

"Yes."

We kept on in this strain and I was nearly asleep from boredom by the time we took the turn past Awetuli. It was there that I saw Tandazele. She was walking slowly, her hide skirt swinging with the movement of her hips, her head erect as though she carried a load on it. She stood still when she saw us and Nicky called to her.

"You are bewitched," I shouted and she covered her face with her hands.

"My dear, what made you say a thing like that?" Colonel Edington asked. "It was cruel. They really believe in mtagati, you know."

"I was only teasing her." I smiled at him. "Stay to supper with us, Colonel. You'd have to take pot luck, but we could play whist afterwards."

"Thank you, my dear." He tried to pat me on the shoulder, but I evaded him and he patted the back of the seat instead. He whipped up the horses and we arrived in fine style with Nicky shouting for joy.

John was on the front steps, pulling on his boots, and he remained with his head bent until we were almost on top of him. He tried to control his rage in front of Colonel Edington.

"What the… What did you come home for, Helen?"

"I got tired of Durban."

"Where's your luggage?"

"I left most of it behind. Aunt Lucy is forwarding it."

"She's a charming girl this daughter of yours," said Colonel Edington. "But impulsive. Youth, I suppose."

"I suppose so. Will you have a drink?" John asked ungraciously.

I got Nicky off to sleep as quickly as I could. Colonel Edington, after his journey from town, looked as though he were ready for bed too, but I played up to him so that he would remain. He lasted out until nine o'clock and he was almost tottering when he climbed into his trap. He made a last feeble attempt at gallantry with a muttered, "See you in my dreams."

John sat through the evening with hardly a word to say; but he was so restless that he sweated and I could see the veins in his temples beating as the blood raced through them. When Colonel Edington had gone, he stood with me at the gate.

"Let's stay out here a while, Helen, I don't think I'll be able to sleep yet."

A shiver went through me. "The evenings are getting cooler. The summer is finished."

"Yes. The cutters will be in next week. They started laying the rails today, so Drew told me. He was over at the mill." He took a deep breath. "You can smell that summer is over. It was the best I ever saw."

I breathed in deeply too. All the scents of summer were there, but fainter than they had been a week before; they came from the guavas and the frangipanni and the moist earth.

"I'm not going to plant the north field this year, no use pulling the inside out of it when we've had such a good season. Drew is on to a Queensland variety, I forget its name.... Are you listening?"

"Yes."

"I'm glad you came home, Helen."

He went inside, but I stayed in the garden. There was a light burning at Drew's Pride, darkness on the other hills. From afar there came the sound of a horse's hooves and I saw a light bobbing on the road. Wheels rattled on the bridge. I stayed until the horse and cart passed by on its way to Drew's Pride and long afterwards I remembered Nancy's laughter rising above all the other young voices.

When I went to my room I found John in my bed with Nicky in his arms. I lay down at the foot of the bed and pulled a rug over myself.

After a while he spoke to me. "Tomorrow morning... that girl Tandazele.... I'll tell her to go back to her kraal."

"Yes."

"Are you comfortable there?"

"Yes, thank you, John."

"I'll stay here. I won't get to sleep if I start moving around."

"That's all right."

"Good night then."

"Good night, John."

The room was full of starlight. A breeze sprang up, stirring the limp curtains and carrying on its breath the scent of the dying summer.

Chapter eight

Nancy and Richard were married in June. I couldn't go to the wedding because at the last moment I caught whooping cough from Nicky. Mrs. Lambert, I remember, hurried to my bedside to find out if I was putting on. One cough from me convinced her and she fled.

She was suspicious of me until Joan was born. You never saw such a fuss made of a child. George and Eric married and had children, but Joan was always the favourite of her grandparents. For a while the whole family lived under one roof with Mrs. Drew the undisputed mistress. Mrs. Lambert egged Nancy on to make the most of her affection for Joan. After a while the only two on speaking terms were Mrs. Drew and Nancy, so Mr. Drew bought farms on the North Coast for Eric and George. That was when Nancy began to grow fat. She had a comfortable time of it, for she had always got on well with Mrs. Drew. She was supposed to be too delicate to have another child, but John said she was too lazy. Only in one thing did she show energy. She was jealous of Richard and she saw to it that he was never alone with another woman.

While the children were still going to school in Westongate, I used to drive them there in the morning and fetch them in the afternoon. That filled in the day for me. We picked up Peter Farrell and Joan Drew at the bridge and we stopped again at the Indian gardens for Leela and her baskets. She always gave us a present, a mango or a banana and once, I remember, some lichees. These were a great treat and I asked her where she had got them from, for there was no lichee tree in the district.

"Mr. Bannerjee buying all lichees on tree from feller by Pinetown," she said smugly. "It making good business. Me giving him one hundred pounds and making two hundred maybe. Lichees to Durban, selling for plenty, plenty money. Mr. Bannerjee getting half, me getting half."

"You'll be rich soon, Leela."

"Very very poor, mama. Alla time paying money. Gotting plenty chiles." She looked sorrowfully at her little daughter Amoya, whom she was taking on her rounds with her that day,

"You certainly would be rich if they were all like Sowa."

"Him good boy that. But Perian spending, spending...." She was choked by bitterness.

I allowed my lichee to lie in my mouth, savouring the rich white pulp until it melted and there was only the polished black stone to which clung the unforgettable taste. Joan gobbled hers and then held out her hand to Nicky. He peeled off the rough skin and popped the fruit into his own mouth, but Peter gave his lichee to Joan.

I looked after the children for Mrs. Partridge that morning. I did this for her every Friday while she baked cakes. The classroom stood next to the kitchen and as soon as she lit the fire the place became hot and we had to go out under the trees. The children were good, lulled by the steaming December heat. The older children worked out sums lying flat on the grass, while I taught the little ones to count with beads. There were as many colours in the garden as there were on the frame. It was Joan who found this out when she slipped away to gather a posy and as she matched each one against a bead, she dropped it into my lap. There were times when you couldn't help spoiling her for her pretty ways, but I tried to be strict.

"You must sit still, darling, like all the others," I said. "It's not as if you knew how to count."

"I can count." She picked up a flower. "One…"

"You must watch the beads."

"I'll teach her if you like," said Peter. "I've finished my sums." He threw the flowers to her and she said the numbers after him as he caught them.

Nicky, too, had finished his sums and he lay on his back watching the tremulous movements of a chameleon that gripped a stick he held. He enticed Joan away from Peter with the chameleon. "Look, Joanie, this will turn any colour you put it on…." Peter pulled the flowers to pieces as he watched them. He was as fair as Joan. His face would have been girlish but for a deep scar that furrowed the length of his cheek; the result of a fall from Colonel Edington's black stallion. Mrs. Farrell blamed Nicky for that because he had been the first to ride the stallion. She blamed him too for Peter's broken fingers. The boys had climbed the Halfway Tree and Peter had caught hold of a rotten branch. Perhaps Nicky was to blame. Left to himself, Peter was a dreamy boy who would rather read about birds' nests than go after them.

I called Joan to my side and set the boys more sums to do. They were going on for twelve, and were really too old for this school and I suspected that they whiled away most of their time teaching the little ones or doing odd jobs for Mrs. Partridge. I knew her of old. Once you were ten you were beyond her. But if Nicky went to boarding-school, what would there be left for me? Long, vain days and the longer nights….

There was a rustle in the hibiscus hedge. A whisper ran amongst the children. "She's there." I saw the flutter of a blue cotton skirt.

"Amoya," said Joan. "Mrs. Partridge isn't here. You can come out, Amoya."

"Joan…" I began.

An Indian child stepped cautiously out of the hedge and sat down next to Joan. She looked greedily at the beaded frame.

"Let her stay," said Nicky. "We're teaching her to count. I'll keep cave for Mrs. Partridge."

It was too hot to worry about discipline. I flicked the beads along the frame. The children stopped staring at Amoya, all except Joan, who pulled the rings from Amoya's toes. Amoya, raptly singing the numbers, wriggled her toes with irritation and made a half-hearted grab for the rings. Joan moved away and taking off shoes and socks, slid the rings on to her toes. She turned her feet this way and that until she caught Nicky's eye and then she lay back in the grass, laughing. The smell of baking cakes floated out to us as Mrs. Partridge opened the door.

"Run, run," the children cried.

Amoya skipped behind the hedge. Mrs. Partridge clapped her hands indignantly.

"Dear, dear, has she been here again? She does distract the children so, Helen. She comes in here the moment my back is turned. Joan Drew, put on your shoes and socks this minute. Why, you have rings on your toes."

"They belong to Amoya."

"This is too bad. Nicky, take the rings and give them back to that Indian. I know her mother, she's an old harpy, she'll make endless trouble. Off with you."

He was away such a long time that Mrs. Partridge had to send Peter to find him and then I went after Peter. I found them on the beach. Amoya was sitting cross-legged in front of them, the rings restored to her toes. She was painstakingly learning swear-words from them.

She ran off when I surprised them, but that wasn't the last I saw of her. Often she would steal into the house and follow me about, until in desperation I taught her to count to a hundred. Then she seemed to sense that my patience had run out and she came no more.

The boys didn't want to leave the beach. Nicky pulled off his shirt. "I'm going for a swim. There's nothing to go back for. She makes us clean the cupboards on Friday afternoons."

"You're not to go into the surf, only in the lagoon...."

They were off across the golden sand-bar, hopping and yelling as the heat bit at them. I found some shade amongst the bushes on the slope and watched them paddle in the water to ease their burnt feet. They looked round anxiously and then slipped off their trousers. Now their taut, thin bodies were silver spears aimed at the sky. They dived flat on the water, skimming like stones flung by a skilful hand. Peter was the better swimmer, utterly fearless in the water. He left Nicky behind in water dark green from the forests of spirogyra that grew beneath its surface, and swam to the middle of the lagoon to float there, breaking the vivid plane of the water. Now Nicky was far from the bank, swimming through the palest tint of green, but he did not reach the clear water, for Peter turned back and they met in a splash of spray and laughter.

Mr. Banncrjee shouted from the hill, "Look out, the policeman is coming." The boys made a rush for their clothes and he hurried down the hill to them. "Go on, go on, enjoy yourselves, I was only joking." He sat down near me with his suitcase beside him. These days Mr. Bannerjee was shabby, for he had been neglecting business for politics. He wore sandshoes and his suit and panama were old; but his name and address had been freshly painted on the suitcase. The same paint must have gone on to his hat, which was as hard as wood, but discretion had prevailed in the matter of the sandshoes and they were a dirty grey.

"You saw my name in the paper, Miss Angus?"

"No. I'm sorry I missed it, Mr. Bannerjee."

"I was mentioned. Amongst twenty thousand, Miss Angus. We were all arrested for crossing the border into the Transvaal." It was difficult to talk to Mr. Bannerjee now, for he believed that Gandhi was God and sometimes he treated you like a benighted heathen for not being able to share this view. He looked at me expectantly, but I made no comment, for this was not a day for one of Mr. Bannerjee's intricate debates. "I have a piece of news for you, Miss Angus. When I spoke of policemen a few minutes ago it was because the thought of the unspeakable police was uppermost in my mind. I had just seen the new sergeant of police step off the train at Westongate. Who do you think it is?" I tried several names, but he shook his head. "Mr. Van der Westhuizen."

"Mr. Bannerjee, are you sure?"

"There could be no mistaking him. A little broader, face of course not so good-looking as some years ago, but...Mr. Van der Westhuizen."

"I can't believe it."

"I am happy that I was able to prepare you. Please be calm, Miss Angus. Would you rather I left?" He got up and dusted the sand from his trousers. "Do you know if Leela had any success with the lichees? I made her my agent, as it were, but Sowa is the brains there. Leela is inclined to miserliness."

"She said this morning they were doing well."

Mr, Bannerjee smiled. "Then when next you see me I shall be more smartly dressed, I hope. And now I see Miss Pimm is on her way here.... It's too late to warn the bathers.... I'll say good afternoon, Miss Angus."

Miss Pimm was in a hurry to reach me. "Helen..." She stretched her lips at Mr. Bannerjee as he passed her. "Helen, who do you think the new sergeant of police is?"

"Chris Van der Westhuizen."

"Oh, you knew. Well, his own aunt didn't and she nearly fainted when I told her a few minutes ago as she was driving past. I saw him on the station."

"Mr. Bannerjee told me."

"Quite a gossip, isn't he? Those boys have got costumes on, I hope."

"Oh yes."

"I'd report them if they hadn't. I like to come down here and collect shells for doyleys when I'm on leave. You get those tiny little purple ones at this time of the year, but I'm terrified to come down here. You never know what you'll see. And the police take very little notice. I can't imagine Chris as a policeman. I'd like to know how he ever got into the force. Mind you, all you've got to have these days is a Van der in front of your name and you can get any Government position...." Nicky elected this moment to dive and Miss Pimm stared in outrage at his glistening buttocks. "Helen, you said they had costumes on."

"I thought they did," I said feebly.

"Well… I'll walk farther along and you can tell them to get out. I'll report them to Miss Partridge…."

There was no need for her to tell on the boys, for Nicky's hair was curling in tell-tale fashion above the line of shiny bristles that stamped the Westongate barber's haircuts and Mrs. Partridge knew at once that the boys had been swimming. The class-room was in an uproar and she was red in the face from temper and the heat of the kitchen. She had not yet finished baking and as she clapped her hands for silence little spurts of flour flew from between her palms.

The shrill voices of the children ebbed and in the silence that followed she became aware of her floury hands. She went out of the room to wash them and we all listened intently to the splashing of the water.

Joan said, "Amoya came and swore at her. She said, 'Bloody old fool.' " Her face bloomed with pleasure.

The children laughed and the gale of sound met Mrs. Partridge at the door. She looked almost frightened, as though she were in a nightmare in which the children took command. Her clapping hands, pink as geraniums, were caught in that storm of laughter and for all the notice the children took of her she might have been applauding them.

That afternoon she sent notes to Mrs. Farrell and John to tell them that it was high time the boys went to boarding-school.

Chapter nine

Mrs. Farrell would have liked Peter to go to a different school from Nicky, but she gave way to his pleas and he went with Nicky after Christmas.

"We'll never be able to pay the fees," she said, as we stood on the station watching the train leave Westongate. "Luke is trying for a job at the mill."

"That's a good idea," I said absently. That seemed to offend her and I hastened to make amends. "I mean, it's worth any sacrifice to give a boy a good education. It's a beautiful school and the Head is such a fine man. Did you meet the matron?"

Mrs. Farrell became agitated. "I clean forgot to tell her that Peter mustn't have desiccated coconut. It upsets him for days.... I wonder if I should send her a telegram."

"No, I'd write if I were you."

The train had disappeared behind the hill and we stood uncertainly on the platform, depressed by the flatness following the rush of getting the boys ready for school. The band of white along the edge of the platform throbbed in the heat and the gravel was burning through my shoes.

Outside the hall across the road a church bazaar was in progress. There were stalls beneath awnings and the bottles of homemade jams looked cool. From that distance the women in charge seemed cool too in their light dresses.

"Let's go over," said Mrs. Farrell. "It will put the afternoon in. I'm going to miss Peter. He's been such company for me since the girls married."

I bought two little paper baskets filled with sweets that I had made, and helped Mrs. Lambert to raffle her embroidery. The needlework stall was indoors and there was no illusion of coolness here. The heat from the corrugated-iron buildings on the station blasted its way across the dusty road into the hall and rose in waves to the shimmering roof. Muslins drooped over rigid whalebone, cane fans fluttered before congested faces. The Vicar gave way so far as to run his finger inside his dog-collar. Mrs. Lambert wriggled in sudden abandon to the heat and then pressed her elbows into her sides in a surreptitious effort to scratch herself. You could trace the moisture trickling from her chin to her neck. From there it plunged secretly between her breasts to spread itself amongst the folds of her constricted body. She had got tired of saying, "Isn't it hot?" and now she was grumbling that the Committee didn't know its business, holding a fete in February. Her complaining voice was a sputter of energy rising above the exhausted drone that filled the hall, and she trotted about fiercely selling tickets with the plain intention of getting the whole thing over and done with. I won a doyley.

The bazaar closed soon afterwards. This was the worst time of the day to go home, for the children were coming out of school and I missed Nicky amongst them. Nancy and Mrs. Lambert were ahead of me and they stopped for Joan.

"Come and have tea with us," Nancy called.

She was acting the part of the rich Mrs. Drew that day and I was in no mood to put up with her airs. "I'm sorry, I promised…" I said vaguely as though I had an exciting appointment with somebody she didn't know. She drove away and I took care to follow so slowly that I would not overtake her.

Leela was walking down the road with empty baskets, her

daughter Chanjaldi beside her. They climbed thankfully into the back of the cart. The girl Chanjaldi had a promise of beauty rare in an Indian; her spirit flowed outwards rather than inwards and this ebullience contrasted like black with white against Leela's serenity. Chanjaldi kneeled, with her arms crossed over the top of the seat. I looked down at her and she smiled at me. Her skin had a trace of gold in it and there was a deep dimple in her chin pressing up her lower lip so that she seemed to proffer a kiss. She had not made the change from childhood to womanhood easily and though she must have been about thirteen now, there was still in her a struggle against ripeness. Leela was anxious to hand her over to her husband and even at that moment she was asking her a question. She was disappointed by Chanjaldi's answer and she threw up her hands in despair.

"This one not ready, mama. I thinking this time, hot hot…. Still no good…." She looked at her sluggish daughter with contempt and suspicion. Her shrewd eyes had not missed the shadowed sensuality in that brown and gold face.

She got off at the huts, but Chanjaldi rode a little further with me. As we crossed the bridge she laughed, for she saw her husband talking to Leela and waving his arms.

"Soon I must going with him," she whispered. "I not telling her…." She held two fingers before her glowing face. "Two times, she not finding out." She put her head back and let the laughter pour from her smooth throat as though she sang. She was still laughing when she ran across the bridge. Ramlagen her husband turned to look up at her. I thought, "He's going to have his hands full with Chanjaldi." He richly deserved whatever was in store for him, because of the terrible hour he had spent with her when she was a child.

Leela married three of her daughters off at the same ceremony from motives of economy. The eldest was the luckiest, for she had had to wait until she was thirteen, the other was eleven, but poor Chanjaldi was only eight. The arrangement was that she should be looked after by her mother-in-law until she was of age for her husband; but Ramlagen wouldn't wait. She was safe enough at night, for she slept with the old woman, but one hot summer's afternoon Ramlagen seized her. Mr. Bannerjee came to her help, but Ramlagen knocked him down and dragged Chanjaldi into the cane. For many months she lay in her mother's house while her body healed, and Mr. Bannerjee spoiled her with sweets and pictures and trinkets. Leela had little time for this troublesome daughter and for years she had been complaining about having to keep her. But Mr. Bannerjee had threatened to report her to the police if she handed Chanjaldi over to Ramlagen before puberty.

The horse plodded through the cane with heart-breaking slowness, yet the sun was still high when I reached home. How quiet the place was. John would be in Maritzburg now or perhaps already on his way back to Durban. He liked that big waitress who worked in the station tea-room. I knew her well now. Her name was Bessie Parker and she had been John's friend for years, even before my mother died.

Nicky might be unpacking. He had gone to school armed with a pattern of behaviour out of *The Magnet,* but Peter would be sure to make mistakes. They had decided not to mention Mrs. Partridge's school to forestall teasing. If Peter became friendly with anybody he wouldn't be able to stop himself from talking about Mrs. Partridge. Truth spilled from him like a fountain; but sometimes Nicky would lie, looking you in the face with such clear eyes that you believed every word he was saying. When you found him out and gave him a hiding he would yell. The yells were another lie, because he scarcely felt my blows. John said he was as hard as a Zulu and as cunning as an Indian. He had picked up a lot of Indian ways when he was a child, for Sowa was one of his first playmates. Sowa was a good little boy and we used to hold him up as an example to Nicky. "Sowa wouldn't do a thing like that, Nicky...."

I began to write out the list of things I would put in his first tuck-box. He would probably starve at that school. I couldn't see them keeping up with his appetite for bread-and-jam alone. John was always saying, "Easy with the jam, Nicky, it's not pumpkin, you know."

I wished now that I had gone with them to Maritzburg; but Nicky had said that he would make a better impression if he wasn't hampered by a woman. When I finished writing out the list of goodies there was nothing to do, unless I played patience like Aunt Lucy did. I should have accepted Nancy's invitation to tea. Perhaps it was not too late even yet. She might invite me to supper if I went up there now.

The sun was almost setting as I climbed the hill to Drew's Pride. There was still warmth in the nagged terrace and in the handle of the french window opening into the sitting-room, for this part of the house catches the afternoon sun. The room itself had cooled. Only a brass gong in a corner was touched by sunlight and even as I watched the shadows slid down the wall and quenched its fire.

The room was empty. Richard's pipe, with a spiral of smoke rising from it, lay on the arm of his favourite chair and on the floor nearby was a picture-book and a paper basket, emptied now of my home-made sweets. Mrs. Lambert's embroidery was on the sofa next to the impressions that her thighs and buttocks and back had made on the tapestry. A cribbage board and cards stood on the table between two chairs; the tea-tray had been pushed aside to make way for the game, and the cups were tumbled one inside the other. The piano was open with music on the stand. They had all been so lately in the room that I had the illusion that they would materialise and take up their positions; Nancy at the piano with her fingers on the keys; Mrs. Lambert working away at her embroidery as if it must be finished within the hour; Richard smoking; and Joan sprawled over the book, reaching for a sweet; Mr. and Mrs. Drew amiably playing cards. The wind slowly turned the page of Joan's book. Almost I saw them look up, smiling with polite approbation because I had come after all. Joan's hair ribbon, still tied in a bow, had fallen on the flag-stones. I put it on the window-sill and went away.

The girl had my dinner on the table and I was obliged to sit down then and there to eat; this to please Zetke, who wanted to go to bed at the first darkness. He was sitting on the wood-box in the kitchen, his blanket in a roll at his feet, for he was to sleep on the kitchen floor while John was away. As soon as the dishes were washed, he lay down with his blanket covering his head and would not speak another word.

I lit the lamp in the dining-room. For a while I read and then I played patience. One of the dogs came into the room, his claws clicking on the linoleum. I patted him, but even he did not mean to keep me company, for he fell asleep at once. The room was suddenly full of flying ants and they dashed themselves down the chimney of the lamp and put it out. Through the darkness I could see a storm coming up out of the sea with a glitter of flame that set the windows alight. Thunder crashed simultaneously with the lightning and I shut the windows, peering out at the cane to see if it had been struck anywhere. Rain started to fall at first tentatively and then with a rush that overwhelmed the lightning. It flushed the cane and poured over the roof and windows. A drip started somewhere, beating at the floor with a plop, plop, plop.

I groped my way to my bedroom to get a candle so that I could put the brass bowl beneath the drip. Now the drops fell with a pinging sound that could eventually drive one mad. I was lost behind the rain. The storm had not disturbed the dog, he slept as soundly as Zetke. Even the flying ants were beginning to die.

I went into Nicky's room. It was austere in the candle-light. The black-and-white of the mattress ticking was too startling, the blankets were folded too neatly at the bottom of the bed.

There was no water in the jug, no soap in the dish. The doyleys had been taken off the dressing-table and put in the wash, the drawers were empty except for squares of brown paper. A little cockroach ran across the dressing-table. I let him go, but I sprinkled borax beneath the brown paper so that the place should not be overrun.

The top drawer was locked. I tried it again incredulously, but it would not budge, and I became obsessed by its subtle challenge. What secrets could a boy of thirteen have? I found the key at last in a pocket of an old coat hanging in the wardrobe.

His collection of butterflies was in the drawer; and his stamps. There were drawings of John, the Buffalo, for whom he had an extravagant admiration; and of Drew's Pride. I remembered that once he told some people who didn't know us that we lived in the big house on the hill. In a notebook there was a tally of the snakes he had caught for Mr. Bannerjee, who now ran a business with the snake-park as a sideline. That year he had earned a pound and with the money he had bought me a box of chocolates for my birthday. I locked the drawer and put away the key.

The dogs had taken shelter on the veranda and now they were barking. Tim who was still inside flew to the front door with a growl. Somebody knocked and I called out to Zetke, but he didn't hear. I went to the window and looked out with the slight hope that John might have changed his mind about staying in Durban.

Chris was there. I opened the door quickly and he came into the room with a surge of movement that was a part of the storm outside and a part of his powerful body. He took off his helmet and the water ran from it into a little glimmering pool on the floor.

"Has there been an accident? Nicky...."

"No, everything is all right. I'm sorry I had to disturb you. I tried tapping on your old man's window, but he must be dead to the world."

"You know he's not at home."

The candle-flame quivered with his laughter. "I didn't know, honestly. I was getting wet and I thought I could put up here for the night."

"Do you want something to drink?" I asked grudgingly.

"Coffee?"

Zetke woke up at last when we went into the kitchen. He stared at Chris affrontedly.

"I haven't come for you this time, Zetke."

Zetke turned his back on us. Chris carried the tray into the dining-room and I saw for the first time that Nicky walked like him, with a controlled vigour that hid his strength. Though his uniform and riding-boots were soaked, I had the impression that inside them his body was dry and glowing, springing independently out of the spurred boots into the wide padded shoulders of the coat.

He sat opposite me, drinking the coffee gratefully. Whatever there was of brutality in him was not marked in his big-boned handsome face but in his hands and I watched them furtively.

He said, "I've been chasing a kaffir the whole afternoon. He was on the hill and he got away into the cane. The rain saved him." He put his hand on some flying ants and the smell of their crushed bodies filled the room. "I'll get him tomorrow. I have an idea that he'll lie up in the cane and then double back. You might know this boy,

Helen. He's the husband of the girl who brought your brother back. She's a nuisance, the girl, she runs after white men, and the boy gave her a hiding and then tried to poison her. You must remember her."

"Yes. Chris, you didn't think I had anything to do with handing you over...."

"Not for a moment."

"I'm glad of that at least."

"What surprised me was to find you here with him. I thought somehow you would have gone away, even married."

"There was Nicky."

"I understand now. I have no bitterness left in me, Helen. But I dislike your father."

"I could almost dislike you too, Chris, for what you've done with your life. The natives say you are cruel. Why couldn't you have done something else?"

"What? I'm the youngest of four boys, you know. After the war there wasn't a place for me on our farm. I did some hunting in Tanganyika, but I became interested in the animals and I spent a lot of time watching them. There was no money in that. I could have gone into my uncle's office in Pretoria, but I didn't fit in there. My mother was beginning to worry about me and I took this job. You say I've a name for cruelty. That's because I'm no good at it really. I begin to take sides; sometimes I'll hate a man for what he has done." He yawned as suddenly as a child.

"I'll make up a bed for you in the spare room. You should have taken off your coat. Hang it up in the kitchen now."

He watched me as I made the bed. When I turned to go he took a step towards me. "Helen...." The word extinguished the candle-flame. He said, "Sorry, I've got no matches ... in my coat pocket." He was close to me and the heat from his body steamed through his damp clothes.

There was the brief gladness of his embrace and then the silence, heavy with secrets. I knew already that there could be no peace between us unless I told him that Nicky was his son. But it was too late to tell him now. Nicky belonged to John. He fell asleep. He had unbraided my hair and he lay with his fingers caught in it. I freed myself with a sharp prickling of the scalp as the strands on his fingers parted. I went quietly into my room, feeling for the furniture in the darkness.

He had gone when I awoke. I stripped his bed and opened all the windows in the house. It was still early and there was nothing to do until the afternoon. Then there would be a meeting of the dance committee. We should sit under the trees at Drew's Pride for two hours deciding whether we should have a sit-down supper or serve tea and sandwiches at the next dance. Miss Pimm would read the minutes of the last meeting….

The housegirl came into the room. I gave the bowl to her, and she carried it out carefully as though it were made of glass. Her face clouded as Chris rode past the gate. A native was handcuffed to the stirrup. There was only a fraction of balance that prevented him from falling and I watched fearfully for the moment that Chris would quicken his horse. If anything he went more slowly. I watched them all the way down the break, sure that Chris would gallop his horse as soon as he was out of sight; but it was a long time before he reached the bridge and then he was still travelling at a slow walk with his prisoner balanced at the stirrup. A constable met him there and took charge of the man. Now the horse sprang away and Chris bent low in the saddle, releasing suddenly the disciplined force of his body. He rode up to the gate and tied the reins to the post.

"You see I got him."

"Yes."

"I could have got him last night if it hadn't been for the rain," he said eagerly.

"I suppose so."

He came up the steps to me. The light touch of his marked hands surprised me. They were thick and heavy and the knuckles were ringed like the trunk of a tree; each one was glazed with blood. He saw my abhorrence and for a second I felt the weight of his hands; but he laughed at me.

"It's not always like this, Helen. Sometimes I help them during floods or in famines and fires…."

"They hate you, Chris."

"They're not smoking dagga and drinking skokiaan, that's why. I'm sorry I couldn't come back to you as you remembered me Helen."

"I'm not the same either," I said humbly.

"Perhaps…."

I shook my head. "It's too late, Chris."

"I'll put my pride in my pocket and come and see your old man."

"Well…. Let me prepare him, give me a few days."

He was smiling as he rode away.

John came home that afternoon. By supper-time he was surly and suspicious. He sat opposite me in the place that Chris had occupied the night before.

"Full of secrets aren't you, Helen ?" he said. "That's what Lucy was like. She had a face like yours and she would look at a man, even her own brother, and make him wonder about her." He got up and walked to the window. "Zetke told me that Van der Westhuizen spent the night here."

"He was caught in the rain."

"I suppose he…I suppose he made love to you?" He had been kicking gently at the wall, but now he sent his foot crashing against it and then limped back to the table. "One day he'll be found in the cane with a knife in his back and good riddance."

"John."

He nursed his foot tenderly. "You know, Helen, I'm not going to run any risks. About Nicky, I mean."

"I can't tell him about Nicky, I wish I could…." "The best thing for you to do is to get away from him. I thought you were cured of it. Why don't you go to Lucy for a few months?"

"John, I love him. There's never been anybody else," He sent cups and plates to the floor with a sweep of his arm. There was a patter of bare feet as the servants ran away. "I'll kill you, Helen. Now listen to me. A week or so ago a man with a grievance came to me and asked me if I would give him an alibi if anything happened to Van der Westhuizen. Like a fool I told him to go to hell. You think that over."

The first attempt on Chris's life was made when he rode out to the farm to see me. He said that he recognised the man, but John and two natives swore that the man had not left our barracks that evening. I told Chris not to come to see me again for I was going to Durban.

Chapter ten

Early one morning I sat with Aunt Lucy on the balcony outside her bedroom. There was no traffic yet in front of the house except a little cart drawn by a sorrowful horse and three cows swaying down the road to a patch of veld nearby. An old Indian, thin as a spider, sat in front of the cart on top of a bag of carrots that spilled with the jolting and fell amongst the other vegetables piled behind him in a mass of orange and scarlet and green and purple. The cart held our eyes until it tumbled down the hill into Durban's streets. There remained still something of its brightness, for some of the carrots had been shaken loose and lay in cones of yellow in the street. Presently the Indian woman who worked in the house next door caught sight of them as she swept the pathway. She gathered them into her sari eagerly as though she were starving.

Aunt Lucy nudged me. "We weren't quick enough. We could have had those." The woman went away with the carrots, but she was soon back again, this time with a little pan into which she scooped the droppings of the cows. "Old hog," commented Aunt Lucy.

The sun was well above the sea now and the street became busier. Ricksha boys plodded up the hill to collect their vehicles from a shed on the outskirts of the city and then went sailing down again, their feet clear of the ground and their bodies rigid between the shafts; a fine sight.

Across the street people were moving about the hospital grounds, Some of the ambulant patients from the men's ward were already in the garden and they waved to three nurses who stood on the veranda upstairs. The nurses, like royalty, waved and smiled. Then they came downstairs and walked through the garden. Rain was threatening and they wore scarlet-lined cloaks that billowed out behind them. There was no slovenliness in their movements and it seemed to me that even the number of steps they must take had been laid down by regulation. I had always liked watching the hospital, but now it fascinated me, absorbed as it was in its own busyness like a hive of bees.

"I've got a good mind to become a nurse."

"My dear, you're not serious surely? Do you realise the things they have to do? Empty… Never mind. And washing men. Think of that."

"I haven't anything to do at Westongate now. I sit there all day with nothing to do."

"When I was your age…. What? Twenty-nine…. I was having… the time of my life. Did I ever tell you about…"

"Yes, you did. Well, I'm bored most of the time at West orngate."

"Nursing is rather common, I think. And yet it would be quite nice for me to have you there. You could drop in for a game of cribbage now and then. I know Matron Carpenter. I'll take you over to see her if you like. But what about John? Surely he wouldn't be agreeable? He's always hoping you might make a good match; you haven't lost your looks yet."

"He'll be agreeable."

That morning I signed probationary papers and at the end of the month I took up my training. John was pleased with me and he turned out the man who had been dogging Chris. When Chris was transferred up country soon afterwards he tried to force me to return to the farm, but I would not go. For the first time in my life my time was fully occupied and I could be sure now that I wouldn't grow like Aunt Lucy. Chris wrote to me at the hospital and I saw him whenever he came to Durban. He had been promoted and Aunt Lucy urged me to marry him. He did not speak of marriage now. Our relationship had become easy and pleasant, without obligation, and he seemed content with that.

It was not until September of the next year that I managed to get leave that coincided with the school holidays. Aunt Lucy had put off her holiday in July and she travelled home with Nicky and me.

The same boxes were standing against the wall and the chocolate machine was still jammed. The same child, surely, was crying beside it. But the advertisement on the hoarding was different. A gigantic, martial young man offered a rifle to the youth of Westongate to mark the year, 1914. Nicky and Peter stood in front of the poster admiringly until John roared at Nicky.

"Come along and hurry up about it."

He was in an evil mood because the cane had been ruined. That was a year of tremendous gales that left the canetops hanging in tatters. The worst was still to come and we spent most of the time indoors, but one evening we struggled up to Drew's Pride for Mrs. Drew's birthday party.

She was nearing seventy and the peacocks were dead, but she was still elegant in a wistful flurry of laces and frills. Nancy as usual was dressed in the same fashion and with her pink-and-white shiny skin she looked for all the world like a marzipan doll.

With a cry of joy she grouped the children about the piano and started them on a round. Nothing would induce Nicky to sing. He caused so much confusion by not coming in on his turn and by wrestling with Peter that from very shame I called him to me. He sat next to me, scraping his boots together irritatingly and when the clock on the landing struck nine he counted the chimes.

"Look at Peter," I said, " He's even turning the pages. Why don't you behave as he does, like a…like a little gentleman?"

"Peter is a bit of a pansy sometimes."

He spoke loudly, but fortunately nobody heard, for the singing had reached crescendo. Colonel Edington, who had become slightly deaf, caught the word pansy, and thinking that Nicky was interested in gardening, engaged him in a long conversation about flowers. I could sit next to the Colonel with impunity now, for I had passed the age that he considered attractive in women.

John was bored and to pass the time he flirted with Miss Pimm. She had been enjoying the music, tapping her foot and nodding her head, but under his bold glance she crossed her arms over her chest, staring with a martyred expression at the wall. John leaned forward, his hand within reach of her knee.

"Who is driving you home tonight, Enid?"

She brought her hands down to her knees to meet the new threat. "Colonel Edington. Why?"

"I thought I might offer," said John, leering at her flat chest.

Now she folded her arms again. "It would be quite unnecessary. Under any circumstances."

His hand was so close to her knee that she gathered herself for a spring. I held my breath. Aunt Lucy, who was sitting next to John, reproved him with a jab in the back and his hand came down heavily on Miss Pimm's knee. She didn't move. She leaned back in her chair and for a moment I thought she had fainted.

John said easily, "Sorry, Enid," and strolled across the room to join the group of men.

"I jerked John's arm, Enid, it wasn't really his fault," said Aunt Lucy, sneering at poor Miss Pimm.

Richard followed John and we were now left with only Colonel Edington and Mr. Farrell. Westongate affairs always ended like this; the women at one end of the room trying to enliven the party, assisted by the less robust men like Mr. Farrell or tame old tom-cats like Colonel Edington. At the other end of the room the men talked about sugar-cane, politics and the war, in an hypnotic haze of tobacco and brandy. That evening Colonel Edington deserted us because he wanted to tell again how they had turned the Boers at Elandslaagte. This made Mrs. Drew nervous, for she was still hoping that Chris would come to the party although it was so late, but the children ran over to listen. Nancy kept on playing in a listless fashion.

Mr. Drew had fallen into a doze and Mrs. Farrell was yawning with sudden gasps politely repressed. Colonel Edington came to the end of his story and Nancy stopped playing. The sound of the wind came into the room.

"Listen to that," said Nancy. She put her hand against the window apprehensively. "Just listen to it."

Mr. Drew sat up and blinked as though he was astonished to find us there. "My God, listen to the wind."

"It could come in and blow us away," cried Joan. She whirled round as though the wind had already caught her.

"I knew a woman who was cut clean in halves by a piece of corrugated iron," said Aunt Lucy.

There was an argument going on outside and presently the Indian servant came in. "Miss Angus…" He looked appealingly at Richard. "Somebody wanting Miss Angus, young Miss Angus." Aunt Lucy sat down again with a snort.

I found Mr. Bannerjee and Perian in the hall. "There has been an accident," said Mr. Bannerjee, "I beg you to come, Miss Angus. It is Chanjaldi's husband, Ramlagen…."

Down at the huts there was such an uproar that John drove on to get the policeman. Mr. Bannerjee pushed a way for me through the Indians who jammed Ramlagen's hut. Some were yelling that a piece of tin had cut Ramlagen, others that Mr. Bannerjee had stabbed him. Women screamed in my ear that they had seen Chanjaldi trying to murder him. Chanjaldi alone said nothing. She lay face downwards on the floor, her long hair trampled by the feet of the crowd. Ramlagen had a savage wound in the neck and a long clean cut across the ribs. I cleared the hut and began to plug his wounds.

Mr. Bannerjee had remained and Chanjaldi crept to him and laid her head on his feet. I had last seen her in a silken sari with a flower in her hair. Ramlagen had come home unexpectedly, and finding her dressed like that he had dragged her by the hair across the clearing to his hut.

"I have listened to her weeping night after night," said Mr. Bannerjee. "But how could I interfere again between them? They are husband and wife and besides Ramlagen, as everybody knows, is a much stronger man than me. I went away to Durban for a week and when I came back this afternoon her sister Amoya told me that she had been tied up in the hut without food and water. He has done indescribable things to her, Miss Angus, but nobody would interfere, for they say she deserves it because she answers Ramlagen back and she must learn to respect him. Only Amoya helped her. She brought her food and water and herself removed the burrs that were tormenting her. A child.... But her mother would not take Chanjaldi into the house. She hates Chanjaldi." He looked down at her in despair. "Miss Angus, you must know she is my daughter.... There was that summer when Leela walked alone in the cane. All Perian's children she loves, but from the first she wanted Chanjaldi out of her house.... This afternoon Amoya brought her to my house and stayed with her there. Ramlagen came to fetch her. I ask you this, how could I stab him, everybody knows how strong he is. A piece of tin fell on him and now he says I stabbed him. This will make a good court case. I have my witnesses, let him bring his."

The crowd was gathering again, for the policeman had arrived. Men and women milled round him like bundles of rags in the wind, each one offering to testify. He arrested Mr. Bannerjee and had Ramlagen removed to hospital. This was the preliminary to the court case that delighted the Indians for many months. Mr. Bannerjee was let out on bail and the case remanded because of the conflicting evidence. In the end Chanjaldi laid a charge of assault against Ramlagen and he was fined and cautioned; the case against Mr. Bannerjee was thrown out of court much to everybody's disappointment. The policeman grew sick of the sight of Chanjaldi, for Ramlagen had only to look at her threateningly and she would have him summoned. He became almost tender in his handling of her.

Mr. Bannerjee built a four-roomed house at the foot of the hill and Chanjaldi moved in there. She had the best room and a servant to do the housework. Mr. Bannerjee became shabbier, but she had many beautiful saris. Sometimes Ramlagen squatted in the house with his relations, twenty-two of them counting infant nephews and nieces, and Mr. Bannerjee would have to get an eviction order against him. Chanjaldi had many lovers, this was well known, but Ramlagen did not divorce her until years later when his family left the district.

It looked as though we were going to be cooped up for the rest of the holidays. The wind showed no signs of abating and we all became jumpy and inclined to quarrel.

"It must blow itself out, it can't keep up like this," said John, looking through the window at the desolate fields.

"You said that yesterday and the day before," snapped Aunt Lucy.

"Anybody would think I had arranged this solely for the joy of being shut up in the house with you, Lucy."

He settled himself in his chair to snooze over a magazine. Aunt Lucy sat at the table with a pack of cards before her. She said nothing, but she drummed her fingers persistently until I took the hint.

"Would you like a game of cribbage, Aunt Lucy?"

"Cribbage?" She looked at me in astonishment as though she had never heard the word before.

Nicky immediately sidled out of the room, but she whipped round on him, her eyes sparkling. "You'd better take a hand, Nicky, it's not much fun with only two playing."

"I've got to do some studying," he mumbled.

"Study during the holidays," Aunt Lucy snorted. "I never heard of such a thing. You must be a dull boy. Sometimes I do think he's a bit dull, Helen." She beckoned me to her side and breathed into my neck. "Do you keep his bowels open? Perhaps he needs a dose of medicine. He always seems so sleepy when I speak to him." She looked at him without affection.

"You're enough to make anybody sleepy," said John.

I could see a row brewing. I said sharply, "Sit down and play at once, Nicky."

"Don't let her stand in the way of his learning," said John. "And Nicky, don't scrape your feet along the floor like that. Are you flat-footed or what? I'm paying out a fortune at that damned school...."

"What is it you have to learn, child?" Aunt Lucy asked. She riffled the cards lovingly between her fingers.

"Latin."

"Decline Amo," she commanded.

"Amo, ama..." Nicky hesitated and then hissed.

"My God," said John.

"You don't pronounce it like that," said Aunt Lucy.

"You can pronounce Latin any way you like, it's a dead language," John declared.

"Now, John, if you remember.... I was always better than you at languages. Don't you remember Father saying..."

"We'll cut for deal," I said loudly.

"Oh, are we going to play?" She beamed at Nicky. "Sit here, my boy, it's a lucky seat."

We began the miserable game. John glared at Aunt Lucy fixedly for a while and then began to nod. Soon he was snoring gently. From the kitchen came the rattle of china, a homely sound against the snarling of the wind.

"I knew a woman once who was cut clean in halves by a piece of corrugated iron," said Aunt Lucy, picking up her cards. Her face brightened and she tapped each card separately as she counted. She discarded, changed her mind and at last threw out the card she had put in the crib in the first place. "Yes, she was cut clean in halves by this piece of corrugated iron."

"You told us that last night," said Nicky.

"Did I ?" She looked into her hand and murmured in a blurred voice, "Fifteen two, fifteen four, fifteen six and a pair is eight," showed her hand with a rapid flourish and put the cards into the pack before we had a word to say. I was sure she had had only six in her hand. Nicky formed the word Cheat with his lips and kicked me under the table while Aunt Lucy pored secretively over the crib.

"You count too quickly, Aunt Lucy," I said tactfully.

"What do you mean by that, Helen?"

"One is apt to make a mistake if one counts too quickly," I explained.

She played a straight game for a few hands after that. The Indian brought the teacups in and John came to life. He stood at the window while he drank his tea.

"Look at it," he said morosely. "Smashing the cane to pieces. I shan't make a farthing this year."

"I can't imagine why you go in for cane, John," said Aunt Lucy, "when you think of all the things that can happen to it. If it's not too much rain, it's drought; if it's not disease, it's wind. I'd lease this and put my money into gold shares if I were you. A person can make quite a lot of money even tickey-snatching."

"You're spoiling for a fight, Lucy."

"You don't even need capital for it," Aunt Lucy persisted. "You can buy on margin. Then you wait for the shares to go up threepence and you sell. You can't possibly go wrong. Then if you make a packet, you can put it into dividend-paying shares and you don't have to worry any more. They simply send the cheques to you."

Nicky, leaning his chest against the table, had lit the matches on the crib board. He watched them flare with a dreamy expression.

"Get out," John roared at him, "maniac. Setting the place on fire."

Nicky hastened to obey him and before he could start quarrelling with Aunt Lucy again, I persuaded him to take Nicky's place at the card table. It was the worst thing I could have done. Before long Aunt Lucy cheated. John hit the table with his fist, sending the cups at the other end into a little dance on their saucers.

"If you please, Lucy, let me see your hand. You had four, not six."

"Six," said Aunt Lucy.

"I say four."

They stared at each other for an ominous minute before they went on with the game. John caught her hand when she tried to cheat again, before she could get rid of the cards.

"Oh no you don't. You've got eight there, not ten."

She muttered at him and then calmly put ten on her score. John pulled the match out of her hand, pegging her down two points. She put them on again, with a tremulous hand. John took the matches out of the board and broke them into little pieces.

"Damn you, Lucy, I won't have this bloody cheating." He scattered the cards. "You've been cheating all your life and I've had enough of it. How did you get Mother to leave you all her money? Cheating and lying. John does this, John does that...."

"I only told her about you and the intombis...."

John threw the cribbage board on the floor and kicked it to pieces. Aunt Lucy shrieked and pretended to faint.

"Get the ammonia bottle, that will soon bring her round," he said, still stamping on the cribbage board.

Thereupon Aunt Lucy sat up. "Pack my things, Helen. I'm going home. And as for my money, John, you won't see a penny of it. I'd sooner burn every share I own. I might leave you some, Helen. Just come and help me with my things because I'm all trembly."

"You'll have to walk to the station," said John, "and this gale will blow you off your feet and good riddance too. You can go now, this minute."

He opened the door and the wind charged in, throwing the cards about the room and tearing Aunt Lucy's hair from its bun. I banged the door. Now the room was peaceful, for we were all stunned by the force of the wind, and I tried to get Aunt Lucy out before they started on each other again, but she had only just begun to enjoy herself. She shook herself free.

"For goodness' sake, Helen, stop clawing at me. There are just a few things I want to say to you before I go, John…."

I left them hard at it. Nicky was in the passage listening to them, astonished by some of the accusations they were hurling at each other. I held up the broken cribbage board.

"Look," I whispered.

We put our arms about each other and danced down the passage into the kitchen. Zetke stared at us.

"Why are you two so happy when the wind blows like this and your elders quarrel?"

"Burn this, Zetke, let it burn until there is nothing but ashes."

The fire blazed more fiercely for a few minutes, but Zetke had no pleasure in it. He sat on the wood-box with his head buried in his hands.

"Have you been drinking skokiaan, Zetke?" Nicky asked.

"I am bewitched in the head," he moaned. "The wind blowing like this makes Zetke as weak as a coolie and I ache from the top of my head to my toes." He looked at me beseechingly. "Give me some of those little white sweets."

"They're not sweets, Zetke, and if you eat them like sweets you will die. I will give you two."

"This is great foolishness," he said as he chewed the aspirins. "Give me more, two are for weak children or coolies or women."

"You're not getting any more."

Zetke bowed his head again. Faintly we could hear the sounds of battle from the dining room. There was a spatter of twigs against the window-pane, the last of the small wood from the flamboyant that writhed naked against the sky. Two big white clouds drove straight for the east window, but before they crashed the wind lifted them up over the roof and whirled them away across the racing canetops. A hen sailed along the yard, diabolically pursued by a paraffin tin. When I ran outside to rescue her, she was nowhere to be seen and there was no time to look for her. A sheet of iron, torn from the shed roof, was falling towards me and as I ran to the kitchen I had an anguished memory of the woman Aunt Lucy had known.

"Keep the door closed," said Zetke. "The medicine is beginning to cure me, but if the wind blows on me it will spoil everything."

Nicky and I tiptoed into the passage. "They must have killed each other," Nicky whispered, for there was no sound now from the dining-room.

Aunt Lucy and John were sitting at the table with the obvious intention of finishing off a bottle of port that stood between them.

The wine made them both sick and the next morning Aunt Lucy stayed in bed although the wind had died down. She demanded a doctor, for she said that the calves of her legs were aching and that she was in for paralysis. I didn't like to remind her that she had had the gramophone going and had danced until all hours. She had danced barefooted, gasping, "Watch the toes, John, watch the toes…. My toes have got music in them."

John recovered sufficiently to walk down the breaks with us to see what damage had been done. We could follow the path of the wind, for the cane leaned over as though a heavy hand had stroked it. On the other side of the hill the cane was ruined. The topsoil had been blown away and the roots obscenely exposed. I felt sorry for John. At first he stood silently, the story of his struggle with the land marked in his face.

Then he shook his fist at the cane. "Jesus," he said in a tone of insult, "Jesus Christ." He pulled a stool out by the roots and trampled it. "I'll pull the lot out. I'll grow mealies, lucerne, anything but this stuff." He kicked the stool and the soil flew out of the roots in a fine powder, as though the cane were giving up the ghost. Without warning, John got sick again.

Nicky and I sat on the bank, decently looking away from him. We could see the beach now that the cane was down. Indians were fishing there and while we watched they brought a big fish in. Nicky jumped up in excitement. Peter was already running down the hill and Nicky went to meet him.

"You come back here," said John, tenderly wiping his mouth.

Nicky did not turn back and John picked up a stick. He watched Nicky and then broke the stick into pieces. I kept well out of his reach until he had thrown the last piece away.

"Let's go along and look at the seed-cane, John. Those plots are low-lying, they mightn't have caught it so badly." I took his arm. The smell of him came to me, but I tried not to show my aversion.

We walked down the hill to the fields that had been so promising a week before, a brilliant green against the older cane. This young stuff had been badly knocked about and John gave it one look before he walked on. I went down on my knees and tried to straighten the tender stalks and to build up the soil around the roots. This cane had not been grown from cuttings but from seed painstakingly gathered. As I cosseted the plants I knew a moment of tenderness for him and I got up to follow him, but he was in the valley by then, talking to Mr. Drew.

The boys were admiring a big salmon. "My father catching him," said Sowa. "Bimeby he giving us some to cook."

"We'll light a fire behind the dunes," said Nicky. "Come along, Peter, we'll go and collect some driftwood for it. You too, Sowa."

The Indians were fishing stolidly. I sat down to watch them. There were white horses on the sea and sometimes a great breaker came for me so threateningly that I scrambled backwards. It was an exciting day and the dogs ran ceaselessly up and down the beach to scatter the gulls as soon as they settled. The boys went by with enough driftwood to roast an ox. Peter's face was already burned, for the sun, like a moon behind the thin clouds, had a promise of summer.

Perian got another strike. "Jaldi," he yelled, and the other fishermen anchored their own rods as they ran to help him, while he played the big fish, for he was too feeble to handle the eighteen-foot rod he held. Already there was the gleam of the salmon in the last breaker, a truer silver than the sea. It was half-an-hour before Perian yelled again. With one accord the men pulled and the fish was on the sands. It lay still for a second and then it leaped again, in a wash of silver from its own reflection in the sand. One of the men gaffed it and we all cried out in triumph with Perian. The sand turned from silver to pink, still beautiful.

"You're going to give us a few pieces," said Nicky.

"No fear. I selling this at hotel. I buying rum with money."

"Give us some of it, Perian," said Nicky, "or I'll tell Leela and then what will you get out of it? Not even one tot of rum."

His friends began to chaff him about Leela and grudgingly he cut off a few steaks. We lit a fire behind the dunes where we were sheltered from the wind. Here the weedy stools of cane straggled to meet clumps of grass that we cleared away conscientiously so that there would be no danger of the fire spreading.

Nicky straightened out a piece of rusty wire and put the fish on it between two stones. While we waited for it to cook, Sowa sang under his breath on one note. He was enjoying himself and he set himself the task of entertaining us.

"In Hindustan frogs are riding on snakes. He giving them good rides so he can eating those frogs." He laughed inordinately and we smiled in a polite way, though we didn't get the point. "I'm telling this story better in my own language."

"You told it jolly well," Peter encouraged him.

"It was frightful, don't tell any more," said Nicky. "You know we ought to get some more fish out of Perian as soon as we have finished this. Why let him waste it on rum?"

"He won't give you any more. He'll chase you."

"I'd like to see him try."

"Here your father," said Sowa, getting ready to run.

Nicky caught him by the arm. "He won't say anything, we've cleared all the grass away."

"What the hell do you think you're doing?" John asked.

"We're cooking some fish," said Nicky sulkily.

"Well, you can put that fire out."

"Sit down and have some with us, John," I said. "It's nearly cooked. Go on, sit down here with us."

"Please doing it," cried Sowa, radiant with a desire to please.

John wouldn't sit down until Nicky asked him. Perian sent up some more fish and it must have done John good because he became affable. The sun had turned before we thought of moving.

"Good God, Helen, do you realise that your aunt has been lying in bed all day without a soul near her?" He kicked sand over the fire and stamped on it. "Come along. We'll give her a game of cards to put her in a good mood. I want you two to be specially nice to her...."

"I'm not playing cards with her," Nicky declared. "I've had enough of Aunt Lucy these holidays to last me for the rest of my life."

"All right, you can stay here. Come along, Helen." As we walked through the cane, he became depressed. "Look at the stuff. I'll be in debt...."

"Perhaps Aunt Lucy will help you out."

"I was thinking of that. I'm going to try and borrow five hundred from her. I don't want to touch a mortgage and she won't expect interest."

"She might give it to you for a present."

"Pigs might fly. Anyhow, be as nice as possible to her. It's a pity I fought with her like that yesterday...."

Some of the boys were already in the garden waiting for their pay. An umfaan was playing a mouth-organ, enjoying the music he made, but Aunt Lucy shrieked at me the moment I stepped into the house.

"Tell them to stop that noise, I've got a splitting headache."

I said delicately to the umfaan, "The chieftainess does not feel like listening to any more music."

He looked at me in surprise, knocked his mouth-organ dry and blew one last sorrowful blast on it before he put it into his pocket. I took a cup of tea to Aunt Lucy. John bathed her temples with eau de cologne.

"They're still making a noise," Aunt Lucy whimpered.

"I'll go and pay them and if one of them makes a sound, I'll break his neck."

"You're suddenly very concerned about me," said Aunt Lucy suspiciously.

John smiled at her with his teeth clenched and went outside to pay the wages. "Rub here, Helen." She pointed to a spot above her left eye. The boys were quiet now and she drowsed beneath my caressing hand. "What's John after? Why is he so kind to me?"

"He's very fond of you…."

"I know what he's after. He's going to try and borrow money from me. He's going to make capital out of these winds. I know."

"You mustn't misjudge him, Aunt Lucy…."

She was almost asleep when somebody began banging the fire-bell. "They're doing it for spite," she screamed.

"No, there's a fire somewhere."

I ran outside. The umfaan, dancing with excitement, blew warning blasts on his mouth-organ. He pointed to a bright red line on the crest of the hill. Aunt Lucy gave up her headache and staggered on to the veranda.

"What's happening?"

"Fire. Look."

The Drews' bell was tolling and presently Richard rode down the hill with a team of his boys behind him. Zetke had stayed to harness the donkeys to the water-cart, but John and the other boys were already far down the cane-break. The boys threw up damp sacks like weapons and sang a song of menace against the fire. "We will slaughter our enemy, we will stamp it into the ground...."

"I think I'll go along too," I said. "You sit here and wait on the veranda, Aunt Lucy, the fresh air will do you good."

"I'm not staying here alone."

"Aunt Lucy, I think the boys may have caused the fire. They were cooking fish down there a little while ago and they might have wheedled some more out of Perian. If John gets his hands on them, there's bound to be trouble."

"Well, it will serve them right. They could be burnt to death. I noticed Nicky with those matches in the cribbage board yesterday, he simply couldn't resist lighting them."

"John might get into one of his tempers...."

"If he hurts them it will serve them right. Boys.... John was a destructive boy, but he never did anything like this."

The fire had been beaten out by the time I reached the field. The Zulus and Indians had dispersed and only Zetke was left. Richard was galloping his horse down the break. He would be cursing the fire, for Joan was to be confirmed that night and they would have to be in Illovo by seven o'clock. John was standing apart glaring at the smouldering trash.

I said, "Did you boys make another fire after we had gone, Nicky?"

There was a faint air of swaggering about him although he was nervous. "Yes. We got some more fish from Perian and then when that was finished we pinched some, at least I did. Perian came after us and I picked up a lighted stick and chased him. The fool ran straight for the cane. Peter was behind me. I don't know, one of us tripped and we fell in a heap. The stick fell on the trash and before we knew where we were there was a blaze, but we didn't attend to it straight away because Perian came at me with a knife and by the time we got rid of him it was too late to stop the fire. We tried to beat it out. Of course, Perian ran for his life and left us to face the music. But I made Sowa stay."

"Does John know who did it?"

"Of course. Peter told, you know what he is."

"These two they won't letting me going," wailed Sowa. "Ma, you telling them I must going."

"We're sure to let you get off scot free," said Nicky. "You're in this just as much as we are."

"I think you'd better hide, the three of you, until I talk to John. He's in a terrible temper."

Nicky whispered to Sowa and Peter and at a nod from me the three boys made a dash for the cane. John caught Peter and when Nicky saw him captured he returned sullenly to my side. But Sowa ran on, shrieking with terror. It wasn't long before Zetke brought him back. Sowa's hands were tied with his own belt and he had lost his trousers.

"This thing I could take and kill like a rat," said Zetke, who held Sowa by the back of the neck. "I could take two fully-grown coolies, dash their brains out one against the other and kill them instantly. When I close my fingers I can feel this weak creature's bones crack." He squeezed Sowa's neck. Nicky aimed a kick at him, but Zetke only laughed. He pushed Sowa to the ground and stood with his foot on the narrow chest.

"John, tell Zetke to let Sowa go."

"You'd better get out of this, Helen," he said. "I'm going to teach these three the lesson of their life."

"You haven't the right to punish Sowa or Peter."

"Get away from here."

"I'm not going." He twisted my arm behind my back and brought me close to his face, bright with sweat and streaked with black.

"John, for God's sake...."

He pushed me into the break. I stood still where he had left me. If I ran up to the Farrells'.... By that time he would have thrashed them. Richard.... I looked up at Drew's Pride. Joan was on the terrace, I could see the flutter of her white veil. Richard and I had been confirmed on the same day....

I sat down on the bank and put my fingers in my ears so that I should not hear the blows fall. What a row Mrs. Farrell would have with him. I took my fingers cautiously out of my ears. There was not a sound to be heard but the whispering of the cane and the surf. He wasn't hurting them after all. Probably he was lecturing them, in a deadly voice that would make poor Sowa faint with terror. A praying mantis climbed to the end of a cane-top and looked at me wisely. Chris would have called it a Hottentot's God. A cricket was chirruping, there was a flurry of movement as a cane-rat shot across the break.

I heard somebody screaming. As I ran down the break John passed me and I saw the bitterness in his face. There was a fire burning in the blackened trash and nearby Sowa rolled like an animal. Peter was hunched up, whimpering, his breath indrawn; but Nicky stood with his blistered hands outstretched, his face as impassive as Zetke's.

Sowa had fainted, but Zetke refused to carry him to the water-cart. "Coolies are cowards, they cannot stand a little pain. Nicky and Peter are men now. Nicky is a great chief, a hunter of lions…."

"'Carry Sowa to the cart, or I'll never give you medicine for your head again."

He picked Sowa up. "He should be thrown into the river and drowned like a rat."

Aunt Lucy gave them each a glassful of wine to drink when I had bandaged their hands. I made Sowa lie down on the sofa with a blanket over him, for he was suffering from shock. Zetke had inspanned the trap and it was waiting at the gate for me, but he had already gone home.

"I'll fetch Sowa's mother. It might give him more confidence if he sees her. I'd better take Peter home first though," I said to Aunt Lucy.

"How did it happen? Where's John? Did they start the fire?"

"John deliberately burnt their hands as a punishment."

"What were you doing to allow it, Helen? I thought you went there to stop him from doing a thing like this. The fool. He'll be put behind bars."

"If I had known he was going to burn them…. But I thought he would give them a hiding. Mrs. Farrell and Leela will probably both go to the police."

"The police. Helen, that boy Van der Westhuizen…. He's high

up in the police force. You could go and see him and explain. You're friendly with him. Wear that blue dress of yours. You could make a complaint against them for starting the fire...."

"Talk sense, Aunt Lucy."

"I was only trying to make a plan. Otherwise we'll have to bribe them. You see what you can do with Peter and I'll work on the Sammy. I wish John was here, he might be able to think of something...."

"He's probably getting blind drunk. He was sorry the moment he did it."

"If only the boys would keep it from their parents. But we can always say John did it for their own good. After all, I remember my mother telling me they had to bite him to cure him of biting people...."

I helped Peter on the cart. "Peter, you shouldn't tell your mother about this, you know. She'll never let you play with Nicky any more...."

I touched up the horse and left her standing there with a sovereign held out enticingly. We were driving away from the sunset towards the sea. Peter knelt on the seat to look back, but for me there was no beauty now. I was aware only of the shape and colour of visible things.

He spoke to me shyly. "I won't tell my mother what happened."

"It would save a lot of trouble," I said unwillingly.

"I know."

"Will you tell Joan?"

He shook his head. We could see the house in the clearing, stark in its ruined garden. Farrell still spoke of moving it nearer the trees, but it remained where it was; nor had he ever got round to painting the front gate. It was a drunken little gate, held by only one hinge and Mrs. Farrell was taking a chance by leaning on it. She raised her hand to wave to us.

"You'll have to tell her, Peter...."

"No, I don't want her or my sisters to know. Or Joan. You see, it wouldn't matter what they did to your father, they'd always feel badly about it. Don't you see?"

"Yes, I think so."

"The worst was when Zetke lit the fire and your father tied our hands up. Sowa didn't realise what was going to happen until they burnt him. But I did. I knew as soon as Zetke started to collect the wood."

I said bitterly, "You don't mind telling me about it."

For all his delicacy he looked at me without comprehension. "No. I don't mind telling you somehow."

He held up his hands as we stopped before Mrs. Farrell. "My hands are burnt, but it's all right, Helen put some ointment on them."

"Oh Peter, Peter, how did you do it?" She was halfway between anger and pity as she helped him down from the cart. "You're always hurting yourself. Now I don't want to be nasty, Helen, but Nicky was at the bottom of this, wasn't he?"

"In a way he was," said Peter. "We were grilling some fish and there was a bit of skylarking. We burnt out an acre of half-grown cane and some seed-cane Mr. Angus had been experimenting with for twelve months. Nicky got burnt too and an Indian boy."

"Don't tell me Nicky got burnt," exclaimed Mrs. Farrell.

I said, "Worse than either of them."

"Well, fancy that. It's the first time I've ever known him to get hurt. It's usually Peter. I thought I heard the fire-bells, but there was nothing we could do; Henry is in bed with malaria. Come in and have a cup of tea, Helen, and you can tell me all about it."

"Peter will tell you. I've got to go down to the Indian huts."

Leela was sitting at her door, puffing a cheroot, too indolent to come to the road to see what I wanted. Serya waddled across the clearing. She was the midwife now and a great gossip if she could find anybody to talk to.

"Perian drunk bastard," she said, showing me a mouth full of betel-nut. It was shocking in that bland face set comfortably in three shiny chins. "Him stealing ring from Leela's toe while she sleeping. She hitting, I thinking him dead." She pointed to Perian, who lay in the grass beside the river.

He was not dead. He crawled forward an inch or two, waveringly, like a chameleon and then collapsed again. Leela walked over to him, looking at him as though she were assessing in pence what he was worth.

Serya settled herself by the roadside for a heart-to-heart talk. "Ma, Chanjaldi lying all the time with mans…."

I shouted to Leela, but she was slow in answering me. She drew back her foot as though she were going to kick Perian and then she shrugged her shoulders at such wasted effort.

"Leela, I've some bad news for you," I called.

She spun the end of her cheroot into the road. There was little beauty left to her; she was old already and sharpened by avarice. One look from her and Serya hastened away.

I leaned down. "Sowa and Peter and Nicky were cooking some fish and they set the cane alight. They all got burnt on the hands."

She asked fearfully. "Why you not bringing him with you?"

"He's frightened. I think he might quieten down if he sees you."

She hesitated. "I not liking to leave Perian. Him hiding ring, bimeby him fetching and I catching him."

"You had better come with me to Sowa. He keeps on screaming. Perhaps in the morning he will be mad."

"What the matter with that boy? Never he is crying."

She was alarmed now. She waited only to set three of her little daughters to watching Perian and then climbed up on the cart beside me.

I said carefully, "Leela, we might have to go to the police about this. My father is very angry, it will cost him a lot of money because the cane is too young to be cut."

Leela was always quick. "What the police doing to Nicky and Peter if you telling?"

"Well, it was mainly Perian's fault, you see, he tried to stab Nicky…."

"That man he making plenty trouble. He stealing ring last night…." She chewed some betel-nut to soothe herself. I couldn't bear the smell of her. "Sowa hurting his hands bad?"

"Just a few blisters. But he keeps on screaming."

"Sowa not doing that," she said reflecting.

Aunt Lucy's voice was a wonder of softness when she spoke to Leela. "The boy seems better, though he still goes off into screams now and then. I can't understand it, he's older than Nicky and yet he carries on like a child. Not a whimper out of Nicky. You see we made him comfortable on that sofa. He had some wine. It might be a good idea if you had some too. Most upsetting."

I could have slapped her. Leela's eyes became brilliant as she followed Aunt Lucy into the dining-room and took the glass of wine from her. She merely passed it before her lips. Sowa held out his hands to her and a storm of Hindustani broke from him.

"He is spilling the beans," I said, and that wiped the fatuous smile from Aunt Lucy's face.

Leela sat on the floor beside the sofa. An intense quiet came over her and I looked closely at her, for she could achieve at will this remoteness when she was hatching a scheme to make money or when she was praying. I hoped now that she was praying. Aunt Lucy fidgeted, slightly taken aback by her stillness. The jewels in Leela's nostrils were twinkling under the light and I passed the time by thinking of Perian creeping upon her to take the ring from her toe.

At last she said, "You giving me fifteen pounds, I not telling the police." She looked at Sowa and he gave a nod like a crafty buyer at an auction sale.

"Fifteen pounds," Aunt Lucy and I said together. Aunt Lucy went on, "If John were only here, he'd knock her flat."

"How much you giving?"

"Two pounds."

A glimmer passed over Leela's face as though deep within herself she smiled. "Fifteen pounds," she said.

"We might go to two pounds ten," Aunt Lucy said.

Pound by pound we crept up during an hour of bargaining and shilling by shilling Leela came down. She might have got more, but Sowa suddenly became nervous of John's return. When the price had reached ten pounds he nudged Leela and she stood up, helping him to his feet.

"We'd better pay," I whispered.

Aunt Lucy paid her in sovereigns that clinked one after the other into the little bag at her waist. Then I had to drive them home, for both she and Sowa were afraid of ghosts.

"I should make you walk, Leela," I said. "You have done a wicked thing tonight and we are no longer friends."

She covered her face with her sari and wailed. When she recovered she stroked my arm gently. "Ma, Sowa not working him hands sore. Better him getting money, police getting money, no good."

"The police shouldn't have come into it, you devil. Don't you come near me again." I could hear her lamentations long after I had left the huts.

As I let myself into the house, Nicky called to me. "Isn't he home yet, Helen?"

"No. Why don't you go to sleep? Are your hands hurting you?" I sat at the foot of the bed in the darkness.

"They're not hurting much. I keep thinking of him, though. I wish he'd come home."

"He'll probably sleep at the hotel."

"You don't think he'll commit suicide."

"Suicide? Him? Oh Nicky, if only I had stood up to him…. But I thought he was going to give you a hiding, that's all."

"He burnt Sowa first and then Peter."

"He made you wait. I can't believe he'd be so cold-blooded and cruel. We'll leave him, you don't have to stay…."

"Shut up, Helen. You don't understand. That's the terrible part of it. He didn't burn me. When it came to my turn, he couldn't do it. He just stood there, holding my hands and he couldn't do it. I put them in the fire myself. He's a coward, Helen."

I sat with him until he fell asleep. Aunt Lucy's voice crackled through the stillness. "Helen. I think I'll have a drink of my tonic, it might send me off. Pass me the tumbler, I've got the bottle under the bed here."

"There isn't a tumbler. You've put your teeth into it."

"Well, go and get one."

"I'm not traipsing about the house. Nicky might wake up. Drink it out of the bottle."

"How low. Give me the soap-dish, that's clean. Give it a wipe with the fresh towel." She held the pink soap-dish delicately between her fingers. "I hate that snivelling little coolie. Of all the sly things. I gave him a five-shilling Sterkspruit share so that he wouldn't say anything to his mother. I said, 'You keep this and one day you'll get a pound for it.' And the moment his mother came in he turned on me." She filled up the soap dish and handed it politely to me. Her voice drowsed sensuously. "When you come to think of it, John is magnificent. Other men...such weaklings...."

Her hair, dyed with henna, shone spuriously in the candlelight. She had dyed too the bare patch on her scalp so that it wouldn't show white. The artful old thing. She began to snore with exasperated little puffs of sound.

The next morning I drove down to the hotel to bring John home. Leela was sitting on the grass opposite the Indian bar. She came over to talk to me, but she kept a watch on the door.

"I not wanting leaving this place, bimeby Perian coming out I catching him," she said.

"Go and get hold of one of the waiters. I'll watch for Perian." Her face became sombre because I spoke to her so coldly.

She went to the back of the hotel at a run and returned with a waiter. He was madly in love with Chanjaldi and he took no notice of me, but began pestering Leela to take a message to Chanjaldi. Leela wasn't interested in his mooning. She took up her position near the bar-room door again.

"Is Mr. Angus inside?" I asked the waiter.

"Yes. He sleep here last night."

"Well, go and tell him that I'm waiting to take him home."

Perian came out of the bar. He danced on the lawn for a few seconds before Leela overcame him. She caught him by the shoulders and, spinning him round, kicked him hard. He ran a few yards before he fell. Leela propped him up again and sent him on his way with another kick.

"Leela, for heaven's sake, you're hurting him," I cried.

"Him spending all the time money. Him taking ring, selling it. Plenty time him kicking me when he sober."

The waiter had come back. He looked with horror on Leela, who was kicking Perian down the road now. Then he shrugged his shoulders. Now he was reasonable and alert for a tip.

"Mr. Angus saying you go home, he sleeping here again tonight."

"Tell him that I shall stay here until he comes out."

For an hour the waiter passed between us with messages, but John would not come home and Nicky went back to school without seeing him.

Chapter eleven

Aunt Lucy lent John the five hundred pounds he asked for, but not a week passed that she didn't write to him asking for payment. At Christmas-time, when Nicky and I went to the farm, she travelled with us and she was still talking about the five hundred pounds.

John was in such a mournful mood that we all felt sorry for him. "I'd join up to get a bit of company," he said. "It's time you came home and did your duty looking after me, Helen, instead of a lot of strangers."

"She's doing an important job now. They'll be able to use Helen as a war nurse," said Aunt Lucy grandly.

She had hired an umfaan to stay near her and watch for snakes and he sat under the table while she ate her Christmas dinner, for the heat had driven us outside into the shade of the flamboyant tree.

"I might as well tell you what I'm giving you for Christmas, John," Aunt Lucy said after her third glass of wine.

"You gave me a tie," said John.

Aunt Lucy carved a piece of turkey and handed it to the umfaan under the table. "I'm giving you five hundred pounds, John." She speared a baked potato for the umfaan.

John walked round the table to kiss her. "Lucy, we'll drink your health. God bless you. It's the most ... I can't think of the word...."

"Princely," I suggested.

"It's the most princely gift."

We all kissed Aunt Lucy. There was a solemn silence broken only by the smacking of the umfaan's lips. Aunt Lucy poured out half-a-glassful of wine for him.

"Don't give him that, you'll make him sick," John warned her.

She put the glass down on the table as though she had made an exclamation mark. "Look who is coming here. Of all the impudence."

Leela was coming through the gate. She began to smile the moment she knew that she was observed. She had on a bright silk sari and she carried a huge spray of lichees and a brown-paper parcel. She put the lichees on the table before Aunt Lucy and the parcel before me.

"Mama, I bring present for Christmas."

"Well, isn't that generous," Aunt Lucy murmured, looking at her present in a fuddled way. "Open your parcel, Helen, I'm dying to see what she has given you." The parcel contained about twenty small squares of silk. "You could make them into handkerchiefs," said Aunt Lucy dubiously. "Here, have this." She pushed the glass of wine over to Leela.

Leela didn't drink the wine, though she took it politely and when she thought nobody was looking, poured it on the ground.

"Silk coming from Sowa's shop," she said.

"Oh, has he a shop now?" said Aunt Lucy.

"Ma, that boy him very clever. Him taking ten...money... and him buying silk. Him walking in Durban selling this silk and everybody buying for Christmas. Him making profits, buying more silk. Bimeby him making one hundred pounds that boy, at night him waiter at hotel, plenty tips. Him buying shop, him getting plenty silk now. You buying there, all Westongate boys they owning this shop." She flicked her hands up and down to indicate thirty.

"Oh, one of those Indian syndicates," said John disapprovingly.

Leela lowered her voice to an insidious whisper, "You going there Sowa giving Westongate peoples silk half-price…."

"I can see Master Sowa doing that," said Aunt Lucy. "But we'll go there and see him. We might even have a few words to say to him."

Triumphantly Leela took some cards out of her money bag. They bore Sowa's name and his address in Grey Street. Aunt Lucy pondered over them gloomily, but there was a jaunty swing to Leela's skirts as she walked down the break.

"I don't think we should have taken it so calmly, Helen. If it hadn't been Christmas Day…."

"What has she done? Just tell me and I'll see to it for you, Lucy." John hadn't yet got over the present of the five hundred pounds.

Aunt Lucy looked cunning. "If I were to tell you, John, it would spoil the whole day, you'd get into a temper. No, Helen and I will go and see this Sowa. Mind you, Helen, we shouldn't go to Grey Street by ourselves. I was reading in the paper only the other day about those two Indians who cut a woman's throat with a sickle and it seems they were hired to do it by a third party who wanted the woman out of the way. It said in the newspaper that they were each paid a shilling to do it. I'll swallow a lot, but I won't swallow that. A shilling to cut a woman's throat." Absently she pulled a cracker with Nicky and the umfaan came from under the table, howling with fright. "Gracious, I forgot about him. It's nothing. See?" She popped a paper cap on his head. "There's a whistle for you too. What does the motto say, Nicky?"

"'He is happiest be he king or peasant who has peace in his home.' That's us," said Nicky.

We all laughed and the umfaan, thinking we were laughing at his cap, crawled shyly under the table. Each time that he blew the whistle, Aunt Lucy gave him a titbit and by the time dinner was over, he was dazed. He was not the only one. The wine and the turkey had been too much for Aunt Lucy. John gave her his arm and led her to the house. She had turned spiteful and we could hear her telling him how she had had to bribe Leela for his sake.

I lay in the hammock and Nicky sat near me on the grass. The shadows of the flamboyant ran away in the breeze, and the stars were moving too. How close the lights of Drew's Pride were…. Nicky was talking about the war, I sat up to listen to him. There was another likeness to Chris in him now, the deep pure voice.

John had noticed it too. He had been crossing the lawn to join us, but he turned round abruptly and went into his office instead. The telephone was ringing. It had been installed since the September holidays and it was still such a novelty that Nicky liked to answer every call. He raced into the house, but John had slammed the receiver down.

"I know who it was," said Nicky, gently rocking the hammock. "It was that beau of yours, Helen, old Van. I heard John say, 'She's not at home to you, you bastard.' Not 'Merry Christmas, Lieutenant Van der Westhuizen,' or anything like that. Simply, 'She's not at…'"

"There's no need to repeat swearing, Nicky. And he hates being called Van."

"I know that. We used to yell it out at him when he was passing and then we had to run for our lives."

I leaned over to cuff him, but he dodged and lay back in the grass laughing at me.

In Westongate people were not judged so much by their morals these days as by their enthusiasm for the war. The ladies were knitting as though their lives depended on it. They brought their knitting with them when they came to visit us on Boxing Day. Miss Pimm finished the socks she was working on and sighed as she rolled them up.

"I haven't an ounce more wool to start another pair. I'm expecting some more wool from Durban after the holidays. That will be my hundredth pair since the war started. I wish I had more wool." She looked at Nancy wistfully, but Nancy kept her head over her knitting, for she had only five pairs of socks to her credit. Mrs. Lambert was the acknowledged champion; she had knitted a hundred and six pairs of socks. "It's a shame," said Miss Pimm. "However…" and she brought out her crochet.

Nancy's dress was caught on the seat and the lace of her petticoat showed. It was a rare and intricate pattern that she had so far managed to keep for her own, but now Miss Pimm, adjusting her bifocal glasses, began stealthily to copy it. By the time Nancy realised what she was doing and whisked her skirt free, Miss Pimm had the hang of the pattern.

"I wish I could find Nicky and Peter," said Joan.

"Don't crowd me so." Nancy was irritated to see that Miss Pimm had already completed the precious pattern several times. " I think it's foolish of us to knit so many socks. Richard saw Colonel Edington in Pretoria and even he says the war won't last much longer and you know what an old pessimist he is."

"I don't agree with him. It's Armageddon," said Mrs. Lambert comfortably. "Everybody will be wiped out."

Joan bent forward to take a biscuit. There was a bulge between her shoulder blades and Nancy first pointed at it and then touched it with the tip of her finger.

"Whatever is this, Joan?"

"It's a piece of calico I tied round myself."

"But what is it for?"

"It's to keep me flat."

"Flat?" exclaimed Nancy.

Slowly Joan's arms came up, crossing over her swelling bosom. With a victorious smile Miss Pimm flicked her crochet-work against her own flat chest.

"You'll do yourself an injury, Joan, you'll just have to put up with it," said Mrs. Lambert.

"But Grannie Lambert, the boys won't play with me any more. They said they weren't going to play with anybody who'd got. . ."

"What did they call them?" asked Mrs. Lambert in an awful voice.

"Did it begin with a T or a B?" This from Aunt Lucy.

"I can't remember."

"The child can't bring herself to say it," said Mrs. Lambert. "Whisper it in Grannie's ear, darling."

She pulled her hair back and leaned towards Joan, but Mrs.

Drew was getting jealous. "Don't bother her like that, Aggie. You sit here next to me, Joanie, and forget what those nasty boys said."

"It was Nicky. He called them..." Everybody leaned forward expectantly, but Joan began to giggle.

"We could ask Nicky; here he comes now," cried Aunt Lucy.

"Dear me, I do hope we're not going to discuss such a subject in mixed company," said Miss Pimm, crocheting hard. "I can't think of anything more embarrassing."

Nicky charged through the gate. "Am I in time for tea?" he shouted. He flung himself on to the seat with a muttered, "Afternoon Mrs. Lambert, Mrs. Drew...Pimm," and began to eat biscuits rapidly, unaffected by the frosty glances.

"My, you do look hot and bothered," said Miss Pimm, smoothing out her crochet so that Nancy would be sure to see how exactly she had copied the pattern.

Nancy went red in the face. She took her temper out on Nicky. "Don't you talk to Joan."

"I haven't spoken a word to her," he said, flabbergasted.

"What have you been doing all afternoon, Nicky?" Aunt Lucy asked in her sweetest tones; and I gave Nancy such a piercing look that she dropped a stitch.

"We've been playing soldiers with the coolie kids," said Nicky. "Peter and I were the officers. You should have seen them drill."

"It would be a good idea if you kept him away from coolies for a while, Helen. Then he might learn to conduct a proper conversation with young ladies," said Mrs. Lambert.

"What have I done?" poor Nicky asked.

"Imagine playing soldiers," mused Nancy. "Do you know, Lieutenant Drew has a boy of your age in his regiment...."

"That Partridge boy," said Mrs. Lambert. "Yes, he's quite a credit to Westongate."

Nicky said defensively," They wouldn't take us. Peter and I went to the Drill Hall and the man said, 'Boy Scouts two doors down.' "

"And yet you must be going on for six feet, Nicky," murmured Nancy. "That's how the Partridge boy managed it, he's tall too."

"I'm going to try again at the end of next term."

I said, "It wouldn't do any good if they did take you. John would have you out the next day, I'd see to that."

"Oh, you wouldn't be such a spoilsport," said Nancy, rolling up her knitting.

Halfway through the term Nicky and Peter ran away from school. We traced them to Roberts Heights in the Transvaal and John went after Nicky. He came back alone. When I met him in Durban, he made such a fuss of me that I became suspicious.

"Did you take Nicky straight back to school?"

"Um. Well, I am glad to see you, Helen. And Durban. What a bleak hole that Pretoria is in the winter. Frost every morning. They had snow in Johannesburg…."

"Where is Nicky?"

"Roberts Heights."

"Have you let him stay in the Army?"

"Mind your own business."

"What regiment is he in?"

"The Transvaal Scottish. The young devils passed themselves off as eighteen."

"I'm going to the War Office…. I'm his legal guardian…. I'll tell them the whole story."

"You can't get him out now so stop your blethering. You'd have done the same. He's so damned keen about it. Anyway, he can go to the Agricultural College when the war is over, better than poring over a lot of books. Now shut up, Helen, I'm tired. I've travelled through from Pretoria without a rest."

I said, "Did you know that Leslie Partridge has been drafted overseas? He's only a few months older than Nicky. Now they've got him they can send him away whenever they like."

"I saw Edington and he advised me to let the boy stay where he is. He assured me that all the active service he will get is a long ride to Windhoek. After all, if the Farrells are going to let Peter take a slap at it…"

"He's older than Nicky. And Mrs. Farrell isn't taking it quietly. She blames Nicky for the whole thing…."

"Oh damn her. Nicky sent you a photograph. He's the smartest kid in the regiment, he'll be commissioned in no time."

By the end of the year both Nicky and Peter were commissioned and sent overseas. I had finished my training and I went home before I took up a post in Maritzburg. Nicky got his second pip in France, before Peter. "Influence," said Miss Pimm. "They're very thick with Colonel Edington and he's a big pot at the War Office, you know."

"That's what she said," Nancy told me. "I said to her, 'Miss Pimm, Nicky Angus was always a clever boy….' "

"Tongue like an adder," commented John.

"You shouldn't repeat, Nancy," said Mrs. Lambert. "Let gossip go in one ear and out of the other, I always say."

I was sewing up a jersey and I jabbed the needle into my finger. I watched the blood ooze from the tiny puncture.

"Look at that. Imagine what a bullet would do or a shell bursting in his face, John."

"Bitch," he muttered. He retreated into his office.

Mrs. Lambert tapped my knee indignantly. "You're getting morbid, Helen. Now pull yourself together. There are millions of young men on the Western Front, millions of them…." She seized her sock and knitted fast to make up for the few seconds she had wasted, as though she intended to make each of those soldiers a pair of socks before the war ended. Everybody had stopped competing with her now.

I worked only for Nicky. All that vast battlefield had narrowed down to him; and he must surely be killed. There was a subterranean madness in me. His discomfort in the trenches, his occasional sicknesses, a piece of shrapnel in his leg; these were as nothing as long as he lived. His letters came regularly for the first six months and then there were lapses. We mustn't worry, said John, there was nothing to be frightened of unless the minister called on you. He meant this as a joke, but it was true enough, and Mr. Skefton, the Vicar, complained that people were nervous of him nowadays.

Joan had had a postcard since he had written to us. The postcard came from Paris, where he had been spending his leave.

"Perhaps he was a little shy about writing to his family from Paris," Mrs. Lambert comforted me. "Gay Paree. My sister visited there and I wish you could have heard some of the stories she told us. She walked out of one theatre. It wasn't that she minded the nude women so much, she said, but when it came to nude men…. That's why he didn't write from Paris, Helen, take my word for it. Too much respect."

"Don't you think he has any respect for Joan?"

"I never thought of that. Why, the young devil…. Look, Helen, who is that on the bridge?"

"Miss Pimm, I think."

"Now what on earth is Enid doing out on a Wednesday? Is it a holiday?"

"No, I don't think so."

We stood up and waited for Miss Pimm. She got out of the cart slowly and then she ran towards us.

She said, "I've a telegram for your father. Mr. Skefton is ill in bed, that's why he couldn't bring it." She took an orange envelope out of her pocket, and a letter. "The letter should have been here a long time ago; there must have been a mix-up somewhere." There was a silence. "'Missing believed killed'—it doesn't necessarily mean he is dead, Helen," said Miss Pimm.

John was in his office. I went in there quietly and put the telegram on his desk. He read it and then sat listening to Mrs. Lambert's voice blending mournfully with Miss Pimm's.

"Get off the place," he shouted through the window.

There was a moment of stunned silence and then they broke into staccato expostulation, but they went away. It grew dark, but we remained in the office, weeping in each other's arms. When the full realisation of what had happened struck us, we drew apart.

"It was your fault," I said.

"Fault…. Yes. I gave in too easily, you mean."

"He should have still been at school."

"Yes. I wanted him to matriculate. It was my fault, Helen." He was shouting now. "He called me a coward and I gave in. He called me a coward because of that time I burnt their hands…. I couldn't hurt him like that…. I gave in, I wanted him to think of me as he did before….."

"There's still hope."

It went on for hour after hour, like a ghastly game. First we would weep together and then I would reproach him. One or the other would say, "There's still hope."

The next morning he went away. He wasn't at the hotel when I called for him, but there was a letter in the post. He had scrawled an address in Point Road across the paper and one other line: "Let me know if there is any news."

Chapter twelve

I took up my appointment, but after a month I broke down. Aunt Lucy brought me out to the farm. She stayed with me during the winter and this was unselfish of her, for I could not settle even to a game of cribbage. At first we haunted the fortunetellers in Weston-gate; the Yogi and the witch-doctor and the woman at the tea-room who could read the tea-leaves, the palm and the cards. But none of their prophecies came true and we stopped going to them.

I would not return to Durban with Aunt Lucy. It was better on the farm away from the sight of young men in uniform. I had a good view of the break from the veranda and as soon as I saw anybody coming I locked myself in the house. Even Mrs. Lambert thought that I was away most of the time. The servants left.

Chris came to see me whenever he had the chance and I used to like to watch him striding along the break. It was easy to pretend that this was Nicky. One afternoon we went to Awetuli and he cut a path through the bush so that we could walk down to the sea. It was the first time I had left the house for weeks and I was so tired that I slept on the sands. The sun was almost down when I awakened. Perian and Mr. Bannerjee were fishing farther along the beach and Chanjaldi was nearby with some children, collecting shells and paddling in the water.

"I brought you a present," said Chris. "It's a necklace, little gold hearts on a chain…." He clasped it on my neck. "See, little gold hearts." The necklace slipped on to my lap. Chris picked it up to examine the clasp. "It's faulty. I'll have to take it back to the jewellers." He swung it ruefully between his fingers so that it shone in the sunlight. The wind was on the sea and the sand and nearby Chanjaldi laughed with the children. She drew nearer and nearer, slyly watching the swinging necklace.

"Put it away," I whispered. "She steals; she'll spirit it away under your very eyes."

Chris laughed and with clumsy, tender fingers fastened the necklace on its velvet bed and clipped the box shut. Chanjaldi lost interest in us now and went back to her game with the children.

"Do you remember the day we first came here, the sea was so smooth?" Chris said.

"I remember it all, as though it were yesterday…." I bent forward and traced the arch of his brows. "Nicky's eyebrows are just like yours, his eyes are the same, his voice and the way he walks too. When John notices the likeness he gets so sulky I could laugh. Everyone says Nicky is like him, but really he has only picked up his mannerisms."

"Helen…"

"That girl Chanjaldi…her mother brought him into the world and nursed him. You remember her, Leela…." There were beads of sweat on his forehead and his eyes were brilliant. "On the night he was born, John shut me up in the room with her and I was frightened because of all the awful stories she had told me, but she meant well. I kicked her right across the room. The other baby died, John's son. I would never have hurt the little thing, I know I wouldn't have, but he thought I was going to and he hit me. The baby fell under me, Chris, and he died. John took Nicky."

I had not expected the anger that shook him. "Why do you tell me now?"

"I've always wanted to tell you, but it was too late when you came back. He was Nicky Angus. He wouldn't have forgiven me and I think he would have hated you."

"You've lain beside me all night and yet you never told me, given yourself to me like a whore. You let your father take him and now he's dead you tell me. How sweet and gentle your voice is, Helen, how sad your beautiful face is. And your hands are so delicate, aren't they? All the other women, they were no good to me once I knew you. I'd sooner love that coolie woman than you."

I ran away from his bitter voice, not caring that Chanjaldi turned to stare at me or that Mr. Bannerjee called out. I saw him again the next morning, walking along the road, but he did not come near me.

As the weeks passed and there was still no news of Nicky, I grew hungry for the sound of his voice and I telephoned him. He spoke to me gently as though he had forgiven me, but he did not come to see me again.

Amoya came to work for me. I remember that it was touch and go whether I agreed to take her on, for she was a wisp of a thing and not even clean. She was Leela's favourite child, then about eleven years old. Leela brought her to me on a summer morning when I sat with a book on the veranda.

I said, "No, she's too young, Leela," and bent my head over my book in the hope of avoiding one of Leela's harangues. She sat down, tucking her feet decorously beneath her sari. The child remained on the step, smiling at me.

"Mama, she very strong this chile," said Leela.

"No."

"Mama, she good chile, she doing what you telling her."

"I said no."

"Never she is stealing." I turned the page of my book. I was about to turn another when Leela said, sighing deeply, "She coming for five shilling a month. We buying all things for her wedding it costing plenty plenty money. She marrying soon, soon."

"Is she getting married?" I stared at the child with a vague jealousy. "She's too young."

"She ready, ma." Leela laughed and pulled Amoya towards me.

The stuff of Amoya's clothes was so rotten that it came apart at a touch, but on her toes she had golden rings and there were garnets and gold too clipped into her nostrils. Ah, to see her standing there in her grimy splendour. She was dressed in a cotton blouse and full skirt, her hair hung below her waist in a thick oiled plait, black and shiny as coal. She had all Leela's beauty and, besides, a radiance from the spirit.

I said cautiously, "Well, I'll give her a try—only for a week or so, mind."

"I leaving her here now," said Leela, rising. "Bimeby you not wanting her going. Guru, Yogi, Mr. Bannerjee they all talking with this one."

When Leela had gone the little girl came on to the veranda and stood by my chair. She was all Indian, even to the smell of her.

"What you need is a wash, Amoya. If you work here, you'll have to keep yourself clean. That's the first thing to learn."

I took her into the bedroom and showed her her face in the mirror.

"My mama washing me this morning. I gotting cold." She rubbed her cheek with her skirt and then slowly turned round, watching herself in the mirror. Then she put her finger-tip on the satin handkerchief sachet that Nancy had given me for Christmas; she held her hand over the silver hairbrush, not touching it.

I put her in the wood-shed with a basin of water and some soap. "Now wash yourself and you might as well wash your clothes as well to start with. I'll give you some other clothes."

She undressed quickly, excitement rippling through her. I rummaged in the old trunk in the shed until I found a tussore silk dress that I had worn as a child. Amoya drew back when she saw it, nodding her head in disapproval.

"What's the matter with you?"

"Not wearing that."

"Put it on." I dumped her clothes into the water and left her. She wore the tussore dress, but she was uncomfortable in it. It hung to her ankles and she plaited a thong from grass to tie about her waist. Then she stood anxiously watching her own clothes on the line as the wind filled them and sent them billowing. A tiny finch hurtled out of a tree and passed so close to her that it brushed her nose. She put out her hands to catch it. It was not so much laughter that was in her face as a passion for living and I saw again the difference between her and Leela.

She put a hibiscus flower in her hair and she had just begun experimenting with a garland when I called her indoors. I showed her how to polish the silver.

"Take your time over them and do them nicely. You're not to breathe on them to make them shine."

Within the hour I saw her on the lawn, fixing frangipanni on to grass stalks.

"You go and finish the silver, Amoya."

"Finish."

I examined her work, but I hadn't a word to say, for it was beautifully done. She had even polished my hairbrush. I set her to unpicking an old dress that I had put aside for dusters. Her hands were quick and unerring, something to watch in that still room.

"You reading that book?" she asked, without glancing up.

"Of course."

"Sowa he reading. He going to school in Durban long time, Mr. Bannerjee he teaching. My mama she not letting Mr. Bannerjee teaching me."

"Sowa is rich. Why do you have to work?"

"He losing plenty money," said Amoya mournfully. "No ships coming with silks. Shop it closing. Now he selling fruit in market."

"I'm sorry about his shop."

Aunt Lucy and I had been there, though Aunt Lucy said that we were fools to patronise the little beast; but he did sell the silk to us cheaply and if we bought enough we should eventually get her ten pounds back. He used to stand behind the counter looking as though he had been born with a pair of scissors in his hand. He smiled as he sent them whizzing down a piece of silk. He had a professional way of making a parcel and as he snapped the string with his finger he bowed to his customer and then spun the parcel neatly in the air before he handed it over.

"Sowa clever, he reading. Gungi teaching me. I marrying Gungi. He teaching me A B C."

"Can you pick them out?" I extended the book to her.

Her finger shot out swiftly. "That L F J…"

"Right. You're quite clever." Her eyes, brimming with intelligence, scanned the page as though the sight of the print was satisfying to her. I closed the book. "Finish your work, Amoya."

She bent her head, but she worked more slowly; and she was so quiet that I forgot that she was there. The flamboyant tree that John used to keep pruned back had spread its arms in freedom and it tapped at the windows on the side of the house as though it would force a way into the rooms to hang its fiery flowers on the walls. Christmas was not far off and the splendid bougainvillea at Drew's Pride was in full bloom, standing out in patches of purple. The tall hibiscus hedge was a scarlet thread dividing the garden from the cane. I could see figures on the tennis-court, like papers tossed by the wind.

"You should go up to Drew's Pride and have a game of tennis, Nicky," I said. "Your white flannels are pressed. It would do you good." I smiled across the room at him.

Somebody touched my arm. I looked down and saw a small brown hand and then I remembered the Indian child. She was not afraid of me as the other servants had been.

"Mama, who you talking to?"

"I was talking to myself."

"No, you talking with Nicky."

Perhaps we are born and re-born. In that unmarked face there was wisdom, and remembered intimacy with suffering.

Leela was right. Amoya was a strong child and every morning at seven o'clock I would find her sitting outside the kitchen door, with a tattered reader in her hands. Gungi had given it to her and it was so filthy that I would not allow her to bring it into the house. Instead I gave her some of Nicky's school books to look through and as she turned the pages I told her stories of his childhood.

I showed her his photographs. There was a photograph of Nicky in a sailor suit and long black stockings; and John, dressed to kill, with his hand dramatically placed on Nicky's shoulder. There was one of the three of us taken in Durban, Nicky by then wearing a straw boater and long trousers. There was the one of Nicky in his uniform. Amoya looked at the photographs politely, and at the christening-robe, but these things were shadows to her. She wanted the grandeur of the battlefield. I read to her all the letters he had ever written to me and she knew by heart those that were written in France.

Sometimes she told the stories back to me and I listened entranced, for she made an epic of Nicky's life story. Her English forsook her as she confused him in her mind with Hindu legend so that the picture she gave was of a Hindu warrior, daring and supple. He carried a lance, he rode on an elephant in pageants; and he was always dressed in gorgeous clothes. All the stories that had been passed on to her through the generations she spilled before me.

I undertook to teach her to read before she was married. There was a preciseness in everything she did, so that it wasn't long before she had developed a flawless copperplate handwriting. She read aloud, imitating the sound of my voice, but when she spoke she reverted to her own nasal, singing tone. Within a few weeks she could write down anything I put before her and I thought I had stumbled on a genius until I discovered that she had a prodigious memory. I tried to teach her slowly, but she strained away from me, asking questions in a quickened voice as though she must know at once everything I had to teach. When two hours were up she was just as avid as when we started, but I would be drained and a little resentful at having had so much information wrung from me. My reward for all this teaching was a reverent devotion that made me feel a hundred years old.

"Why don't you send this child to school instead of making her get married?" I shouted at Leela one day.

She had come with Chanjaldi that morning, not so much to sell me vegetables as to show to Chanjaldi that Amoya was getting on in the world.

"Better she marrying. She waiting she lying round with plenty plenty fellers."

"Miss Angus not marrying," said Amoya. Both Leela and Chanjaldi looked at me speculatively.

"Give her a chance. Let her go to school, Leela," I said.

"Derika going school. All time that girl's husband kicking her."

"Perian kicks you and yet you never went to school," I said triumphantly.

Leela brooded over this. Then she spoke in Hindustani to Amoya.

Amoya said dutifully, "My mama is saying I must tell you I want to marry Gungi. I am loving Gungi here and here." She touched her throat and her stomach. There was desire now in the plastic face.

"Always he is kissing her," said Chanjaldi. Leela cuffed her when she realised what she had said.

Amoya comforted her by taking her into my bedroom to show her the treasure on the dressing-table and Leela chewed some betel-nut to calm herself. As it took effect she expanded.

"This Gungi gotting plenty plenty money, not drunk, not shouting. Always talking nice his peoples. I gotting five girls gotting good mans." She smirked over this rich reward for her efforts. Chanjaldi's voice came rapturously from the bedroom, but Leela chose to ignore the existence of this wayward daughter.

I took her down a peg. "There is Chanjaldi...."

Instantly she was miserable. "Like... like Perian that girl. Wanting all time playing not working." She lowered her voice. "No chiles that girl. Me I praying.... Mama, bad in here...." She pressed her hands against her breast.

The object of Leela's sorrow stood in the garden trying first one flower in her hair and then another. She had gone out of the house by the back door and she did not come on to the veranda again. There was a purpose in this presently to be revealed. Amoya began her lessons again and Leela followed Chanjaldi down the break. She returned almost at once and beckoned Amoya to her with great secrecy. Chanjaldi was screaming with disappointment and I saw Leela pass my hairbrush to Amoya, who went in through the back door to return it to the dressing-table. They must have thought I was blind and deaf.

Chanjaldi often came to join in the lessons and to listen to the talk about Nicky. If she took anything Amoya always brought it back. She liked best Amoya's stories about Nicky. As she listened, her face would open passionately and her hips move with the schooled ecstasy that had been part of Leela's teaching. When I noticed this I sent her packing; but she had already stolen two photographs of Nicky and Amoya could not find them to bring them back to me.

The day of Amoya's wedding was nearing and I went with her across the river to see the jewellery that was to be her marriage settlement. She had kept me posted with the stages of the haggling between her parents and Gungi's. At one time it seemed that the affair would be called off, for Gungi's mother became obstinate and hid three bracelets and a ring. It took Gungi a week to find them. Then she said that Perian had borrowed money from her and this would have to be taken off the settlement. She and Leela wrangled for so long that the children became desperate and planned to run away together.

Leela won the day. She squeezed a hundred pounds' worth of jewellery from Gungi; brooches, rings, bracelets and anklets. To look at Gungi's parents you wouldn't have thought they had a sixpence to their name, for they were shrivelled with meager living and their clothes were dirty and threadbare. If Gungi was stronger and cleaner it was because he had been working at the hotel for three years. Leela was not deceived. Piece by piece she prised the jewellery out of them. By this time Gungi's mother wasn't on speaking terms with her and she followed me into the cane-break to warn me to beware of the whole family: they were thieves. Somehow Leela had found out that they had a share in a banana plantation near Pinetown.

But on Amoya's wedding day Gungi's mother blossomed out in a new sari and wore jewels that she had hidden from Leela's rapacious eyes. I went to watch the ceremony, but Amoya that day was far from me, a Hindu amongst the Hindus. I took off my shoes and entered the hut.

She stood with Gungi beneath an archway of palms, her eyes

downcast. The priest hung a garland of marigolds on Gungi's breast and Perian gave Amoya's hand to him. It had been Leela's great fear that Perian would disgrace them all by getting at the rum, but he had been guarded carefully and he was respectable if a little mournful. Now the priest was chanting while Amoya slowly paced with Gungi. The prayers went on interminably and I lost interest and putting on my shoes walked away. Whatever there had been between the Indian child and me was finished now. Standing there in her yellow sari she belonged to a way of life that was complete in itself, that would enfold her more fiercely as she grew older. I was sad for her early flowering because it carried the seeds of an early death.

Music started, anaemic and without texture. Now there would be dancing and a little delicate eating of vegetables, there would be the singing of more hymns. Not until the third day would the feasting begin on poultry and mutton and goat's flesh. And Gungi would be allowed to take his Amoya. I hurried down the break, away from the smell of the incense. The alien music died behind me.

Mr. Bannerjee caught me up as I reached-the gate. "I saw you leave...."

"Why aren't you at the wedding enjoying yourself?"

"I came to tell you that I saw your father. I have a little restaurant in Grey Street now. People send in for lunches, you should taste the curried trotters.... I have a good cook. In time I might take Sowa in with me, he's had bad luck that boy, almost ruined by the war. But business will pick up. I kept telling him that he should go in for hardware, but he loves the silks. It's not altogether the money with Sowa, he differs from Leela in that respect. As I was saying, I saw your father, Miss Angus. He came in for lunch."

"What would he be doing in Grey Street, Mr. Bannerjee?" "I think you should go to Durban and bring him home, Miss Angus. That's why I followed you. I am seldom in Westongate nowadays and this is the first opportunity I have had to speak to you. There was another thing. I want to ask you to do a great favour for me."

"Certainly, I'll do anything within my power," I said, matching politeness with politeness.

"It's Chanjaldi. Would you take her to a doctor? Leela can't be persuaded. But I think if something could be done for Chanjaldi, if she could have children for instance, then she might save herself."

"I'll take her if she'll go to a doctor, Mr. Bannerjee."

"And your father? You wish to contact him?"

"Not yet. Perhaps in a few weeks' time when I feel stronger."

He brought out a shabby wallet. "Here is money for the doctor, Miss Angus, and my address in Grey Street." He bowed and left me.

Amoya had helped me. I didn't want to sit alone any more. The next day I walked up to Drew's Pride. There were four young officers spending their leave there. Nancy played ragtime and tried to get me to flirt with them. I wrote to Aunt Lucy for the first time in months, and I began to eat regularly so that I should be fit for duty soon. I even summoned up enough energy to persuade Chanjaldi to go to the doctor. Mr. Bannerjee had wasted his money. There was nothing to be done for Chanjaldi and she would never bear children.

Chapter thirteen

John had said, "Watch out for the minister, he'll tell you soon enough that Nicky is dead." I wanted to hide when I saw him getting out of his car in front of our gate, but Zetke said, "This is a man who brings good news." He had come that day to start the ploughing.

I went slowly down the step to meet Mr. Skefton. He clasped my hand with strong, soft fingers.

"Nicky is alive, Helen. He has escaped from the Germans and he is interned in Switzerland...." Then he said distractedly, "I should have brought one of the ladies with me," and fanned me with his hat.

I shouted, "He's found again, Zetke." He gave a great laugh and picking up the hammer, beat the firebell to send the tidings across the hills. I took the hammer from him and sounded out the notes myself, while Mr. Skefton stood silently watching me. My hair came loose and streamed behind me. Zetke was singing a wild and beautiful song. Across the river the prayer-flags on their bamboo poles sent the message to a Hindu god. Three clangs and a pause. Who would remember?

Richard remembered and brought champagne and Mrs.

Lambert brought a turkey that we roasted in the oven. Mrs. Farrell brought some of her matchless cakes. While we waited for the turkey to cook we sang hymns, Zetke harmonising in a voice of muted thunder that gave to our singing a barbarous power.

I went to Durban the next day to find John. Aunt Lucy and I called first at the address in Point Road, but there was nobody in the house except a thin, grey woman who ushered us defensively to the gate while she spoke.

"He doesn't live here any more. He has moved to another place out of town, I think." She hurried back to the house and banged the door, but just as we were walking away, she opened it again. "Try the station."

"That waitress. It's like a spy-hunt," said Aunt Lucy.

Bessie was not at the tea-room. "She's in the cloakroom now, dear," a waitress told us. "Her legs were giving her trouble and she took an easier job."

We went to the cloakroom. Bessie was knitting a khaki sock and she looked up warily. "John Angus's daughter, isn't it?"

"Yes. Do you know where my father is?"

"No. Not now." There were pennies in a saucer on the table and she moved them with her forefinger, reflecting. "The landlady wouldn't have him in the place."

"Don't you know where he went?"

"Somewhere out of town. I can't say. I don't mind giving a helping hand, but some things I won't be mixed up in. You look upset. I wish I could help you." A thought struck her. "If you want to use the convenience, don't bother about putting a penny in. I've got the keys," and she jangled a bunch of keys.

"Well, that's very kind of you," said Aunt Lucy. Bessie ceremoniously unlocked a door. We got nothing further out of her, she was as tight-lipped as the woman in Point Road had been.

"We'll have to go to Mr. Bannerjee," I said as we walked towards the steps. "He's got a restaurant in Grey Street. I have his address."

"I hope it's not too far down, Helen. It's a great place for murders. Keep your gloves on. I once heard of a woman who had her finger cut off for the sake of a ring. She was dead fortunately and didn't feel anything. On second thoughts I won't go with you. I'll sit in the tea-room here and have a snack, I'm exhausted."

I left her ordering tea and toast. The restaurant was easy to find, but Mr. Bannerjee was out. I left a note with the waiter and returned to Aunt Lucy.

"I'm going back in an hour's time," I told her. "You'd better go home, you look worn out."

"Be careful where you go, Helen. Remember there is such a thing as white slave traffic. We might never hear of you again. Both those women were peculiar about John. I hope he hasn't been murdered."

When I returned to Grey Street after seeing her home I found Mr. Bannerjee waiting for me outside his restaurant. He carried his suitcase. "I've brought something to eat, we can simply warm it up when we get there. I hope you don't mind, Miss Angus, we'll have to catch an Indian bus," he said, as we hurried along Grey Street. "They'll let us sit in front."

"You know I don't mind," I said politely.

Mr. Bannerjee pushed his way confidently through the crowd that was struggling to get on the buses at the stand. In those few minutes I was thrown first into the arms of a turbaned Mohammedan and then pressed against the bare ribs of a Hindu dhobi who seemed to me the most optimistic of us all, for he carried in each hand a bundle of washing. A raw Zulu girl who smelt of wood-smoke screamed as I stood on her foot. Mr. Bannerjee opened the door of a bus.

"Move up," he commanded a coloured girl. "Sit on your friend's lap and this lady can have the other seat."

The girl snarled at him. "I'm not going to. We were here first."

"I don't want any arguments," said the driver. He sat behind the polished wheel, unmoved by the desperate battle that raged about him.

"We'll pay you double fare," said Mr. Bannerjee, as cool as the driver.

The driver said promptly to the coloured girl, "Move up or I'll put you off."

The girl sat sulkily on her friend's knee while I took her seat. As soon as the bus moved away both girls began to push against me, but still I considered myself lucky to have got on at all, for the dhobi had been left sitting on the pavement, his bundles of washing beside him like two big white balloons, and the Zulu girl was staring after the bus in a bewildered way, as though she couldn't even yet believe that she hadn't managed to get on. When Mr. Bannerjee saw that the girls were pushing me he put his arm over the partition between us. He had somehow squeezed past legs and insinuated himself between bodies until he had placed himself behind me.

"Keep your arm away from me," said the girl, who was wearing a hat covered with artificial violets.

"You mind your manners, then," admonished Mr. Bannerjee.

"Dirty coolie."

Mr. Bannerjce was silent for a few minutes before he retaliated. "Her name must be Violet for sure," he said to me.

"Is your name Violet?" I asked in the hope of establishing more pleasant relations.

"No, her name is Violet. Mine is Pansy."

"You wouldn't believe it unless you heard it with your own ears," Mr. Bannerjee remarked.

Violet had thick rippling hair, a rare auburn. She wore it loose with a mauve ribbon tied through it. Her khaki-coloured face looking from this frame had a nightmarish quality, of which luckily she seemed unaware. She tossed the hair back and it hit Mr. Bannerjee full in the face.

"I like auburn hair," he said when he emerged, "especially when it goes with a milk-white skin and blue eyes like yours, Miss Angus."

"Be quiet," said the driver.

Violet said shrilly, "Dirty no-good rubbishing coolie."

The driver flicked a look at Mr. Bannerjee. "Be quiet now."

Mr. Bannerjee was not as easily quenched as that. "Two coffee, one milk," he said cheerfully.

Then I saw why the driver was afraid. Violet drew a long shiny hatpin from her handbag.

"Now, Violet, you got six months for that last time, remember," said Pansy. "You don't want to spoil the evening, man. Look, there's the boys waiting for us."

The bus came to a stop. Pansy and Violet, all smiles now, pushed past us to join two fresh-faced sailors who stood outside a tumble-down house close to the road.

Somebody at the back of the bus was eating an orange and the smell of the peel put a tang into the fumes of petrol in the close little cabin. The journey was becoming almost pleasant, for we had left the town behind and we were racing through groves of mangoes and guavas towards velvet hills.

Mr. Bannerjee and I got off as the bus began to climb into these hills. I followed him to a whitewashed gate and along a narrow path bordered by big white boulders to a small cottage.

"Mr. Angus," he called.

The door opened. For a few seconds we stared at each other. Everything that he was lay in his face.

"I've come to take you home." I kissed his cheek. Standing so close to him I could smell the dagga on his breath. We went into the house and sat down.

I said, "Here's the telegram about Nicky. We had a party when I got it and I rang the fire-bell like this." I beat the time on the table.

Mr. Bannerjee had gone into the kitchen. I heard him yelling for the umfaan. John put the telegram into his pocket and went out of the room. I found my way into the kitchen where Mr. Bannerjee was banging pots about. The kitchen was filling with smoke.

"This is a terrible chimney," said Mr. Bannerjee.

"I wish I'd known, I'd have come sooner."

There was no answer. Mr. Bannerjee had stopped his clatter of work and the evening stillness came into the room. I turned to look at him. He stood with a dish-cloth in his hand, beyond the circle of light thrown by the lamp, with a halo of moths spinning before him.

"You've been looking after him…."

He flung the dish-cloth on to the table and the circle of moths wavered and broke up. "I hired the umfaan and came out here once or twice a week with some food."

181

"I'll have to stay here and get him right before I take him back."

"You can't stay here, Miss Angus. Wait until you see him under the influence. See that tree over there?" His outstretched hand spoilt again the dizzying rhythm of the moths.

"It's too dark to see anything."

"He smashed it last week, smashed it without knowing what he was doing. Only a week ago. I locked myself in the house, or he might have got me too."

A memory came to me of dagga-mad Zulus, glimpsed as they ran down the break past our bungalow, smashing at the cane with their sticks.

"Where does he get it from?"

"From the ricksha boys, I think."

"Oh, Mr. Bannerjee, why didn't you let me know?"

"I was hoping he would be all right soon."

I said, "Thank you, Mr, Bannerjee, for looking after him."

"He doesn't sleep...." He lifted the lid of a pot, "You like curried trotters? They're your father's favourite dish."

"Yes, I like them. When I was nursing, I saw a man cured of drugs. I might be able to do something for him."

"The police nearly got him once. He went into the Indian Market to buy some mutton and he attacked the shopkeeper. He could have killed him, I managed to get him away...."

"I wouldn't like anybody at Westongate to know...."

A wintry smile crossed Mr. Bannerjee's face. "I thought not. Would you like to serve up? I'm going to sit outside, it's hot in here. I'll take my plate now, please."

I tried again to thank him, but he had gone outside, carefully carrying a chair and a plate. Now the moths took up their dance again and I heard John moving in the house.

Mr. Bannerjee went back on the bus the next morning, but he promised that he would come out again. I stood at the gate, watching until the bus was out of sight. The hills here were dark beneath banana plantations. They were quiet hills and I missed the sound of the cane.

I went into the house. The umfaan had tidied the place and there was nothing to do but write a note to Aunt Lucy. I was sealing the envelope when John came into the room. He walked round and round the table with feverish, purposeless haste.

I said, "I've written a note to Aunt Lucy...."

"Lucy. The things I could tell you about Lucy." He snatched up the letter and crumpled it. He marched round the room again. His whole body was crackling with the energy that the dagga had released in him so that he looked like a young man and his voice was loud with this bursting energy. He was good-humoured enough that day, except once when he stumbled over a chair. He kicked it to pieces while I sat still and silent, afraid that he would turn on me next. The brilliant stream of the dagga ran its course quickly. Soon he sagged into a chair, with his eyes half-shut as though he saw voluptuous visions.

I found the box of dagga and hid it in the shed under a pile of sacks; but he had another hoard. It was on the morning that he gave me this secret hoard that the battle seemed won, and lost again when he walked to Durban for a fresh supply. He spent the night away, in that horrible little place down the road, I think, for he gave me a gross description of the girl Violet the following evening when we were sitting together in the tiny dining-room. He had been smoking and the dagga was pungent in the room, for I had locked the doors and windows so that he should not get out again.

"Her hair is just like yours, Helen."

The words hung on the air between us. He knew I was afraid of him, as an animal might have known. I had been writing to Nicky and as he got to his feet I lifted the page suddenly and flicked it over the lamp chimney. The darkness dazed him and he blundered across the room. I felt my way to my room and closed the door quietly, turning the key without a sound. He had found the front door and he tried it. I put my hands over my ears so that I should not hear what he was saying, for he thought that this was my door. He battered it and there was the crash of splintering wood as it gave way. He must have hurt himself, for I heard him fall, but I was too much afraid to unlock my door until morning. He was sane then, but in an ugly mood and I could not prevail on him to give up his stock of dagga.

Mr. Bannerjee came that day. I had hired an Indian carpenter to repair the front door and he stood at the gate watching the man at work. A bus was tearing down the road and he turned suddenly to run for it. I thought he had lost his nerve, and I couldn't blame him, for I, too, was afraid now. I decided I would put John in a hospital and I waited for his temper to improve before I discussed it with him. I packed my suitcase, ready to leave before nightfall.

In the afternoon a car drew up before the gate and Chris got out. I went slowly down the path to meet him.

"How did you know where to find me?"

"Mr. Bannerjee told me."

"I thought he had taken fright. John is asleep...."

"You know you're risking your life. He'll have to go to hospital, he ought to be in gaol."

"I thought I could manage it. I didn't know it would be as bad as this."

The Indian carpenter was waiting for his money. While I paid him Chris swung the door backwards and forwards.

"I'll help you, Helen. The first thing to do is to find the stuff."

"I've looked, but I can't find it."

"They're always cunning. But that's where I can help you, it's part of my job."

He did find John's hoard, in a box beneath the flooring boards. He burnt it outside. He stayed with us that night and his presence made John pull himself together for a few hours. It was the beginning of the cure and Chris did more to help him than I could have done. We never knew when his car would draw up at the door, and he always came in uniform, a subtle menace that John understood.

Once I said to him, "You've been generous, Chris. You could have arrested him. It would have been your duty as well as a sweet revenge."

He gave me a strange look. "I've already had my revenge, Helen, but it wasn't sweet."

In that nightmarish house friendship grew between us warm and strong.

John was gaining ground. Within three weeks he had reduced his smoking to one cigarette a day; and this he never gave up. To the end of his life, except for those three days that he lay dying, he smoked a dagga cigarette at five o'clock. Zetke would leave a little calabash full of dagga on his desk once every three months.

When he was almost cured Aunt Lucy came to stay with us. It was curiosity that prompted her, but I was glad enough to have her with me, for though he was over the worst of his craving I was still afraid of him. She was, I think, rather disappointed at not having seen him in the grip of the drug and she looked on its gradual reducing as something of a game.

On Armistice Day we locked the house up, and paid off the umfaan. Chris drove us to Durban. We left Aunt Lucy there and went straight through to Westongate by train, for I wanted John to avoid the excitement of the celebrations.

It was early afternoon when we crossed Awetuli and stood for a while on the bridge watching the waterfall. A honeybird called to us deep in the ravine.

"I'd like to follow him," said John. "When I was a boy, we were never without honey in the house."

He took my arm and we went slowly up the steps into the cane-break. Now and again he stopped to pick up a handful of earth or to look critically at a stool of cane.

"There's a lot of stripe about," he said.

He walked with his head up now. We turned the last bend in the break and saw the house. Golden Shower spilled from the roof to the ground. There were poinsettias blooming along the fence.

"That flamboyant needs pruning back," said John, unlatching the gate.

Chapter fourteen

The flamboyant tree was shapely again and the fields newly planted when Nicky came home. John drove Aunt Lucy and me to the station in a spanking new motor-car. There was a brass band on Westongate station and banners that made a splash against the sky: Welcome Home and Well Done Good and Faithful Springboks. As the train steamed past, the boys looked solemnly out at this lively display. I saw Nicky. John was roaring beside me. Then everybody began to shout and to wave Union Jacks; all except Mrs. Townshend, whose son had been killed. She collapsed on a bench and Colonel Edington had to take her home, leaving the Reception Committee uncertain of the next move, for he was to have addressed them. Everybody then turned on Miss Pimm for having allowed her sister to come to the station and Miss Pimm kept shrieking, "It's funny, she's been so brave all along."

The boys had entered into the spirit of the thing and joining hands they swung down the platform towards us. The band was playing the Missouri Waltz and now all the ladies were crying. Nicky was on the end of the line and he was the first to break away. I was swept into dizzying, pagan bliss as I touched him and for a moment he was all things to me. Then he had left me and turned to John and Aunt Lucy, whose wig he helped to adjust before he kissed her.

There was so much confusion now that we thought we would be able to escape the speeches at the hall, but Miss Pimm took charge and we had to sit through an hour of long-winded enthusiasm. This was one of the prices we paid for victory, John grumbled.

At home the yard was swarming with Indians and Zulus, for John was providing a feast; beef for the Zulus and mutton for the Indians, packets of sweets for everybody. The Zulus danced before Nicky as though he were a prince. Chanjaldi placed a garland round his neck and Mr. Bannerjee made a speech. In return Nicky told them the story of his adventures. It was a fine story of Germans flying before him and Nicky chasing them now with a rifle and now with a bayonet. Zetke told the story again in song.

The chanting died away. Darkness came on early, for the sky was overcast. I moved close to Nicky so that I had only to reach out my hand to touch him.

"Tell us what really happened," I said.

"Well, to begin with, I had pneumonia when they picked me up. I was in hospital for a month. I had a flesh wound on my arm. See?" He rolled up his sleeve. "Nothing much…."

"It left quite a mark," said Aunt Lucy.

"To cut a long story short, a Belgian orderly who was working in the hospital organised an escape and he picked on me because I was pretty fit once I got over the pneumonia. There were two others. He gave us clothes and an address in the town. We were near Munich. The idea was to get to France, of course, but that fell through and we had to make for Switzerland. We might as well have stayed in Germany for all the good it did us. When everything was cleared up the War Office came to the conclusion that some smart Alec had taken my identification disc off thinking I was dead and that's why you didn't get news of me for such a long time. He never handed the disc in, probably because he came back and found me gone."

Aunt Lucy was disappointed. "Well, that is a tame story, I must say. I'd like to have seen you let loose amongst them, John. You'd have given them something to think about."

I moved over to the window to watch the rain that had begun to fall. The light from the lamp splashed the cement path and as the raindrops hit the path they flew up again like little silver soldiers. Aunt Lucy went to bed. Soon afterwards we heard the popping of a cork.

"Aunt Lucy is just the same, she still likes the bottle," he said.

"Nothing is changed...."

"Nothing is changed, Helen? Why, we have a motor-car. And there's Chanjaldi, she was a child when I last saw her. And Amoya is married and well on the way.... And look at Joan. She's not ashamed of her whatsanames any more...."

"You at least are the same horrid boy."

The next morning I went into his room to unpack his clothes while he was out on the lands with John. I found the picture of a dark-haired girl. She was plain and I wondered why he kept the picture until I came across a letter she had written to him. Her name was Phyllis and they had spent a week together during his leave in Paris. There was another photograph of an older woman who was beautiful, but there was nothing to show what she had been to him. He had begun to tear up this photograph, but had thought better of it. In his writing-pad there was the beginning of a letter: "Darling, if you marry me...." That would be Phyllis surely. I looked again at the photograph that he had wanted to tear up. The suitcase contained nothing more except the cork from a champagne bottle and a drawing of a man with a bayonet through him.

The door opened. Aunt Lucy must have been drinking her tonic while she lay in bed, for she was tipsy. She rocked herself from her heels to her toes slowly in an effort to balance herself, closing one eye as though that helped.

"Helen." She came into the room at a run and pitched on to the bed. "You're reading that boy's letters."

"I'm not, I'm unpacking for him." I tried to snap the case to, but she had already seen the photographs.

"Who are the girls? Let me see."

I passed the photographs to her. "You'd better not let him know you've seen them. You know how sensitive boys are."

"Sluts," she said, giving the photographs back to me.

189

She stood up and then she turned deadly pale and fell to the floor. I thought that the drink had been too much for her, but it wasn't that. The influenza epidemic had struck Westongate and Aunt Lucy was always able to boast that she was the first to go down.

Walter Drew and his wife died during the epidemic and Joan inherited Drew's Pride. Nancy's feelings were hurt, but Richard had expected it and he had a house planned on the adjoining farm which was his portion. Nancy had no intention of leaving Drew's Pride and she entrenched herself in the east wing, where she had a small kitchen installed so that she would be impregnable when Joan married.

The question of whom Joan would marry fascinated Westongate. Nicky and Peter were considered to be well in the running, but while they were away at the Agricultural College Joan was seen with so many boys that speculation gave way to gossip.

She had a reputation for daring, but that meant nothing, for she achieved this by following the fashions. She was the first girl in Westongate to have her hair shingled and she came to exhibit herself to us one afternoon soon after Nicky left the College.

"Miss Pimm says I look fast. I wish you'd cut your hair, Helen, and that would give me an air of respectability."

"What about the skirts?" said Nicky. "Helen would have to shorten her skirts by four inches at least."

"Miss Pimm and my grandmother are putting up a fight to keep short skirts from Westongate," said Joan. "They're talking of getting up a petition signed by the returned soldiers saying they didn't fight to see womanhood desecrated. Poor Leslie Partridge then told them of the desecration of womanhood that he had seen in France."

"Did they leave?"

"Lord no. They hung on his words. They liked particularly that part about bayonets."

"Corpses piled to the ceiling," Nicky murmured.

He stood with his back to us. The branches of the flamboyant dipped gently in the breeze and the great inflorescences, scarlet and yellow, hovered within reach, but just as he tried to take one it was carried up again out of sight. Chanjaldi and Amoya were in the garden, for I had given them leave to take some flowers for their festival. Chanjaldi walked about like a child who has had a surfeit of goodies. The corner of Amoya's sari was full of frangi-panni, but when she saw the flamboyants she reached out with both hands and captured one. The other flowers spilled on the grass. Nicky helped her to break the branch. He left her looking at the flower as though she didn't know what to do with it now that she had it.

Joan said, "Womanhood, black or white, would never be desecrated with Nicky about. He is a credit to you, Helen."

"Even Miss Pimm approves of me." He touched her hair. "She doesn't know that I've bought a bottle of whisky. Will you have a drink, Joan? Helen?"

"Not for me," I said tartly. "And since when has Joan taken to drinking whisky?"

"An heiress like Joan can drink whisky and choose the husband she fancies."

"Smarty," said Joan absently. She watched the girls, who were making a wreath about the flamboyant. "The smaller one is a beautiful girl, Helen. How old would she be?"

"Amoya? About seventeen. You should remember her, Joan, you stole her rings from her toes and you were so happy when she swore at Mrs. Partridge. She has two children now."

"I remember her. I suppose she will have a dozen before she is finished. She'll be a white-haired hag by the time she is twenty-five." She swallowed her drink at a gulp and shuddered.

I said, "Joan, how can you?"

"She doesn't enjoy it unless she shudders," Nicky gibed, but he touched her hair again.

She hiccupped. "I was saying, Nicky, that Amoya will be a white-haired hag soon."

"Perhaps. But Chanjaldi won't. She has nothing to do all day but beautify herself. She lives in Mr. Bannerjee's house and queens it over his servant. The old dames of the village gnaw their nails when they hear Chanjaldi laugh, such a singing laugh...."

"Oh, Nicky, hearts and flowers. But remember the flowers would be marigolds."

"Shut up, Joan. It's come to a pretty pass when even a whisky doesn't sweeten you up. Here, have another one."

I felt suddenly angry with him. "Stop giving Joan drink. Do your parents know about this whisky-drinking, Joan?"

"Oh yes. But not Grannie Lambert, she'd have a fit." She hesitated and then swallowed the whisky as though it were medicine.

John came out of his office. "Ah, whisky," he said and poured himself a stiff drink.

"Have a heart, John, that's mine," said Nicky. "It's about time you bought a bottle. Returns from the mill should be good this year."

"They could be worse," John admitted. He raised his glass to Joan. "Here's to your bonny blue eyes, Joan, and your bonny legs. My God, it's not so long ago we couldn't even mention legs, never mind look at them…."

"Except on Zulu girls," said Joan innocently.

John filled his glass again and Nicky corked the bottle. "It's a better world since the war," said John. "The ladies' skirts have gone up and so has the price of sugar." He laughed over this and repeated it. "I must remember to tell Pimm that one."

"She's quoting the Indian women as models of propriety," said Joan, "and that makes me wonder what Amoya would look like in a short skirt, or perhaps it's Chanjaldi Nicky would like to see."

"Chanjaldi is the flighty one in that family," said John. "She's so modern that she has been divorced and she has no children."

"I hate the sight of her," I said. "She isn't intelligent like Amoya and she's not even as pretty."

"I bet she's a lot more fun though," said Nicky, and John guffawed.

"You do admire her, don't you, Nicky?" Joan reminded me suddenly of Nancy. "I've just thought of something. I'll wear a sari to the fancy dress dance and I'll say that Nicky Angus admires Indian women as much as Miss Pimm does, but for different reasons."

"Oh do that, Joan, and I'll love you forever," said Nicky. "Think how it will liven everybody up. But you're too fair."

"I'll stain my skin and hire a wig."

"Do you think your grandmother's heart will stand it?" I asked dryly.

She said joyfully, "I'll do it, shall I, Nicky?"

John looked at her with approval. When she had gone home he helped himself to more of Nicky's whisky.

"There's a girl. If I were a young chap like you, Nicky, I'd snap her up before anybody else. What more could you ask for? Good looks, spirit, charm. And land. Miles and miles of sugarcane."

Joan did wear a sari to the fancy-dress dance that week. "This is what she said to me, and you can believe it or not," Miss Pimm reported. "Nicky Angus admires Indian women as much as you do, but for totally different reasons. I really felt as though I was going to faint, hearing a thing like that from a young girl. She must have meant it as a joke, but I thought it wouldn't do any harm for you to know about it, Helen."

I said easily, "Joan is one of these modern flappers, she thinks it's smart to talk like that. They had an argument about short skirts, it was something to do with that...."

"I suppose Nicky was disgusted with the way she shows her legs. Still, I'd have her up if she said that sort of thing about my brother."

Miss Pimm handed the post to me as though she were delivering the summons. When I reached home Nicky was paying the daygirls. Joan was on the veranda and she followed me into my bedroom.

"I've got a headache. I think I'll lie down."

"It's all that hair, Helen. Wait, I'll put a damp cloth on your forehead."

"Joan, you must be careful what you say to Miss Pimm. I know her and in a few months' time she will still be talking about you in that sari and twisting the whole story...."

"It was a joke. Nicky was in it too."

"It was a nasty joke."

"But Nicky doesn't care what Miss Pimm says. He laughed like hell about the whole thing."

"Well, then, he is as much to blame as you are because he should have been offended. You people are losing all sense of proportion."

Joan made a face at me and I put my hand on the shining cap of her hair. Amoya came to the door. She came often to visit me. She sat down on the floor near the window.

"I keep sweets for you," she said and from a tobacco bag she spilled bright yellow sweets on the table. I knew the taste of them well, so awful that it clung to your palate for hours afterwards no matter what you ate to get rid of it. Joan and I both refused, but Nicky chewed one up when he came in for tea. Joan looked at him in admiration.

"Miss Drew, did I show you the calendar I make?" Amoya asked. "I painted the picture myself."

"No, but let me see it now."

Amoya took out the calendar that had been folded into a square and put away with the sweets in the tobacco bag. "I count," she said, pointing inexorably to the numbers, "First, second, third, fourth, fifth, sixth, seventh...."

"Oh for goodness' sake, Amoya," Nicky groaned.

"It's a pretty picture," said Joan. "You've done it very well."

"Don't encourage her." Nicky leaned over to shake Joan by the shoulders, so close to her that his face touched hers. He whispered something to her and then went out of the room. Joan sat still. Pink bloomed on her bronzed skin, not only on her face but on her neck and arms.

"It's a pity you can't go to school, Amoya," I said. "So many Indian girls go nowadays."

"No good," sighed Amoya. "Gungi always say one day he will send me to school, but he not let me go for five minutes. He grabs me two, three times in one night. We are loving each other like... like..."

"Like mad," said Joan.

"That's right. We are loving each other like mad and there is no time for school. He say there will be plenty time when I am widow." There could be no world without Gungi and she laughed, subtly infecting us with her happiness.

"Amoya, you mustn't tell us your bedroom secrets," Joan protested.

"Miss Drew?"

"She means you mustn't tell us about Gungi making love to you," I said.

"It's not like that now, Miss Drew," Amoya said reassuringly. "Now I got a baby, that finish."

"How long before your baby is born, Amoya?" Joan asked when the shout of laughter had died down.

"Soon maybe." Amoya looked with pleasure on her fullness. "I am having son this time. My mother and I pray every day and giving offerings. Then Gungi will be happy and my mother-in-law will love me."

"She's the fly in Amoya's ointment," I told Joan.

I knelt down and put my hand on Amoya. "It won't be long, perhaps a week. I can feel him moving." Amoya touched my hand and smiled into my eyes. I said uneasily, "She has a hard time with the babies. I think at the last moment the old midwife frightens the wits out of her. This time I'm going to help her."

Nicky's shadow fell on us. He said, "Joan, my father has opened a bottle of whisky, this is our great chance."

They went out of the room and we heard them laughing with John in his office.

"It is good that your brother marries such a kind and pretty girl, Miss Angus," Amoya consoled me. "And she is rich too. That is good." She sat there until the sunlight slipped away from her and lay in a band of gold on my dressing-table. "I go home now," she said, picking up the tea-tray, "I come again when my baby is born."

"I hope it's a boy for you and Gungi."

The room was darkening. I heard the chugging of Peter's Tin Lizzie in the break. He had the headlights on already and as he came round the bend in the break they shone on the walls of my room.

The white basin and jug on the washstand and the white scarf I had thrown over a chair were lifted from the shadows. The noise of the engine swelled to a roar, wavered and died. Now the wash-basin and jug and scarf settled down sedately into their places.

Peter had joined the party in John's office. They all sounded a little drunk. I got up and began to dress hurriedly. Nancy had taken to putting white rice powder on her nose and chin, she was even talking of having her hair-bobbed when she had persuaded her mother. I plaited my hair and wound it over my ears like headphones. The new styles did not suit me, I was not thin enough. Miss Pimm of us all would have looked her best, but she refused to change her way of dressing and she looked rather like an advertisement from an old magazine these days.

Joan and the boys had gone on to the veranda, but John was banging the wall of his office. That meant he wanted his cigarette. I put only a pinch of dagga in it that evening because he had been drinking. He listened-in while he smoked. Nicky and he had made the wireless set and it was a boon in the house. Nothing had ever kept John so quiet. Sometimes Chris telephoned me at this hour. I waited for the bell, keeping close to the telephone, for John would be bound to say I was out if he got to it first; but there was no call for me that night.

"Wonderful," John said when he took the headphones off, "I got a wonderful reception."

"What were they playing?"

"Oh, it wasn't music. Somebody talking about gardening, how to grow dahlias. That's the first time I've had such a clear reception. Growing dahlias. You ought to try your hand at them, give you an interest." He stubbed his cigarette and chewed a peppermint.

Joan and Nicky had crammed into the front seat of Peter's car. I called out, "Aren't you three going to the bioscope? Mr. Bannerjee said he would keep seats for us in the back row as long as we weren't too late."

"We're just taking Joan home," said Peter. "We'll have to hurry because I promised to drive my mother to the hall."

I frowned at Nicky, for he had hold of his bottle of whisky

and he was making motions of drinking from it. "I'm only taking it along for safe-keeping, Helen. John might get at it."

The car roared down the break and then we heard it stop. I said, "They're drinking that whisky. You'll have to talk to Nicky, John…."

"Probably engine trouble," said John. "That old tin can of Peter's is always giving trouble. You'll hear them go off again just now like a packet of crackers."

As we sat down to supper we heard the motor again. They could not have gone twenty yards before the crash came. Peter had run the car into the Halfway Tree. He was the only one hurt and we took him to the doctor to have some stitches for the cuts on his face before we let Mrs. Farrell see him.

It was unfortunate that Mrs. Lambert should be visiting Mrs. Farrell that evening. They were waiting for Peter to drive them to the hall when we brought him home. Mrs. Lambert detected the smell of whisky at once and she came to each one of us sniffing like a hound on the scent.

"You've all been drinking," she said. "It's a disgrace. I could smell it on Peter too."

"The doctor gave us something to drink to steady our nerves," said Nicky promptly. He breathed heavily towards her.

"None of your impudence, Nicky."

"I don't care whether you were drunk or sober," said Mrs. Farrell, "I've had just about enough of you, Nicky. I'm not going to allow him to see you again. This has been going on ever since you were children, one accident after the other. Anybody would think you did it deliberately…."

John lost his temper with her and we hustled him out of the house, leaving Mrs. Lambert to console her. We took Joan to Drew's Pride after I had tidied her up and made her eat something.

"Do you think it would be too dreadful if we went to the bioscope?" said Nancy plaintively. "After all, it's not as if Peter was in any danger, is it? I did so want to see Douglas Fairbanks in this picture. Mr. Bannerjee was telling me about it…."

"We're going," said John. "She's got a hope if she thinks we're going to sit at home. Besides, what good would it do Peter?"

Nancy smiled at him and went upstairs to get her coat.

"I don't feel like going," said Joan. "I think I'll go to bed. I'm getting a headache."

Nicky put his arm round her. "Come along to the bioscope. You'll get the horrors sitting alone here." She had always given in to him too easily and she couldn't deny him even such a small thing. She ran upstairs to change.

The bioscope was shown in the hall and the only good seats were in the back rows. These Mr. Bannerjee fought tooth and nail to keep for his regular customers. He had been successful that night and we seated ourselves smugly behind the Drews. Sowa, collecting the money at the door, gave everybody a sparkling smile with the ticket. He and Mr. Bannerjee were partners and their standing was none too secure, though they paid handsomely for the hire of the hall. Mr. Bannerjee had to explain every detail of the picture to Mr. Skefton before it was shown. Miss Pimm, as a great favour, played the piano. When we came into the hall she was giving the Westongate choir an airing. The lights went off so suddenly that we might well have imagined that we had been struck blind. They had to be switched on again, for the members of the choir had been left stranded at the top of the hall. Boos and yells followed them while they found their seats. Off went the lights again.

The screen remained blank. A bedlam of derision broke loose and Mr. Bannerjee must have become flustered, for nothing appeared except the words, Part Four, upside down. The noise reached a crescendo, but luckily for Mr. Bannerjee he managed to start the picture and the audience calmed down into a mere stamping of feet and shrill whistling. Once Sowa had had to hand back the money, but tonight everything went well until Douglas Fairbanks kissed Mary Pickford and then Miss Pimm rose up and tried to block the view by spreading out her arms. We all yelled, "Shame!" and an audacious hand pulled her down into her seat; she refused to play the piano after that.

Mrs. Lambert arrived during the interval. She made Nicky give up his seat next to Joan and he had to stand for the rest of the time; I could hear her giving Nancy and Richard a hurried account of Peter's accident. "Smell Joan's breath," she finished triumphantly. "He's been giving her drink." She turned round and glared at Nicky.

Richard patted her knee several times. "Later, later," he kept saying, but he had no effect on her low, hoarse voice.

Mr. Bannerjee had trouble starting the picture up again and as the mob howled I leaned forward and tugged Mrs. Lambert's hair. She gave me a long, steady look when the lights went on again.

Chapter fifteen

Leela was sitting outside her hut, mashing curry-paste with an oval stone.

"Where's Amoya?" I asked.

"Sick three days, ma. Screaming all the time. You going looking bimeby?" A muscle tensed in her calm face. "Gungi lying in hut, crying like silly fool. Making chiles crying."

A prolonged scream broke the afternoon stillness and made itself visible in Leela's face. I ran to the hut that had been set apart for confinements.

Amoya stood in a corner of the hut, her lips pulled back in a snarl of agony. Serya was in the opposite corner. As I came to the doorway, she bent her head and charged Amoya, butting her in the stomach. The rhythm of Amoya's body ceased for a moment and she screamed again. Serya turned to me, her face haggard and sweating. She cried out in rage and bewilderment and went for Amoya again, but this time I pulled her back. Amoya, her eyes blazing with pain, squatted down.

"You must be patient, Serya, you must wait...."

"Too long she waiting, bimeby baby him finish."

I tried to turn the baby, but I was unsuccessful and the only ease I could give Amoya was to keep Serya from her. I made her lie down and gave her a bag of warmed salt to hold against her. For an hour we waited, Serya sulking behind an evil-smelling fire, and muttering incantations like a witch's curses. Slowly, as though he knew the futility of his effort, Amoya's son came feet foremost into the world. He did not cry and with a glance at the dark purple of his face Serya put him aside on the floor; but I picked him up and swung him and smacked him until he cried. Serya, all officiousness now, took him from me. Amoya raised her head from the dust to look at him.

The close little room was darkening, there was slime on my hands. I went down to the river and trailed my hands in the water like a child, for the pattern of life seemed simple and joyful when I thought of Amoya's son.

We were going to have a storm. The wind was in the canefields and the clouds and in the racing shadows. It blew from the sea, but it could not conquer the smell of turmeric and spices and garlic that came from the huts.

I stood up hastily. Mrs. Lambert and Miss Pimm were crossing the bridge and they were astonished to see me there playing with the water.

"Whatever are you doing?" Mrs. Lambert called out.

I joined them on the bridge, wiping my hands on my handkerchief.

"I've just been helping the midwife to deliver Amoya's baby."

They looked at each other. "Well, I am always forgetting you took that course in obstetrics," said Mrs. Lambert jealously. "When anybody sends for me again, I know what I'll say to them. Send for Helen Angus. I'm getting too old to chase around the countryside. Seventy-three this week."

"Coolies. I suppose a nurse learns to put up with anything, Helen." Miss Pimm's eyes brightened. "Isn't Amoya the girl who works for you?"

"Yes."

"Oh. You do take an interest in her, don't you?"

"We came for some lichees," said Mrs. Lambert briskly, "and we'd better hurry, Enid, there's going to be a terrible storm; just look at that sky." She shouted to Leela, "Have you got lichees, Mary?"

Leela did not answer her. "I don't think she heard you, Aggie. We'll have to go down. Besides I'd like to see the baby. I've never seen a new-born coolie baby."

"They won't let you in. The old midwife is superstitious…" I said.

"They let you in."

"I was helping."

She went down the slope at a run and Mrs. Lambert and I followed more soberly. Leela was short with her, for she was close-fisted and she took as much pleasure from bargaining as any Indian. When she asked to see the baby, Leela nodded her head in refusal.

"You not seeing now. Bimeby you seeing."

"Well, we didn't come to see the baby," said Miss Pimm, wrinkling her nose. "We came to buy some lichees."

"No gotting." She took no more notice of Miss Pimm and began to mash the curry-paste again.

"I can see we're not wanted here for some reason," said Miss Pimm. "There's a bit of a mystery if you ask me. It's most peculiar," said Miss Pimm. "People are usually only too glad to show off a new-born baby."

"It isn't an hour old, the mother had a hard time and the midwife is superstitious about people coming in," I explained.

A spatter of rain quelled Miss Pimm. "We'd better go or we'll be drenched. Are you walking back with us, Helen?"

"I'll wait here. Nicky is in Westongate…."

"Ah, he will be calling in here, will he?"

"No, but we could wait on the bridge and we should catch him there."

They wouldn't hear of that. I could see that Miss Pimm was only too anxious to get away now so that she could talk about the preposterous idea that had come into her head. She never knew how close she came to being butted by the sacrificial goat. He was tethered to a stake set in the grass on the river-bank and he charged at her retreating buttocks, but the rope brought him up short before he could reach her.

I laughed and Miss Pimm raised her voice spitefully. "The Anguses…. They're all like that…. I wouldn't be surprised if Nicky…" She passed out of earshot.

Leela said, "I giving you present. I giving you two fowl."

She spat a long stream of red that narrowly missed the curry-paste. A lean rooster that had been scratching in the dirt nearby rushed forward, but I kicked some earth over the spit before he could gobble it up.

Leela sparkled. Sowa must have been doing well out of the travelling bioscope, for she had two fine rubies clipped into her nostrils. Her sari, too, was expensive and in the dim hut beyond I saw several new pieces of furniture.

"You're getting rich, Leela," I said.

"Bimeby you Angus richest peoples here," she retorted. "When Nicky him marrying. Sowa him making money. Bimeby next year him building big big house where Zetke living. Him marrying rich girl in Durban. Must giving her plenty plenty things. Him buying that land for cash, but Zetke not wanting going. Bimeby Sowa going police. Sowa building big big house, big like Drew's Pride."

"You'll have a job getting Zetke off; he has lived there all his life."

"Sowa owning that now, every day I telling Zetke," she said complacently. She spoke more softly. "Ma, you looking Perian bimeby, me I thinking that man sick, him go two nights not drinking rum, no cane-spirit. That man working two days. Me I not liking, mama. Why for him not running in bar?"

"Perhaps he has reformed, Leela." Before I could explain to her what I meant I saw the car on the road and I ran to meet it. As I crossed the clearing the wind dropped suddenly and forked lightning cracked the clouds apart. There was a roar of thunder and I saw flames take hold of the cane on the hillside. Almost at once the rain quenched the fire. Nicky had driven on without seeing me.

Leela pulled me into the hut out of the rain. She offered me some holy water to drink and took a mouthful herself when I refused.

Then she lit a lantern. Now I could see the new sideboard and the carpet on the floor. All round the walls were spritely holy pictures. Small idols stood about like ornaments with offerings of flowers before them. It was a cheerful place. This was the living-room and beyond I could see Leela's wonderful new bed. Under the mattress were several big bunches of bananas placed there for ripening.

Leela began placidly to prepare cakes, ladling ghee into a pot with sugar. She returned again to the phenomenon of Perian, but she could not believe in his reform and begged me again to see if he was sick when he came home. He had been working on the shop that Sowa was building between the native and Indian settlements. It was to be a grocery shop and he would catch the trade from both. Now that Sowa was to be married she was happy indeed, for only in this one thing had he been a bad son; most of the jewels she wore were in safe-keeping for his wife and besides he had a bag full of ornaments buried in a secret place. She knew why Sowa had risked putting off marriage; he was able now to speak for a rich girl whose father had influence. In all things Sowa was clever.

There was a movement in the thatch and I looked up to see a puff-adder threading a tenuous way through the ceiling of banana leaves. Something, diamond-eyed, leaped to the floor. I ran outside.

"Rat," said Leela chuckling.

"There is a puff-adder up there."

"It good. It eating rat."

The rain had stopped. Now there was even a little sunlight on the turgid grass. Fowls came out of their sheltering places and began to scratch and peck with fury to make up for lost time. Leela gave me a dollop of the curry-paste and Chanjaldi ran out with some sweets for me and began to cry when I hesitated at taking them. Gungi from a distance was bowing to me, Mr. Bannerjee stood on his veranda and made a speech. From the top of the hill I looked back at them all and saw them as illusory, colourful shadows.

Battalions of clouds were massing, there were gulls flying in from the sea. I hurried down the gloomy break through high cane that rode with a song on the wind. Before I reached home the rain had started again. It came with the maddened wind that threw it up in thin sheets before it ever reached the ground. Soon the rain mastered the wind and began to beat steadily on the canetops.

The rain lasted for twelve days and we grew used to the sound of it. When we did awake to silence the sky was still heavy with clouds. Zetke had turned up, bursting with news. He was trying to light the fire, but his mind was not on what he was doing, for he was feeding sodden wood into the stove. I was surprised to see him there, for he no longer worked for us. His sons were on the farm now.

"You'll smoke us out of the house, Zetke. Why don't you chop up some of the packing-cases in the shed?"

John came into the kitchen. "I suppose the law will say that I must pay your sons for sitting at home these five days. Has much damage been done?"

"The bridge is gone, the big bridge. Awetuli bridge still stands, for it is bewitched. I had a ride in a boat from the policeman. The water is all over the country, it covers the hills." A grin overspread his face, as was necessary while he told bad news. "Two of your cows are bogged, that's what I came to tell you."

John controlled his voice carefully. "I've got a good mind to kick your sons out for good."

"I cannot blame you," said Zetke. "All they think of is buying goods from the coolie and making him rich. The cows are at the head of the lagoon. My sons are with them now. We must go quickly, for the river grows mightier every hour." Now he smiled with enjoyment. "Many of the coolies have been swept away in their houses and drowned. Some are sitting on the roofs waiting for the policeman to take them off."

I lit the Primus, for Zetke had given up the fire and stood with folded arms waiting to lead John to the cows.

"You'd better go down to the river and see if you can give a hand there," John told Nicky. "I've got to go and see to the cows these fools left out."

I went with Nicky to the river. There was not a timber to mark the bridge and of the dozens of huts on the bank only eight remained. The policeman and Richard were plying boats between the huts and the shore in an effort to get the Indians to safety. Richard gave his boat up to Nicky and went with Mr. Skefton to arrange lodging for some of the Indians at his barracks. Peter came down afterwards and stood with Joan, sulkily watching, for Joan stopped him from joining Nicky because he had had a touch of pneumonia after his accident and he was still pale and thin.

We were fascinated by the goat that swam desperately for the bank, for at that moment he seemed to be the only one in danger, having jumped from the roof of Leela's hut. At last Mr. Bannerjee waded into the water and pulled him to the bank by the rope that still dangled round his neck. The goat ungratefully tried to butt Mr. Bannerjee and on being foiled rose on his hind legs in an effort to reach the canetops.

Amoya's hut was gone, but she was safe on the tin roof of Leela's hut. She sat patiently beside her mother. Perian and Gungi, Gungi's parents and the children were there too, so that there was not an inch to spare even for the fowls. These had been crated and hung about a foot above the water. As the wind swayed their box they set up a wild cackling. The women shrieked, but their voices had no power against the wind, so that their danger in those first few minutes seemed unreal to me, although the river slunk all around them.

Nicky brought his boat alongside the hut and there arose a great argument amongst them, for they could not decide on the best way of climbing down to him. To show them all how easy it was, Gungi, putting his little daughter into the circle of Amoya's arm, clambered down the side of the hut, using the fowls' crate as a step. It gave way beneath him and he fell headlong into the racing current. He and the crate were swept from sight. His mother sprang after him and she, too, was lost.

Sowa stood opposite the hut, his smart suit ruined by the water. There were brilliant globules like an adornment on his hair and his face too sparkled but from the tears that slid down his cheeks. Beside him Serya and Chanjaldi shrieked to the women to stay where they were, but Mr. Bannerjee and Sowa were quiet. The policeman rowed over to help Nicky and he added his voice brutally to the noise, shouting to the Indians to take a chance and jump for it. The hut lurched.

"It's going," breathed Joan.

"You will be drowned, Amoya. Jump, jump," I cried.

Sowa was down on his knees, his arms outstretched to them. Chanjaldi had covered her face with her sari. Leela took a step forward as the hut moved slowly into the middle of the river. It gathered speed at once and all along the bank our voices rose in a terrible sound; but those on the hut seemed calm. Amoya gathered her two children to her. Perian took Leela in his arms and hid her face against his breast as the hut whirled downstream. Their white hair mingling flew out behind them like a cloud and a corner of Perian's dhoti fluttered loose, so that for a moment there was something gay in their swift flight.

The wind was blowing fiercely now and a gleam of sunshine showed on the water, darkened by mud to the colour of black tea. The policeman turned his boat and began to drag the remaining Indians off by force when he could reach them; but Nicky's boat was in midstream. I called his name and he looked towards the bank. The boat had already been picked up by the current and it was making for the sea with the hut.

"Come on," gasped Joan. "We'll get to the hill by the time they reach the lagoon." A prayer was falling from her as she ran and I joined in, "Our Father Which art in Heaven..." Sowa, a little way in front of us, was calling on his god in a loud voice. Mr. Bannerjee was left far behind.

Down the dripping breaks we ran, with the wind behind us. Although no rain was falling, we were wet through from the cane-tops that swished water on our heads and from the grass that drenched our feet. Nothing stirred in the sodden trash except swarms of midges that eddied like vapour in the sunlight. In the hollows near the river where only the tops of the cane showed through, seagulls were riding like little white boats.

From the hilltop we could see the distorted course of the river, the lagoon and the surf. The three had merged into an undivided body of water, for the sandbank was gone and breakers thundered in to meet the swiftly flowing river. John was still working with Zetke and the umfaans to save the two cows bogged in the mud at the foot of the hill. They dragged one of the cows clear, but before they could rope the other the boat and the hut came in sight. They encountered the last line of breakers and spun round and then rose on the crest of the wave, rocking from side to side before they were caught again by the current.

We ran on down the slope to the water's edge, sliding in the mud and pulling ourselves up by the tufts of coarse grass. John was in the river waist-deep, yelling for Nicky like a man gone mad.

A great wave curled out of the sea. It came in smoothly, carrying little foam, but when it crashed the spume shot up thirty feet high. The hut was smashed, but as the wave spread itself over the lagoon the boat bobbed up again. There was nothing else to be seen except a bright sari caught on a board. The boat swung round and then I saw Amoya clinging to a plank, her baby still tied to her back.

Peter plunged into the water and swam towards the boat, His blazer lay in the mud beside me and automatically I picked it up. He reached the boat and Nicky helped him in over the stern.

They were making a try to save Amoya, for she had been thrown clear of the current and they moved the boat towards her inch by inch. I waited stonily for the waves to take her, for while she was there Nicky would not give up. They left the boat to the wind and the current, but when they were within a few yards of Amoya they began rowing again. Nicky bent over and took her by the hair, lifting her clear above the water into the boat. At last they started for the shore. John and Sowa were standing ready on the rocks to drag the boat in, but before it reached them it was swamped again, caught by the force of the current and a big wave. As the spray cleared we saw it again. Peter was not there. Amoya lay with her arms crossed over the gunwale and Nicky was bending to the oars. He edged into deeper water that eddied in swirls, carrying the boat to the rocks. I saw with wonder that Zetke had freed the other cow and the umfaans were unconcernedly driving both up the hill; but Zetke at least did wait to see if Nicky was safe.

Sowa lifted Amoya from the boat. She shook herself free and took her baby from her back. As she held him up, his head lolled as though his neck were broken. I took him for her and laid him face downwards on the sand. I worked over him for half-an-hour, but it was no use. It was John who picked up the baby and gave him back to Amoya.

"Finish," he said.

She looked from her son to the wide sea as though she asked a question. There were grains of sand on the baby's cheek and with her forefinger delicately she brushed the sand off and then traced the outlines of his features. It was sad now to see that likeness to Gungi, for whose soul in the fullness of time he should have prayed.

The sorrow in Sowa's face had given way already to acceptance. He touched Amoya's arm.

I said, "Take her to the barracks. There's an empty bed in the end room, Sowa. Give her something hot to drink."

She went away quietly, carrying her baby. They hadn't gone far before Mr. Bannerjee met them. He picked Amoya up and with his head bent plodded across the sand dunes to the cane. We watched the sea for an hour and then we went home.

Mr. Skefton left John to settle some of the Indians in our barracks; the others were already at Drew's Pride. Then I went with him to see the Farrells, for one of us who had been there had to help break the news and I thought I should be more acceptable to her than John or Nicky. We wrapped the blazer in brown paper so that she should not guess at the disaster before Mr. Skefton had time to prepare her. It was Mrs. Lambert who opened the door to us.

"Oh, Mr. Skefton and Helen. Come in out of the wet. We're just busy with the pig. Henry killed it this morning when the weather fined up. It's good weather for it, mind you, pretty cold. They're expecting her relations…." She stared at us. "Something has happened."

"Yes."

"Henry. He was going across the river to catch the train to Durban, he wanted to go to the dentist. He's been suffering agony with toothache during all these floods. Is it one of the girls…? Henry…?"

"Peter," said Mr. Skefton. "He was drowned rescuing an Indian woman and her baby."

"A coolie Mary and her baby," exclaimed Mrs. Lambert. "Oh, I can't believe it. Nobody could be so selfish. He should have thought of his parents first...."

"Please tell Mrs. Farrell I should like to see her," said Mr. Skefton mildly.

Mrs. Lambert had disturbed his poise. I couldn't see that he would be equal to the occasion. He swooped on the cat that had been rubbing itself against his leg, stroking it from head to tail as though he were glad to touch something alive; but the cat got away from him. It moved stealthily across the floor after some prey that was invisible to us. Mr. Skefton crouched down and snapped his fingers.

He straightened up as Mrs. Farrell came into the room, her face alert. Mr. Skefton was, after all, equal to the occasion. The harshness and fatigue left his face, he had the right words ready for her. "Peter is at rest...."

He signed to us to go out of the room. There was only the shed where we could shelter and I followed Mrs. Lambert there. Portions of the pig's carcass were hanging from the rafters. There on the table were Golden Syrup tins filled with lard.

"Peter is at rest," she said, mournfully beginning to stuff sausages. "Don't think this is a terrible thing to do, Helen, and Peter dead, but this will go bad unless it's finished today and it will come in useful at a time like this. I like to give practical help.... Tell me what happened, my dear...."

"He swam out to Nicky...."

"Ha, I thought he wouldn't have been doing a thing like that on his own."

"It wasn't Nicky's fault in the least. A wave swamped them and he was washed out of the boat. It seemed to happen in a second."

"It's a pity he was with Nicky, it will cause a lot of bitterness." The pig's head was on the table and his trotters stood neatly in a row in front of his snout. The stare of alarm in his dead eyes didn't worry Mrs. Lambert. She finished the sausages and picked up the head, holding it affectionately under her arm while she scraped off the hairs. "Yes, she'll find this useful with people popping in and out all the time to condole; I always say you're never at a loss with a bit of pork in the house." She paused to wipe her eyes. "It's a funny thing, when she wrote over and asked if I would help with the pig this morning I was on the verge of saying no. But then I thought, I've never let Susie down yet when she has killed a pig and she would do the same for me. What is friendship if we can't help each other? And wasn't it a blessing that I came? She would never have been able to get through this and it would have lain here rotting." She drew a long steady breath as she placed the pig's head beside his trotters.

"His coat is in this parcel."

"Put it down over there, Helen. Poor boy. I can see him now, standing in that doorway asking her if he could go down the break for a walk. If you promise to look after yourself and don't go near that Nicky Angus, she said, and being so busy with the pig, she let him go, but she wasn't easy about it. 'But you can't keep him cooped up for the rest of his life,' she said. Here, take these tins of lard, Helen, they'll come in useful and you might as well have some of the sausages."

"No," I said wildly, "no thank you, Mrs. Lambert. I don't want them."

"Oh do."

"Oh no, I couldn't."

"Well then, I'll put them in the car. The Vicar can take them home to Mrs. Skefton, they're partial to pork. Are you sure you don't want any, Helen?"

Mr. Skefton was calling her. She put the tins of lard into my arms and tearing off a piece of the brown paper from Peter's coat hastily wrapped up some sausages. She made me take these too.

Mr. Skefton said, "Will you go to her now, Mrs. Lambert, and stay with her until her husband comes home? No, Helen, don't go in. I told her a little of what happened. It may be better if you speak to her later. Now...now she is somewhat...ah...unreasonable."

I crept round the house, embarrassed by my hateful burden. Mr. Skefton started up the car. He was silent and listless as though he had used up all his power, but he was still observant. He looked questioningly at the Golden Syrup tins and the parcel.

"The pig?"

"Yes. Mrs. Lambert thought you…"

"I don't want them."

"Nor do I." With an excess of fury I flung the tins of lard far into the cane.

"Oh, don't waste…"

We were passing the Farrells' barracks and he held out the parcel to an old Indian woman who was leaning on her hoe watching us. When she did not take it he called out "Catch," and tossed the parcel to her. The paper flew off and she caught the sausages neatly on her hoe. She looked at them with repugnance.

"Not beef. Pig," he shouted.

"Huh?"

"Pig."

"Perhaps she's a Mohammedan."

She frowned at us and Mr. Skefton made a grunting noise. That seemed to terrify her and she threw the hoe and the sausages from her and ran into her hut. Fowls came streaking across the clearing and a mynah alighted arrogantly amongst them. The Indians' dog, a rakish creature with a scarred back, slunk forward on its belly and then sprang amongst the fowls. It wolfed the sausages.

"There are times when I don't understand Mrs. Lambert," said Mr. Skefton.

In each of us was the belief that if we could recover some of the bodies we would gain a meagre triumph and we searched for many days. Even Zetke searched, though not one of the Zulus had been drowned, and even Miss Pimm, whose life was marked in such definite channels that she fretted if she drank one cup of tea more than she was accustomed to. We searched in groups or separately, walking along the sand with our heads bent against the sunlight as though a craze for collecting shells had swept Westongate. Sometimes we remained on the hilltop and watched from there.

So I sat late in the afternoon with Zetke beside me. Behind us the heavy cows lowed for milking-time and an umfaan twanged a Jew's harp on a single mourning note. A group of Indians passed us. They were praying, not loudly, but with the sound of humming.

The clouds were coloured by the harsh light of the thwarted sunset. The swollen sea, purple and silver, was hushed, for the tide was at the full. There were gulls over the rocks. As they swooped we saw something move in the water beneath them.

"Behold," shouted the umfaan.

Zetke sprang to his feet. "Watch the cattle so that they do not stray into the cane," he said, and the little boy sank philosophically on to his heels, playing again his dirge on the Jew's harp. I could hear it half-way down the hill as I followed Zetke, but on the rocks I heard only the timeless beating of the sea.

It was Leela who lay there. She was caught by a skeleton foot in a crevice of the rocks. The tide had turned now and the water was already tugging at her. She resisted its pull, waiting to be taken from the sea for the last rites and to make her accounting with Sowa. The rubies in her nose glowed so that there was still something of life in her. Naked and breastless as her poor body was, her face was still untouched. Zetke had no pity for her. He seized a piece of driftwood and with one swift stroke he loosened her from the rocks and sent her floating out on the tide.

"Oh, Zetke," I cried, "oh, Zetke, she will come to you in the darkness and there will be a terrible bewitchment on you. She came back to her people so that they might burn her. And to give her jewels to her son."

Zetke flung the driftwood into the sea. "I am not afraid. Every day she said to me, 'The police will chase you off your land because it belongs to my son.' Coolie woman, Zetke laughs at you now."

But there was no peace for him or for me. He sent the umfaan on with the cattle and came with me along the beach in an avid search for more of the dead. It was almost dark when we came upon three bodies lying in a row on the sand; Peter, Gungi and an old woman whose face was unrecognisable. Zetke's courage had failed now that night was coming and he did not touch the Indians. I sent him running to the Farrells with the news and presently Farrell and Richard came to take Peter away.

Amoya haunted the hilltop for days after the funerals had taken place, thinking that even yet her father and mother might be washed up. Early one morning Mr. Bannerjee came to my window to beg me to bring her home.

"She has sat there through the night watching and still she will not leave. She will come for you, Miss Angus, for you are her teacher. It is Sowa's fault, he blames her and says she is cursed."

He took me to the place where Amoya sat and then waited for us in the break. She looked at me vaguely as though she were in a trance when I helped her to her feet.

"What is the use of sitting here? You will never find them now."

"My mother, Miss Angus, she will come back for a funeral. To her these things were all; the wedding and the funeral, the sons, the goddess…."

Not for Leela the washing and the lying in state, the three garlands in the coffin, the prayers and the funeral pyre on the river-bank. She must follow the lonely sweep of the ocean and come at last to rest where none knew her.

Amoya wept. "Not yet I know that Gungi and my children are dying. I will cry for them not one year but always. And for my mama. When I am a child she took me once to Durban because I never see the temple and the gods, or a big boat close by. We are poor and she had her train fare but none for me. She hides me beneath her sari and I am knowing when the conductor came for the tickets because her legs are sweating. But he did not find me. And I sat in the temple and learned there. I saw the big boats. We went to the market and she buys me five sweets."

I put my arm about her and helped her to walk. The sun was clear of the sea now. In the east the sky was blue and gold, illuminating the clouds above the horizon, while clear across the west there rose the splendid are of a rainbow. The bright clouds and the rainbow had no meeting place in the sky, for between them lay a heavy grey mass from which fell elusive mist. It was a paradox, for the brighter the east became the harder the rain fell, and though we stood in golden light we were wet through.

"You tell me the rainbow means promise of no more rain," said Amoya.

"You could hardly call this rain. It's not real."

"Nothing is real," she said.

I put my hand over hers, but not so easily could I penetrate her solitude.

Chapter sixteen

There's an iceberg off the coast," said John, shivering beneath the touch of the wind.

I closed the front door, but he was still cold and I brought a jersey to him, hoping to sweeten his bad temper by my solicitude. The Indian women had already washed up the supper dishes and as they made their way to the barracks they screeched and yelled to frighten away the devils.

"I wish they would shut up. I'm sick of them," John complained. "I wish to God the water would go down and they could get out of the barracks."

"They're yelling to frighten away Peter's ghost," said Nicky, who was standing at the window. "You'll hear a din tonight. They've got a priest from Durban and they're going to sacrifice the goat and lead Peter's spirit down the break...."

"What damned rot. I wish they'd lead old Mother Farrell down the break...."

The Farrells were leaving Westongate. There was a notice, For Sale, next to their gate and there was no work done on their farm, for their Indians had fled because Mrs. Farrell went through the breaks calling for Peter.

The floods had hit us hard, for most of our lands were low-lying and the cane had been ruined when the river broke its banks. Still, John planned to buy the Farrell's property after he had made Nicky and me promise that we wouldn't spend a penny unnecessarily. He had been to see Farrell that afternoon to make an offer.

"What did the Farrell's have to say?" Nicky asked.

"I never got past the gate. You should have heard her. She cursed you, Nicky. Practically said that you pushed Peter out of the boat. Anyway, she won't sell to us, or to the Drews, not even to Mrs. Lambert. What a bitch. I think she can read my mind because I'm standing there thinking I could get Richard to buy for me and she said' 'You needn't think I'll sell to anybody here who'll act as a go-between.' 'Oh well, keep your damned property and I'll keep my money,' I said." He mixed a glassful of brandy and water and clapping the earphones over his head shut himself off from the world.

Outside the Hindu priest was chanting and I looked anxiously at John to see if the noise was disturbing him, but he seemed happy enough. Nicky and I began a game of draughts. Presently the quivering notes of a flute sounded.

"That's the priest, looking for Peter's spirit, said Nicky, jumping two of my men.

The music came nearer and nearer. We looked through the window to see the priest approaching the gate; behind him his followers had started a commotion that worked the dogs into a frenzy and they rushed about snapping at the heels of those on the outskirts of the crowd. The roosters in the yard were crowing in a passion of bewilderment.

"God, what's that noise?" cried John, snatching off the earphones and then looking through the window, "It's an uprising...."

"No, they're looking for Peter's spirit," I reassured him. "They say he's haunting us."

"Oh, is that all? How am I supposed to hear the wireless?"

"He's got it now," said Nicky. "Look, they're turning back.

They're going to lead him down the break and nail him to the Half-way Tree."

"Well, I wish they'd hurry up and do it," John said. "Finish your game of draughts and I'll take you on, Nicky. I'll give them half-an-hour to stop their mumbo-jumbo. It's a sort of persecution. A man takes them in and gives them shelter when they're down-and-out and then he's got to put up with this sort of thing."

"They think they're doing us a good turn," I said.

"It's an insult to Skefton. He buried Peter in a Christian manner, didn't he? I've got a good mind to put a stop to it."

"They're coming back, they must have lost him." Nicky left the draughtboard and went to the window. "Ah, he's got him again...."

"Come back and finish the game,"' said John.

Nicky beat him. He drank some more brandy and went to bed.

The noise continued throughout the night and several times John got up to threaten the Indians, but they took no notice of him.

For three nights the priest hunted Peter's ghost, and on the night that he nailed it to the Halfway Tree Nicky went down the break with the Indians.

When the water dried up some of the Indians built their huts again on the river-bank; but others bought land at the foot of the hill as Sowa had done. The bridge was reconstructed and the foundations for Sowa's big house were laid. Before the end of the year the shadow of the masonry had fallen across Zetke's kraal.

There had been an outbreak of enteric after the floods and I had my hands full, for many of the Indians in the barracks went down. Amoya learned the rudiments of nursing so easily that I went to see Matron Carpenter and got her a start as a probationer.

She came to say good-bye to me one April afternoon. She wore no flowers because of her mourning and she was so thin that I wondered whether she would be able to stand up to nursing, yet she would not sit idle. She polished the silver while she talked to me.

"This is like when I first come to you, Miss Angus, when I am still a little girl."

"It is not so long ago."

"Then I am very happy."

"Yes."

"We will not talk about that time again. Mr. Bannerjee saying I am lucky to have sweet memory. Yes. Now also it can be happy. Sowa he forgives, business is good. He will give me a place to live and find me another husband. He knows many people. I am telling him that to be happy like that, it is not what I am wanting." She smiled. "He saying, 'You thinking you man, girls must not go away from their people.' Bimeby he saying I am not wearing sari. . . "

"Ask him why he doesn't wear a dhoti and work in the fields like his father did."

Now she laughed. "I ask him that and he is angry."

I walked with her as far as Awetuli and on the bridge we said good-bye. I gave her a pound for a present and she gave me a calendar that she had made, but she was not satisfied and looked in her bag for something else to give me. She had only her marriage jewel and I could not have that. Then she saw Chanjaldi coming down the steps to the bridge, and she ran to her to beg one of her trinkets from her. Chanjaldi, in a glittering sari, was on her way to meet a lover and happiness flowed from her. She bent down so that Amoya could unfasten the clasp of a necklace. It had been mended with fine wire and it took a few minutes for Amoya to get it loose. She embraced Chanjaldi and then brought the present to me. It was a necklace of little golden hearts. Chanjaldi went on her way laughing.

"Not this," I said to Amoya. "Give me a flower, one piece of fruit rather ... I know this necklace, Amoya."

"She taking it, Miss Angus?"

"It is her own, but throw it into Awetuli and then it will not bring us bad luck."

"It is waste," said Amoya, but she threw the necklace over the bridge into the pool.

That evening I telephoned Chris. I heard the click that meant Miss Pimm was listening-in and so I said only one word to him:

Chanjaldi. Night after night she was in my dreams running from me with golden laughter.

Nicky often left the house at sunset and did not return until nearly dawn. He quarrelled with John and me when we asked for an explanation and left the house for several days. He stayed at the hotel and John went there every day to beg him to come home.

At last he came to me. It was a moonlit night and I saw his ravaged face clearly. I ran to him and drew him into the house.

"Nicky, what is it?"

"That girl Chanjaldi...."

He stifled my scream with his hand. "John will hear you, for God's sake be quiet." He brought some water to me. "I'm sorry, I didn't mean to give you such a shock."

"What has happened, Nicky?"

"She's going to have a child."

This time I fought back the wave of faintness. "That's a lie. She can't have children."

"She swears it's true. Helen, forgive me. It was after Peter died. I couldn't forget him. Remember we used to think the cane was whispering 'Peter, Peter, Peter.' And then that night they laid his ghost.... Chanjaldi..."

"She has had other lovers. Coolies."

"Helen. Oh don't, Helen. It began a long time ago, when I came back from the war, the very first day. She put a garland round my neck and she said in Hindustani, 'You are my god.' I used to watch her.... I remember one day she made a wreath with a flamboyant flower, it was for me, she said. She had a photograph and she used to put flowers in front of it every day."

"She stole that from my album."

"She used to tell me stories...."

"She stole those from her sister."

"Helen, she won't let me go."

"How can she keep you? Don't be such a fool."

"If she has this child...."

"I'll strangle it. But she can't have children, she's trying to trick you. Go and bring the car round. We can coast down the hill. John won't hear, he's been drinking like a fish ever since you left home."

"What are you going to do, Helen?"

"I'm going to make quite sure that she's lying to you."

I left him sitting in the car in the cane-break and crossed the quiet clearing to Mr. Bannerjee's house. A dog barked, but I slipped in through the fence before he could bite me. I knew where Chanjaldi slept, in the front room of the house. The window had been left open and I stepped into the room. Chanjaldi was lying on her back. I moved over to her and pulled the coverlet from her. She was naked. The moonlight fell on her beautiful body, sleek-skinned with careful tending. I bent over her.

I might have been a lover, she awoke so languorously. When she recognised me she kicked out wildly and snatching up the coverlet fled through the house; but I knew what I had come to find out. I was out of the window and across the clearing in a few minutes with the dog snapping at my heels all the way to the car. Nicky drove the dog off with a stick. He laughed and swore in turns when I took the stick from him and beat him with it.

"She was lying to you. If you ever go near her again I'll kill her." He had nothing to say as we drove home.

I washed myself and made some tea. We drank it in the kitchen speaking in whispers so that John would not awaken.

"I'll have to get out for a while, Helen."

"Yes. You'd better go tomorrow."

He went to Durban the next morning and I thought he was free of her. Afterwards I wished that I had stabbed her as she slept.

Joan and Nicky were married in a Registry Office in Durban. They sent wires to all of us and casually went for a honeymoon to Cape-town. They were away for six months, to give us time to cool down, said Richard. Even John, delighted with the match, thought that we should have had all the trimmings to mark the occasion. Miss Pimm made Nancy's life a misery with her innuendoes. When it was learned that Aunt Lucy had been one of the witnesses Mrs. Lambert's fury broke all bounds.

There were brown patches on the hill where the cane had been cut and we had shorter, sunny days, with a bleak wind blowing at times. One windy day shortly after Nicky's marriage I drove to Mrs. Lambert's bungalow to have tea with her. I was a little nervous, for her note had been stiff.

"Did Joan surprise you too?" I asked as I led the horse behind the shed out of the wind. "I didn't have an inkling. I thought she might have confided in you."

"That's what I wanted to talk to you about, this hole-in-the-corner wedding, Joan could have had her photograph on the front pages…."

There was a solitary fly in the sitting-room and she plodded after it patiently with a swatter. It rested on the cups and the sugar and on the iced cake standing ready for tea.

"Drat the thing, you'd think it would light on the table for a minute." She sighed deeply and I thought she had given up, but she went after the fly persistently until she killed it.

"I'm sorry Nicky did a thing like that, Mrs. Lambert, but after all, Joan must have been in complete agreement."

"I know she hates a fuss. It wasn't that I wanted to talk about exactly."

She straightened the lace doyley beneath a vase and pulled off a withered gladiolus petal which she flicked through the open window.

"Oh my goodness, here comes Enid Pimm," she cried. "The last person I want to see. She'll stay here for hours and do nothing but talk about Joan. Of course I might have known she would come, it's Saturday afternoon and she'll wonder why I'm not at the Jumble Sale." In a great flurry she wrote on a card 'Out, back at five.' She pinned the card to the front door, locked all the doors and windows and pulled the curtains. "Don't think I'm strange doing this, Helen, but I have a good reason. Thank heavens your horse and cart are behind the shed. Shush now."

Miss Pimm's narrow feet pattered up the wooden steps and we heard her say, "Out. Why, I could have sworn…"

"She'll go round to the back," Mrs. Lambert whispered. But a long pause followed. "Look through the keyhole, see what she is doing, Helen."

I removed the key carefully; and found myself gazing straight into Miss Pimm's eye.

"Aggie," she said, "are you there, Aggie?" She tried the door. "I wonder what's the matter with Aggie Lambert. She drinks. I've always thought so, you can see it in her nose. Peering through keyholes. A secret drinker."

It seemed a long time before she went away. "Fancy Enid Pimm saying a thing like that about me," mourned Mrs. Lambert. "You wait, Enid. Oh dear, what a predicament. Do you think she'll go round saying that I drink?"

"Of course not," I said. "A postmistress would hardly admit even to herself that she gazed through the keyhole at her best friend."

Mrs. Lambert was comforted. "You have quite a brain, Helen, I never thought of that. It was most unfortunate." She cut into the cake with a sudden vicious stroke of the knife. "I couldn't let her in, she has the habit of staying the night. There's something I've got to say to you and the sooner the better. I'm an old woman now and my heart isn't what it was." She poured the tea. "Helen, have you ever told Nicky that he is your son?"

"No."

"Don't shout at me, dear. I thought you hadn't. I've written to him and Joan together to tell him the truth. And don't look at me like that. I've thought about it and it's my duty. I'm not going behind your back. I haven't even posted the letter yet. I thought if you wanted to write, this would be your chance to make everything clear to him. You should have told him long ago, but it was none of my business. I was waiting for him to become engaged to Joan and then I would have taken them both aside, with you present, of course, and told them in a nice way. That would have given Joan a chance to decide. This way is more unpleasant for all concerned. . , ." There was no sound in the room but the swishing of the cane as it tossed about in the wind. The colour in Mrs. Lambert's face deepened. "What a wind," she said unsteadily. "What a wind. Do you think Enid Pimm saw your cart? It's possible. My, it's getting close in here." She crossed to the window and began to struggle with the catch, her breath harsh in her throat. "Helen, help me, I can't get the window open...." She sagged against the window-sill. The ugly colour grew more vivid as she turned her head towards me. For a second more she was afraid and then there was nothing in her but the will to live. "Air...medicine...a brown bottle..." Her eyes met mine,

I went swiftly to her. The window yielded slowly. Now the wind was pouring over her. I found the brown bottle at her bedside.

It was not until late that night that she was able to talk. I had taken over from Nancy and as I took her medicine to her I saw that tears were coursing reluctantly down her cheeks. "Lambert used to say to me that his pet name for her was Peach-blossom, she was so pretty," she whispered. "She sounded so nice the way he used to describe her. But she isn't nice, is she, Helen? She's selfish through and through." A smile pierced the tears. "You are like he thought she was. Even the first night we were married he talked about her. Lucy, Lucy, Lucy. You're a good girl, Helen, a good, good girl. That letter.... You can tear it up. Look in my handbag on top of the wardrobe." When I had torn up the letter she went to sleep.

I thought that night that she was broken, but within the week she was on her feet again. Her animosity towards me returned slowly and sometimes she stared at me balefully as though she were remembering that I had frightened her almost to death in that closed room.

John and I went to Durban to find out from Aunt Lucy the details of Nicky's wedding. She had written us two letters, but not one of them mentioned Nicky, they were full of some obscure trouble that had overtaken her.

"Sounds as if she's got cancer," said John.

We found her in bed.

"Well, this is a fine time to get ill," said John. "We've come to celebrate. The only wedding this family is likely to see for many a year unless Helen surprises us. Tell us all about it, Lucy."

Aunt Lucy refused the brandy he offered her and drank her wine instead. "I've got something more important to tell you, but I'll get this over first. Nicky simply came in here one morning and said, 'Put on your best dress, Aunt Lucy, I'm going to be married.' So I got dressed and gave him a cheque for…never mind. We waited outside the Courthouse and along came Joan. I thought she looked rather pathetic walking alone like that. She had taken off her hat and she looked like a child in that shapeless dress, all the rage of course, and the sunlight in her hair, so pretty. And then she stopped by an old coolie flower-seller and bought two roses. Nicky ran down the steps and said, 'I sent flowers, Joan, didn't you get them?' She said, 'I've been out walking, I didn't go back to the hotel.' I began to cry and Nicky was quite rude, after the present I gave him too. Anyway he took her arm and they came up the steps as happy as happy could be and got married, sent the telegrams. Then we went to an hotel and had something to eat and drink. And off they went on the train to Capetown. That's all. I got the idea somehow that she was sad. I suppose she would have liked a big wedding like all girls do, but he can twist her round his little finger, he always could. But it's not important now. They're married and happy, spending that money I gave him. Something terrible has happened to me."

"What?" we both asked.

Aunt Lucy did not answer. She pulled a dressing-gown on and thrust her feet into slippers. Then she combed her hair and faced us tragically.

"Do you smell anything?"

We sniffed. "Curry," said John appreciatively.

Aunt Lucy looked triumphant. "There. Now come with me and I'll show you something."

We followed her on to the balcony outside her bedroom, overlooking the house next door. There were about ten Indian women sitting on the grass with their children. They were well-to-do, for they wore many jewels and their saris were costly.

Aunt Lucy shrieked, "Did you ever see anything like it?" Her voice carried clearly across the garden. A woman sewing on a machine stopped her work to look up at us. "Count them, John."

"I make it twenty with the children."

"I've seen as many as sixty, goodness knows how many, go in there to sleep. Sixty, now put that in your pipe and smoke it." She staggered back to her bedroom. "I'm staying in bed, I can't stand it."

"It's a blow," said John feebly.

"It was bad enough when Appleton made his house into a nursing home, but this is the last straw."

"You'll have to do something about it," said John.

"All I can do is move away." She gazed at us dolefully. "Imagine that, I'll have to move away. Even if I could put up with the thought of them as next-door neighbours, there's the smell." She held her nose.

"Don't be vulgar, Lucy."

"Vulgar! I've got to give up my home and you say I'm vulgar."

"Why don't you buy them out?" John suggested uneasily.

"And buy all the surrounding property? Oh no, the solicitor told me that's just what they want."

"You'll have to do something. Go and see your Member of Parliament."

"A fat lot of good that will do," scoffed Aunt Lucy. "And the noise. The other day they had a coolie Christmas and you should have heard the din. On and on all night until I nearly went mad. Tom-toms and a sort of fife thing and singing like this." Aunt Lucy sang drearily through her nose. "I've got to face it, I'll have to sell out. There is no other answer for it."

John was appalled. "You've been here for fifty years, Lucy. You can't leave now. And do you realise you won't get anything like what the place is worth?"

"I know that."

"Then surely it would pay you to buy them out," John argued.

"How often must I tell you, John, that the solicitor said not to do it on any account? He says that I'd have to buy all the property round here to make myself safe because as it happens this isn't a restricted area. And Matron Carpenter says that the hospital might have to go, Helen, or be converted into a non-European hospital.

Oh, I've heard all sorts of tales. There was a man who had to pay out thousands to get them out of shanties because he had built a big house at the top of the Berea. There's a lot of trickery going on. Some big financier is buying property, a white man, and putting coolies in and then when the people sell out next door he clears the coolies off and sells both houses to white people at a big profit. No, I'm going to save what I can. I'll sell out. And that means, I suppose, hotels for the rest of my life...."

"You could come out to the farm, Lucy...."

"Amongst the snakes. Oh, you needn't look like that, Helen, I shan't foist myself on you."

John frowned. "We'll have to think a way out of it, Lucy. It's a problem."

"All very well for you to say it's a problem, you people should have thought of this when you brought them out. Sitting up there on your hill...."

"They're all around us," said John suddenly. "Hundreds of them. Hundreds of coolie kids. There was all that loss of life during the floods, but our barracks were chock-a-block with them, the same at Drew's Pride. That's what caused this, they have so many children...."

I said, "Don't worry about that. Half of them don't see the first year out."

"A good thing. Perhaps the floods weren't such a bad thing after all, though the cane is ruined and I thought we were getting well established with the good prices and the subsidy." He looked at Aunt Lucy benignly. "Mind you, I'm more optimistic about sugar than I've ever been. They are talking of setting up an Experimental Station. It shows you what the country thinks about it. It might be a good idea for you to put the money from this house into land round Westongate. The Farrells' property is up for sale and I could work that into a nice little farm for you, Lucy. She won't let me have it, mind you, but there are more ways of killing a cat...."

"Don't talk about property to me, John. I'll never put another penny into real estate, not a penny. You see, John, the land doesn't belong to you even if you hold the title deed, not while they can live right next door to you."

"They can't buy on our side of the river, so we're pretty safe."

Aunt Lucy did not sell her house, for the price that she was offered was so low that she became angry whenever anybody talked about it. She took out her treasures and shut the house up. Everything was brought out to the farm and wherever you looked there were elephants. When Nicky came home he said that we should paint them pink and then Aunt Lucy might be prevailed upon to give up the bottle. She settled down with us and even spent the summer on the farm with a bodyguard of two umfaans and the dogs.

Chapter seventeen

A few weeks after Nicky's wedding the Farrells sold their property. Mrs. Lambert couldn't get to us fast enough with the news. She drove in state now, for she had bought Peter's Tin Lizzie and she had hired an Indian to drive her. You could hear her coming a mile off, for above the motor she would yell, "Mind the bumps, Sammy."

She sprang out of the car and ran up the pathway, nearly tripping in her hurry to bring the bad news.

"You ought to be more careful at your age. Break a hip and you're finished," said Aunt Lucy gloomily. "What's the matter anyway?"

"My dear, I can't tell you what has happened. I never thought Susie Farrell had a vindictive bone in her body. Do you know what she has done?"

"Put 'Killed by Nicholas Angus' on Peter's tombstone," Aunt Lucy hazarded.

"What ideas you get," grumbled Mrs. Lambert. "Of course not. That would be libel. You wait until I tell you. This affects you, it affects every one of us. She sold her property to that rich Indian."

"Sowa?"

"That's right."

"Is it true or just something you heard?" I asked cautiously.

"It's true enough. Thompson the land agent told me this morning. Helen, your father will be angry."

Aunt Lucy tapped on John's office window with her stick. "John, come here. You ought to hear what Mrs. Lambert has just told us."

"I'm too busy," he shouted.

"It's about the Farrells' property."

That lured him out. "Well, what is it, Lucy? Afternoon, Aggie. What's the news?"

"Tell him," prompted Aunt Lucy.

"Well, John… This morning I was having a chat with Thompson outside his office and he told me that Susie Farrell had sold her property to that Indian, the rich one…. What's his name again, Helen?"

"Sowa."

"For goodness' sake be careful, John," exclaimed Aunt Lucy. "Don't take it like that, you'll have a stroke." She fumbled in her bag and brought out smelling-salts, but when she waved them under John's nose he pushed the bottle away so violently that it fell to the floor. Everybody's eyes watered. John coughed and cursed.

When he recovered he stood looking across the river at the big house that Sowa had built. "Sowa. How the hell did he do it? A few years ago, what was he? A snivelling little coolie without two shillings to rub together. How did he do it?"

"They live on the smell of an oil rag. And I can tell you what he's going to do now," said Aunt Lucy with penetrating shrewdness. "He's going to try and sell the place to you, John, at a profit. You mark my words, I've had all this explained to me by a very clever solicitor."

Aunt Lucy was right. A week later John received a letter from Thompson. It was Thompson who was responsible for the building of the new hotel to which fast young men and women came from Johannesburg for their holidays. ' Selling land to Indians was just about what everybody had expected of him, said Miss Pimm.

I went to his office with John with the hope that my presence might prevent a violent scene. Thompson showed no signs of coming to the point. He opened the folders he had prepared for the season.

"Westongate is Nature's gift to the tired business man," he read out enthusiastically.

When he received no encouragement he began to play noughts and crosses on the folder. There came a sharp knuckling on the door.

"Come in," said Thompson, growing nervous under John's stare.

Sowa, too, was nervous. He sat lightly on the chair to which Thompson waved him. He was well turned-out and as he pulled up his trouser legs he revealed purple-and-gold socks. His hair was glossy as a cap of patent leather and indeed everything about him shone, from his shoes to the ruby in his tie-pin. But this sheen of wealth did not take from his face the eagerness that poverty had marked there and he was as thin as ever.

"I'm thinking of selling out the bioscope," he told us ingratiatingly. "I'm back in the silk business, you know."

"What do you want for the Farrell property?" John asked.

"What was the figure we arrived at, Mr. Thompson?"

Even Thompson bent his head at this display of cowardice. He played a game of noughts and crosses before he mumbled, "Six thousand pounds."

"I paying the transfer fees. The property is still in Mrs. Farrell's name, but I holding… hold… the deeds."

John got up and struck him across the face. "You must be stark raving mad. You wouldn't have paid more than two thousand for that lot. You thieving …"

"Mr. Angus," implored Thompson.

Sowa had already stumbled out of the room and I sprang before John. Thompson was waving his hands as though he fanned away hot air. "That's not the way to do business, Mr. Angus. A little talk, perhaps we could have arranged something."

"He's getting no six thousand pounds out of me," said John. "Good day to you, Thompson."

We expected Sowa to summons John for assault, but he played a different game. The house stood empty for a while. The notice 'For Sale' was still next to the gate, which had achieved a sort of respectability at last because it was wired up. Zetke was the first to see the two Indian families that Sowa had put into the house. Early one morning he shouted, "Behold, coolies."

We stared across the valley, shading our eyes against the rising sun. Then we looked at the Indians through the binoculars. John went inside for his revolver and Zetke began to stamp his feet to work himself into a fury. "Who is it that cheats us when he trades with us? The little coolie, the skeleton. Who is it that takes our land? The little coolie, the skeleton. Who is this rat that walks like a lion amongst the Zulus?" His umfaans chanted back to him. "Rise, oh Zulus, kill...."

I got the revolver away from John and shouted to Zetke to stop his foolery, for the grown men were joining him now.

"It wouldn't be a bad idea if. . ." Aunt Lucy began, but John had come to his senses and was telephoning the police.

The Indians were arrested that day and it seemed strange that clever little Sowa should have made such a mistake. The land on our side of the river was restricted to Europeans and the police sergeant told us that no Indian could spend a night there, even if there employed. Mrs. Lambert sacked her driver and replaced him with a reckless Zulu youth. Everybody followed her example and turned away their Indian servants.

We soon found that Sowa had made no mistake. Within a few days there was another Indian family in the Farrells' house. These Indians, too, were arrested and in all, six Westongate families were imprisoned. Then strangers came into the house and we realised at last that we were in for a fight. I quarrelled with Mr. Bannerjee; John was fined for assaulting one of the strange Indians. But sometimes I met Amoya on Awetuli bridge and we talked about nursing. I came to know when she would have leave and I would walk casually to the bridge to meet her; we were secretive about these meetings, pretending to each other that they were by chance. Once she, too, crossed the bridge and was arrested.

When Nicky came back from his honeymoon, he gave us a solution. "The only thing to do is to beat them at their own game. Take no notice of them if you're not willing to pay the six thousand."

"They can whistle for it," said John.

"Well then, leave them there. Don't report them to the police."

"What do you mean, just let them take over the whole place?"

"No. I think if we could get rid of these strangers, we'd be in a better position. They're all town men and organised. But they can't stay forever. If we leave them there, they'd go eventually of their own free will."

"Then others would take their place."

"They'd be Westongate Indians. And they have their own affairs to attend to. They'd get tired of seeing their gardens and businesses going to pot."

"There seems a bit of sense in that," John admitted.

"It will take patience, I'm warning you, but it's the only way to beat them."

It was almost a year before the Indians left. "Now is the time to make a deal with Sowa," said Nicky.

He and I went to see Sowa in his new house. Joan had gone to Durban with her parents for a week's holiday and she was expected back the next day. I remember that I wished that she would stay away longer, for Nicky had been having his meals with us.

Chanjaldi opened the door to us. She had been laughing and when she saw Nicky her face bloomed again.

"I didn't know you lived here?" I said.

"Staying here till Mr. Bannerjee coming home. He going Durban, bimeby he taking me India with him, today him buying tickets. Please what you wanting?"

"Is Sowa home?"

"Him not coming till four-o'clock train."

Nicky looked at his watch. "It's ten to. I'll wait for him at the station."

We turned to go, but she nodded her head and put out her hands in a lovely gesture. "Please you coming inside. You seeing this house."

Nicky walked away, but I followed her into the house, curious to see if the stories of Sowa's magnificence were true. The floors swept before us like vivid green grass, the rooms were full of expensive furniture and brass ornaments, the curtains were made of silk. Everything was sumptuously new. Through the window I saw another acquisition, a big Alsatian dog with red mange on his back. I wondered who had defiled their hands to treat him with sulphur and lard until I saw Amoya. She was out of mourning now and she wore a flower in her hair.

"What, are you on leave again, Amoya? They do treat you well."

"No, no, Miss Angus, I tell you. The clinic sends me here with Sister Johnstone...." She introduced me to a big woman whose patronising air reminded me of Mrs. Lambert.

"We're proud of Amoya," she said. "She topped Natal in her last examination."

"Look, I show you what we do." Amoya went out of the room and came back with a leather bag and a book. "We go along the South Coast and Sister shows the midwives what to do and gives them a bag and a book." She opened the bag and showed me bandages and scissors and castor oil and antiseptic. "They pay two pounds. This is for Serya. I buy it for her, she won't pay. Always she fights with me because I am a widow. I have to tell her what is in the book, she does not understand what Sister says."

Serya had come into the room and she seated herself on the floor with a supercilious air. She was not a good pupil and I did not envy Amoya her task. She looked sideways at the illustrations in the book to show her contempt, but she coveted the shiny black bag which she had on her lap now, opening it from time to time to peep at the contents. She burst into a flood of argument with Amoya, and Chanjaldi joined her. Amoya slapped the page and shook her fist at Serya, but Serya would not be convinced. Chanjaldi laughed, writhing with enjoyment as Serya put her fingers in her ears and closed her eyes, so that she could neither hear Amoya nor see the illustration. Amoya tried to pull her hands away and then with a flash of inspiration Sister Johnstone snatched the bag from her. Serya knuckled down after that and seemed to become almost interested in what Amoya was telling her. She tucked the book into her sari at the waist and picked up the bag.

A stirring went through the house and a girl came into the room, beckoning Serya. "It's Sowa's wife," Amoya told me. "She has her first baby. Twice she has false labour and Sister Johnstone says she must go to the hospital in Durban if the baby not born by tomorrow. Sowa is saying all right she can go." Sister Johnstone and I went over to the hut to look at the girl, a delicate child of about thirteen. After a great argument Serya allowed Amoya in too.

Nicky honked the horn of the car. "The train will be an hour late, Helen, I'm going to have a drink, I'll pick you up just now," he called.

He had not returned by the time we left Sowa's wife and went back to the sitting-room. I left a message with Amoya for him, for it was growing late and I wanted to be home by five to give John his cigarette. Just as I was leaving a stone crashed through the window and hit Chanjaldi's hand. A spot of blood sullied the gorgeous carpet. Chanjaldi was out of the house in a flash. She caught the umfaan and slapped his face. He was one of Zetke's grandsons and Zetke came for her with a knobkerrie. Chanjaldi fled inside and locked herself in. Zetke sat down outside the gate, twirling the knobkerrie and swearing that he would not leave until he had hit her.

Far down the line I heard the train whistling and I hurried away, for I did not want John to search for the dagga and find where I had hidden it. It was a cool sparkling afternoon and the cane rode on the breeze with a song of promise. We were going to reap a bumper crop. The cutters were already in stripping the cane on Mrs. Lambert's property and as I approached the semicircle of men, some of them straightened up to greet me and then, seeing the others forging ahead, set to again with prodigious sweeps of their knives. The tops fell with a long hissing sound about them and they stood on a carpet as fine as Sowa's. There was a sweet smell to the fallen tops and I remembered that once when Richard and I were children I rode past him on a cane-truck and knocked his hat from his head. He pulled me from the truck and we went rolling over and over in the canetops.

The induna struck the iron railing in a tree. "He has hit," the men shouted and they straightened up, swinging their knives high. Mrs. Lambert was in her garden, staring passionately across the river.

"Come here, Helen."

"I'm in such a hurry, Mrs. Lambert...."

"Just look over there for a minute outside that rich coolie's house. Don't tell me he's got a motor-car now. I asked the induna boy, but he says it's Nicky's car, but what would Nicky be doing there, for goodness' sake?"

"It is Nicky's car. Sowa has just come in on that train; it was an hour late, and Nicky must have come back with him to bargain over that land of Farrells."

"Oh, so that's what it is. I couldn't believe my eyes when I saw a car there, I really thought the coolie had bought one. A lot of them in Durban flaunt round in motor-cars nowadays. Let's hope he comes to some agreement with Sowa, he's the best one for it. Nicky understands coolies, I will say that. I was thinking, if he can't beat him down, it would pay us all to buy the land between us rather than let them get a foothold. I saw it happen in the Transvaal. They're much stricter with them there, but the coolies would move in on the Europeans and simply by being there bring the property down."

"Oh, I think he'll be able to beat Sowa down. If he had gone there in the first place everything would have been settled now. You know how hot-tempered my father is."

"And when all is said and done Nicky did save this girl and she's the sister of the rich coolie. The one there was all this talk about. Of course he'd be grateful...."

"Nicky wouldn't throw it up at him, of course."

"Oh, of course not."

She walked a little way down the break with me and I had to run the rest of the way, for it was growing dark.

Aunt Lucy met me on the veranda. "I gave John his cigarette," she said conspiratorially. "I found the stuff in your top drawer. Just a pinch of…you know what…and the tobacco, that's right, isn't it?"

"Yes."

"It seems to buck him up. He's in a wonderful humour. We're going to play Nap for money tonight."

While we were playing cards I listened for Nicky's car in the break, for I had expected him to come to supper with us, but I did not hear it and I thought he had driven straight to Drew's Pride.

It was Mrs. Lambert who told Aunt Lucy and me that he had not been home all night.

"I want you to come up to Drew's Pride with me, Helen, and have this out with Nicky. His car didn't leave that coolie's house until this morning at five o'clock and then he came out with an Indian woman."

"I told you, he went to see Sowa about Farrells' land," I said, but I began to tremble and Mrs. Lambert noticed it.

"He wasn't with Sowa when he came out of that house. My eyes are not as good as they were, but I could make out the sari. Don't you forget, Helen, he's married to my granddaughter."

"You're not trying to make insinuations against my nephew, I hope," said Aunt Lucy, putting on her grand air.

Mrs. Lambert was unawed. "There was a lot of talk about Nicky and that coolie girl and she's back here with Sister Johnstone, they're giving a lecture on Indian Welfare in the hall. Enid Pimm always said that it might have been a good thing that that baby was drowned during the floods or goodness knows what would have come out. I remember we weren't allowed to see the baby…."

"It's a wonder your tongue doesn't drop off, some of the things you say," retorted Aunt Lucy.

"Well, I'm not one for gossip and what's more I never make mischief, as Helen has good reason to know. But I do know men, Lucy. I'd like a shilling for every man I've seen go off the rails. That's why I want an explanation from Nicky. I wouldn't tolerate it if I thought he had anything to hide, but believe me I wouldn't want to upset John with a lot of idle speculation."

"The only thing to do is to ask him," I said, as calmly as I could. "You'll find he was bargaining with Sowa, and if the girl did walk to the car with him it might have been only out of courtesy."

"It might be. I'll admit they're polite. We'll go up there and see him, shall we? And no hard feelings. In any case, I want to do a bit of tidying up before they get there and bake a few things for afternoon tea. Nancy enjoys a home-made tea when she has been staying at hotels. I won't make a scene, I'll be tactful."

"I'll come with you," said Aunt Lucy, joyfully. "Though goodness knows I'll be black and blue after a ride in that old boneshaker of yours."

Nicky was still in bed when we reached Drew's Pride and the three of us sat in silence waiting for him to come downstairs. He knew by my face, perhaps, that something was wrong, for he became wary even before Mrs. Lambert spoke.

"I've come up to tidy up the place, Nicky, I hope you don't mind."

"Sorry I wasn't down…."

"I didn't expect you to be, Nicky, not when you've been up all night." Mrs. Lambert gave a false laugh.

"I saw you coming out of that rich coolie's house…." Mrs. Lambert prompted.

"Oh yes. I went to see Sowa about that land of Farrell's."

"You couldn't have been talking about that all night."

"We were. I was trying to beat him down to three thousand." His voice was gaining more confidence now.

"I can quite believe that it would take all night," said Aunt Lucy. "You know how they go on about threepence, never mind six thousand pounds."

"And what was the outcome of it, Nicky?" Mrs. Lambert asked, watching him intently. "Did you beat him down?"

"Yes. I'm to meet him at eleven o'clock and we're going to Thompson's office to finalise things. I'll have to get a cheque from John, of course."

Aunt Lucy giggled. "See? She thought you had been carrying on with a coolie woman, Nicky."

"I thought no such thing. I wanted things cleared up and I didn't want any trouble if I could avoid it, but you must understand a grandmother's feelings, Nicky."

"I do," said Nicky vaguely. "But that's what happened."

"It's nearly eleven now," I said.

I would have gone with him, but Mrs. Lambert said smoothly, "Please stay and give me a hand here, Helen. We might as well all have lunch together. I don't suppose Nicky will be more than an hour or so arranging the business this time. Will you, Nicky?"

"I'll have to find John first," said Nicky.

"Oh, he's down on that field on my boundary, I saw him this morning," Mrs. Lambert told him. "Bring him up here for lunch, Nicky. One o'clock sharp." It sounded like an ultimatum.

"We'll all help," cried Aunt Lucy. "I love going into other people's kitchens, don't you, Mrs. Lambert? They always seem so interesting."

Nicky returned with John before one o'clock. They were both in a jovial mood and I suspected that they had been drinking.

"Look at that," said John, slapping down a paper on the table. "Receipt for three thousand pounds from Mr. Sowa Naidoo. Nicky got the better of him, even if it did take him all night." He stared at Mrs. Lambert.

Mrs. Lambert was impressed and a little chastened. She served Nicky with the choicest piece of the chicken; and the meal went off so well that Aunt Lucy, primed with stout, was calling her dear before it ended.

The train was punctual that day and as soon as Nicky heard it whistling down the line, he went to meet it. John was still talking about the sale of the property when Nancy and Joan and Richard came into the sitting-room, already beginning to tear open the parcels to show us what they had bought.

"I'll bet Sowa made a nice little packet out of it all the same," said Richard, sinking into his favourite chair and lighting up his pipe. "I've never seen such a live wire in my life."

"He's got a new shop in West Street, a huge place like a bazaar," said Nancy. She began to try over a new jazz piece that she had bought in Durban. "We saw him last night in the window fixing up a display. They're opening with a sale tomorrow. We saw such a wonderful musical comedy and as we were walking to the hotel, lo and behold we see Sowa working away there at half-past eleven at night. No wonder he's rich."

"I thought he was going to rush out and drag us in to buy some silk," said Richard. "He tapped on the window and went through quite a pantomime, bowing and smiling to us...."

There was a silence in the room now. Mrs. Lambert put down the plate of scones that she had been handing round.

"It couldn't have been Sowa," said Nicky. "I was with him all night haggling over this property. It must have been one of his brothers."

"I could have sworn it was Sowa...."

"One of his brothers," said Aunt Lucy, picking up the plate of scones and holding it firmly under Mrs. Lambert's nose.

"They all look alike to me." Nancy had got the hang of the piece and she played it loudly.

Mrs. Lambert pushed away her cup. "I have to go to Weston-gate. I almost forgot, I promised Enid Pimm.... There's something on at the Church Hall."

"It's only a lecture by Sister Johnstone on Indian Welfare," I said quickly.

That evoked a bleak smile from her. "Well I must go all the same."

"I promised to go, too."

"Are you really interested, Helen?"

"Professional jealousy," said Aunt Lucy, grimly bright. "You go along, Helen."

Mrs. Lambert said not a word throughout the drive except, "Jim, mind the bumps," when the driver sent the car rollicking down the road. He was so much surprised when she told him to pull up at Sowa's house that he stopped in a clatter that shook us from head to foot.

Sowa came to meet us. "A happy surprise," he cried. "You are liking to see the house, you two ladies?"

Mrs. Lambert followed him into the passage gingerly. "You've spent a lot of money."

"Yes, hundreds of pounds in furniture," he agreed enthusiastically. "Bimeby when Zetke going at the end of the month this a good place. I making gardens." He swept his hand towards the windows. The sitting-room was full of Indian women, clustering about Sister Johnstone. She greeted us cheerfully. Mrs. Lambert sat down on one of the purple-plush chairs as though she were sitting on a nest of ants. Sowa bent down and picking up a fragment of glass dropped it through the window.

"These natives, always breaking windows," he sighed. "They doing this last night, and that Zetke he wants to catch Chanjaldi, he sitting there all the time. Chanjaldi frightened last night. Amoya she going to help Serya and Chanjaldi...."

I knew that he was about to say that Chanjaldi was alone in the house all night and she knew it too, for she began to talk at the top of her voice in Hindustani. Sowa looked alertly towards Mrs. Lambert.

"I would like a word with you in private... some business ..." she said.

"You coming in here, please, I got little office, got plenty samples of silk."

She preceded him down the passage, her nose a danger signal in her white face. Sister Johnstone had been yelling something at me above the babble and now she moved across the room to me.

"Isn't it a good thing that Sowa's wife is having such a difficult first confinement? I've been able to get Serya on my side. I don't mean I'm not sorry for the poor girl, of course. I've persuaded him to get her taken to Durban to the hospital. This is only false labour, but only Amoya knows that. If we move her tonight.... What was I going to say to you? I can't think in all this noise."

"The clothes," said Amoya. "You were going to ask for clothes."

"Oh yes, baby clothes, we do need things so badly. Sometimes we have to wrap the babies in newspaper. Anything would do, the women could make them over..."

"Yes, I'll bring a big bundle down and Mrs. Drew will have some things." I answered her sanely and it seemed a sort of miracle that I could, for at this moment Sowa would be telling Mrs. Lambert that Nicky had been alone all night with Chanjaldi.

Sister Johnstone began to tell me how she became interested in Indian welfare as though she were testifying at a revivalist meeting. Sowa came back into the room with Mrs. Lambert. She nodded to Sister Johnstone and cut short the flow of words.

"I have to go now, Helen. Are you coming with me?"

"Yes."

In the flurry of farewells and promises of support I still saw Sowa's face. It was cold, but beneath the coldness anger was beating like a pulse.

"It was his brother all right," said Mrs. Lambert as we bounced along the road on our way back to Drew's Pride. "I can't tell you how relieved I am, Helen. I asked him straight out, one of the worst things I've ever had to do in all my life. But he said no, it was his brother. I won't say too much at the moment," and she stabbed her forefinger at the driver.

Nicky came to see me that night. He told me that he had forced the sale of the Farrells' property by reminding Sowa that he had risked his life to save Amoya and that he had tried to save Perian and Leela too. There was no need to worry about Chanjaldi, she was going to India with Mr. Bannerjee at the end of the week. I sat alone for a long time after he left me, looking towards Drew's Pride with something like hatred, for I had the foolish notion that it was the big house that had stolen his honour.

Chapter eighteen

Aunt Lucy stared at her game of Patience angrily and ruffled up the cards. "I don't know why I play, I never come out." She prodded the umfaan with the tip of her elegant shoe, for he was on the verge of falling asleep. "Watch out for the inyogas."

He recognised the word inyoga and conscientiously looked under the garden seat before subsiding into a doze. Aunt Lucy's eyelids fluttered. The place was so quiet that I could hear the rustling of the wind in the border of everlastings beneath the veranda.

The gate clicked and Sowa came down the path. He was wearing a blue suit this afternoon and new patent-leather shoes. Aunt Lucy awoke slowly and, seeing him there, moaned a little and turned her face away.

I said, "You're taking a chance coming here, Sowa. If my father were to see you, he'd break your neck."

He sat down, carefully removing a dried leaf from the seat. "I saw your father driving to get the post, Miss Angus. What I am saying is not taking long. That property of the Farrells was worth six thousand pounds to your father. He would pay it if I waited long enough. Do you know why I am coming down to three thousand pounds?"

Aunt Lucy asked alertly without turning her head, "Why?"

"Please send the umfaan away."

"He doesn't speak English."

"Please send him away."

He waited until the umfaan had gone down the steps. "Nicky is coming into my house yesterday morning and he putting the cheque for three thousand pounds on my desk. I am just off the train and I am still holding my hat in my hand. 'You must coming with me to Thompson now and put the sale through for Farrell's land.' 'My price is six thousand pounds, Nicky,' I tell him. 'For me it is three thousand pounds, Sowa, because I am risking my life for your father and mother and your sister Amoya.' 'Nicky,' I am saying, 'You tell me this and I give in straight away. That is Sowa Naidoo. Always he is paying his debts. That is good business. Take the property.' No argument, I give in when Nicky asks me."

"Nicky told me this," I said.

"I want another three thousand pounds, Miss Angus." "Three thousand pounds." At last Aunt Lucy sat up and faced him.

"That is due to me. Nicky worked a trick on me. Chanjaldi is telling me today that he is there all night with her. They are…these two are…" His face was lit from within by a white-hot rage that beat into his voice, "Amoya must go to the hut to help Serya with my wife and they are alone these two, Nicky and Chanjaldi…."

"He would not be the first with Chanjaldi," I flashed at him. "If this is Amoya, he gets a knife in his back. But for Chanjaldi I wanting the money he tricks from me. 'I am your friend, Sowa, I am saving Amoya and she brings credit to you now, I am risking my life for your mother and father. I am your friend, Sowa.' Mrs. Lambert she knows he was there, but I am saying at once I am not in Durban because Chanjaldi tells me. 'But Mrs. Drew and Mr. Drew and Nicky's wife they seeing you in the window of your shop,' she is saying to me, 'but Nicky says it is your brother, and he was here all night talking business with you.' Then I am knowing what Nicky has worked out. 'Madam, it is my brother you are seeing, I am here with

Nicky all night.' You pay me three thousand pounds, Miss Angus, or I go to Nicky's wife with Chanjaldi and she is knowing we tell truth because she sees me in the shop window."

"I'll write out a cheque for you now," said Aunt Lucy too promptly.

"Cheque is no use to me," said Sowa. "You giving me gold shares now, Miss Angus."

"I am not going to do it," screamed Aunt Lucy. The umfaan came to the steps to see what the noise was about. He picked up the wig that Aunt Lucy had thrown at Sowa and looked at it in wonderment. Sowa got to his feet nervously.

"I going now. I fetch Chanjaldi and we go straight to Nicky's wife."

I followed him to the gate. "Sowa, give me time. I can persuade Miss Angus. Just give me time, she'll do anything for me."

"I give you time and you go to the police, Miss Angus."

"No. I'll get the shares for you, even if I have to take them. But you must give me time."

"In one hour I go to Durban with my wife."

"Tomorrow then…."

"Tomorrow you make plan, Miss Angus, perhaps you are even telling your father and Nicky and they are hitting me. No."

"I'll try and bring them to you before you go to Durban."

"Don't coming to my house, Miss Angus, too many peoples there, perhaps Sister Johnstone you show her what you bring and then she is witness. You not coming in my house."

"Where then?"

"Bring them to Awetuli." He looked at me closely. "No. Maybe you are bringing your father and Nicky, maybe they are hitting me."

"Send Chanjaldi then," I said scornfully. "They would not hit a woman. But I will not tell them, Sowa."

He smiled briefly. "Yes, I send Chanjaldi."

"Then six o'clock, Sowa? That gives me two hours to persuade Miss Angus."

"By six I am going to Durban."

"Sowa."

"I doing it then for you, Miss Angus. Six o'clock Chanjaldi she comes for the shares." He became nervous again and hurried away down the break and across the bridge.

I went back to Aunt Lucy. "He's got us again. But he says he'll wait until six tonight. Oh, Aunt Lucy, give me the shares to take to Chanjaldi, she'll be on the bridge at six o'clock."

"They're not getting them. Was Nicky mad? He deserves horse-whipping. A coolie woman...."

I knelt beside her. "Give me the shares, Aunt Lucy. You've always said I could have them."

"Not until I die and they're for you, not for that stinking little coolie. If we did give in, they'd keep blackmailing us."

"They didn't when John burnt his hands. Besides, they've got to go to Joan at once, or she'll never believe them. Sowa knows this."

"I don't care what happens, I'm not parting with my shares to that coolie."

She drank some wine and I left her drowsing on the veranda while I walked to the huts to see Amoya, for I thought she might intervene, but she was at the meeting in the hall. Mr. Bannerjee had not yet returned from Durban. Chanjaldi was sitting with a group of women on the veranda and when she saw me she came to the gate. The police patrol rode by, turned and rode back again in front of Sowa's house.

"They doing that for me," said Chanjaldi, "but Zetke he run away now. Bimeby I must getting parcel from you, Sowa he saying, plenty money. Miss Angus, you seeing Nicky you telling him Chanjaldi..."

"I wish Zetke would cut your throat."

She began to mutter incantations against the evil eye and I felt some satisfaction in having frightened her. When I reached home, Aunt Lucy had the shares tied up in a bundle. Her eyes were puffy with tears and she broke down again when she gave them to me.

"There, take them, Helen. Oh, this is an evil, evil family. There's not one of us...not one of us..." She cast herself on to her bed and began to scream.

I gave her some wine and before she could change her mind I set off for Awetuli. John's car was on the road, but she had not seen it yet. There was still some time to wait before Chanjaldi came. I decided to go on to Sowa's house before Aunt Lucy told John of what had happened.

As I walked through the dense bush towards the road, I saw Zetke. "Why do you hide here like a thief, Zetke?"

"She thinks the police have frightened me away and soon she will come out of the house. I will wait here two days and then she will not be frightened any more and that is when Zetke will catch her."

"I can help you to get your hands on her."

"How?"

"She will be out of that house just as the sun goes down, on her way to Awetuli. Wait for her here, she will come alone. Swear to me that you will not let her pass."

"I swear by my sister."

Awetuli was already in shadow and there was no sound but the ceaseless rush of the waterfall. The trees growing at right angles from the bank cast shadows of strange shape on the bridge and at this time of the evening it was easy to believe in the ghosts that haunted Awetuli. I had climbed to the top of the steps when I saw John coming towards me. I plunged into the cane, for I was afraid of this old man who walked as though he were young. He carried a cane-knife and slashed at the cane as he passed it. He went on to the bridge, and drove the cane-knife deep into the trunk of a tree growing from the bank. Before I ran from him I saw him throw up his arms as the full glory of the dagga coursed through his body. I was glad then to think of Zetke beneath the trees on the other side of the ravine.

Aunt Lucy would not take the shares from me. "Oh, Helen, what have I done?" she wept. "I shouldn't have told him, but I was beside myself. He smoked two of those cigarettes and he had been drinking in Westongate. Helen, I didn't think the dagga would have that effect on him, I thought it would just buck him up. He said he was going to kill her…"

The clock in the house chimed six and the notes filled the

dusk with laughter. When she did not come, would he go across the bridge?

"Telephone Nicky," Aunt Lucy gasped. "He might be able to do something with John. Helen, I thought he would kill me too when I tried to stop him from going at the last moment."

I waited until the clock struck the quarter before I went to the telephone. I had just picked up the receiver when Aunt Lucy came to my side.

"He's coming back now, Helen," she whispered.

We saw him in the half-light, a shambling figure at the bend in the cane-break. Aunt Lucy pulled me into her bedroom with her and pushed the chest-of-drawers against the door. He went into his office and we heard the turning of the key. All night long we listened to the tramp of his feet. The only time he stopped was when Aunt Lucy and I begged him to let us in. Then the stillness behind that closed door became so frightening that we were glad to hear again the tramp, tramp of his feet.

Aunt Lucy drank some more of her wine and fell asleep. It was almost dawn then and I tried the door again.

"John, let me in."

"Where is Lucy?"

"She's asleep."

The door opened slowly. I stepped back when I saw him.

He said, "Helen, my face. Look at my face."

Beneath his skin the blood had congealed into a purplish mass that hung like over-ripe fruit on his cheeks and forehead and chin. He had taken off his shirt and he wore only his trousers, his feet were bare; but I found when I touched him that he had no fever, he was cold.

He gasped as though a hand choked him. "I've got to get outside. I'll be all right if I can get some air into my lungs."

I let him go. I had seen death so often that I knew already that he was finished, but I telephoned the doctor, speaking softly so that Aunt Lucy should not awaken.

He sat under the flamboyant tree rocking himself backwards

and forwards as a consuming restlessness seethed through him. I tried to still him with my hands.

"You must keep quiet, John. Lie down, keep still. Oh, try to keep still…."

"I'm thirsty. I'm dying of thirst."

I ran to the demijohn on the veranda and poured a glassful of water for him, but he threw the glass to the ground. He put the demijohn to his lips and drank as though he would never be satisfied. He banged the demijohn down and stood still to get his breath back.

"Look at my foot, Helen. Take off your shoes and feel how cold it is. I want you to press your foot hard on mine, I don't think I've got any feeling left in it." I bent down and touched his foot. My hand was warm against its iciness. "Part of me is dead already, Helen." He walked about the grass tenderly. "But I can still walk, I can still walk as well as I ever could."

"You mustn't walk about, John, you must lie still."

He sat down, rocking himself violently again, as though he were driven by the blood that showed in his temples by a thunderous beating. Then he was up again, striding along the path. Reaching into the flamboyant, he broke off a stout branch that he cracked like a twig in his hand, as though testing his strength. He broke it up into small pieces. I could look at him no longer.

The stillness of the morning had deepened into breathless noon. Aunt Lucy still slept. One or two curious servants had come to the edge of the garden, but when they saw John they ran away.

I looked down at the ground and I could not see even the movement of an ant. Beside the path the flowers stood unstirring and beyond the cane was still and smooth in the sun. There were no birds to be seen, but I could hear the throb of their calls beating steadily against the heat. Not even a cloud moved across the sky. It was not his violence that was the offence, it was the stillness of the unfeeling landscape that was the offence to the spirit. I longed for a bitter storm and a thunderous sky. split by lightnings, for a wind that would shake the cane from its lethargy. It should have been so.

He flung himself into the hammock and lay there with his head on his arms, kneading the canvas with his toes. I knelt beside him and he put out his arms to embrace me, but with such force that he knocked me off balance. There was still strength in his hands as he pulled me to my feet.

I said, "Listen, there's the doctor's car now. Can you hear it? You'll be all right now, John."

He sprang out of the hammock. This was the last effort of his body. He stood as though he awaited an enemy, his chest racked by his breathing, his blood hammering against his veins and lighting up his eyes with red fire. It did not seem possible then that he could ever die.

Doctor Stewart sat on the veranda with us after he had been an hour with John. The girl brought tea and he drank some before he spoke.

"You'll be able to manage the nursing, I think, Helen."

"Yes. Mrs. Lambert will come in the daytime and I'll take night duty."

"There's a little hope, isn't there?" said Aunt Lucy.

"It's no use beating about the bush. John is a very sick man. His heart, his kidneys ..."

Aunt Lucy was crying again and I left Nicky to soothe her when I walked with the doctor to the gate.

"How long, doctor?"

"Perhaps a few days. You can't tell. If he comes out of it, paralysis...."

"Yes, I know."

I watched his car until it passed into the cane, but I picked it up on the bridge and followed it along the road until it turned the bend to Westongate. Zetke came quietly to my side.

"The Buffalo is sick?"

"He will die soon."

"I will have the bones thrown for you today." He paused for a decent interval. "She did not come."

"Chanjaldi? Perhaps it was as well."

"Only the Little One passed me, but I hid myself and she did not see me."

"The Little One?"

"They call her Amoya."

Chapter nineteen

On the third night they lit the funeral pyre on the river-bank and burned Amoya's broken body. I had taken some flowers in the afternoon and left them outside Sowa's house hoping that some-body would make a garland of them. Mr. Bannerjee saw me standing by the river where the place had been prepared for her.

He said, "You are praying for her, Miss Angus?"

"For myself too."

"Do not cry so bitterly. It is not here that we find perfection. As for me I will think that she has ascended into heaven in a rain of flowers. You think that perhaps Chanjaldi…. Next week she goes to India with me and to you it will be the same as if she died. Do not grudge Chanjaldi her life; the adulteress, the thief, the liar. Some day you will say, 'One there was, Amoya, whom sin did not touch, who loved and was kind….' "

"So many words, Mr. Bannerjee. She had work to do."

"What? To make the coolie clean?"

The cane was restless that night. It rippled in the moonlight, supple as a python. I fancied that the wind brought to me the chanting of the Indians, but the sound I heard was the beating of the drums at

Zetke's kraal. Far down the cane-break I heard too a stirring of Zulu voices, deep and strong and passionate. The men from our barracks were abroad and I thought they must be going across the river to drink beer at Zetke's kraal, for he had harvested his mabela. There was no sound inside the house but John's stertorous breathing.

"They're burning Amoya's body," I said.

"What was the verdict at the inquest?"

"I told you. Accidental death. They thought she was frightened of the shadows and lost her footing…."

"That's what did happen. I wouldn't have hurt her, I thought it was the other one. She sprang backwards when she saw me,"

Perhaps she had thought him a demon spawned from the shadows as he came towards her with the upraised knife. He was silent for a long time and when he spoke again there was the shadow of mockery in his voice.

"They wait until the head goes off with a bang and they go away as happy as kings, laughing and chattering…."

The beating of the drums had ceased. There was a glow now on the hill and I watched it for some minutes before I realised that a fire had broken out across the river. It was Sowa's house that was burning. Soon there were more fires along the foot of the hill, in the newly built houses of the Indians, and then the huts went up in flames. I drew the curtains across the window.

"Pull those curtains, Helen," John said irritably, "I want to see the cane. It's a good crop, isn't it? A bumper crop…. What's that glow in the sky, the funeral pyre?"

"No, it looks like the Indians' places."

The ghost of a chuckle came from him. "Old Zetke always said he would burn them out. Open the windows wide, I want to see this."

I left him watching the fires while I went into Aunt Lucy's room to see how she was. She had fallen asleep, a glass of wine still in her hand. It slipped from her fingers as I came into the room and the wine drenched the air with its sickening smell; but the glass was unbroken. I set it on the dressing-table and the tiny sound awoke Aunt Lucy.

"I fell asleep. How is John?"

"He's much the same. You spilled your wine." I opened the windows to let out the fumes.

"Don't do that. Snakes travel at night, they say. One might crawl in."

"You must get some air in the room. I'll stand here for a while and see that nothing gets in."

"Is there a fire? What's that light?"

"There are some fires across the river, the Indians' places. I think the Zulus have risen."

She screamed faintly, but I had to leave her, for I heard John moving in his room. He had struggled out of bed. I pushed him back again.

"Do you want to die?"

He pointed speechlessly through the window. At first I could see only the inferno across the river and then I made out the thin orange line running through the cane on the border of the ravine.

"There's nothing to worry about, John, there's Drew's bell ringing, they've seen it already. Promise to lie still and I'll go outside and organise the labour."

He nodded and turned his face to the wall. There was no answer to the fire-bell and apparently no answer at Drew's Pride or on any of the other farms, for the fire was spreading unchecked through the cane around Awetuli.

I telephoned Drew's Pride. It was Joan who answered me. "I was just going to ring you up. There's hell broken loose. Nicky and Dad have gone to try and get hold of some labour to fight the fire. The policeman has just left here. He says there is no danger from the Zulus if we just sit tight, they're after the Indians. How's John?"

"Just about the same."

"Nicky brought Grannie Lambert over. She's had another of her heart attacks, but she seems better now."

I put the receiver back. I went to John and told him that Nicky and Richard would soon have the labour organised. Then I telephoned Chris. It was almost an hour before I heard his voice, as clearly as I heard it that first time at Drew's Pride.

"Helen, are you all right?"

"Chris, will you come out? You'll be able to manage them, the very sight of you will bring a lot of them to their senses."

There was a pause. "I'll get there as soon as I can manage it."

John had long since realised the magnitude of the disaster and he lay silent, but Aunt Lucy came tottering out of her room. Smoke was seeping into the house although the windows were closed. The Zulu women brought their children out of the barracks and laid them beneath the water-cart, turning the stopcock slightly so that their faces were eased of the scorching heat from the approaching fire. The wind, grown vindictively strong, sent it on us in a towering sheet of flame. A burning stalk twisted through the air and fell on the thatched roof of a hut, but one of the women climbed up and beat it out. She was a strong woman and she formed a line to fight the fire as it leapt the break and so the house was saved.

The dogs had caught a cane-rat on the steps and they missed the streak of a mamba's flight across the veranda; but Aunt Lucy had seen. I put my hand over her mouth to stop her screaming and took her to her bedroom. I shut her up there with an umfaan and one of the dogs for company.

There came a sound of running footsteps. Sowa leaped the gate and flung himself flat on the veranda. There were two more Indians behind him, but these were caught by the pursuing Zulus. I saw Zetke with his face a-shine with sweat, a half-smile on his lips, pick up one of the men by his neck and crack his skull with a knobkerrie. He flung him into the burning cane; the other man fell beneath an assegai. The Zulus dragged his body with them as they ran on in search of more prey.

I gave Sowa some brandy to drink. He was so crazed with fright that he could not speak and I had to support him into the house. John made me bring him into the room to tell him what had happened that night.

"So they got your fine house, Sowa." His words slurred voluptuously through lips like purple grapes.

"Yes, master."

"Tell me how all this came about."

"When we seek Amoya I ask Zetke if he is hurting Amoya." He broke into Zulu. "No, but if I find her body, little coolie, I will do the same to her as I did to your mother when I found her. I tore her loose from the rocks and gave her back to the sea, and I will do the same to your sister if I find her. I will cut the face of the other one and no man will look at her again." He began to sob.

"Get on with it. Be a man, for God's sake."

"Then I am going to the police and laying a charge for trespass against Zetke and asking twenty pounds for the time he stays on my property. The Sergeant says this is fair and he is giving Zetke three days to get off my land. And that day we are finding Amoya and she has fallen and broken her neck and her legs, everything. Chanjaldi she was frightened to go out of the house because maybe Zetke will be hitting her and she telling Amoya…." He turned his bloodshot, beaten eyes on me. "She is telling Amoya she must go for a parcel you bring, Miss Angus, and she saying to Amoya that it will be babies' clothes like you promising her."

"Go on," John said into the silence.

"When we are lighting the fire for Amoya, the drums beginning to beat and soon there are plenty of Zulus. Chanjaldi she has gone already on the train and they are looking for her everywhere. Some have got cane-knives that they keep back from work and some have got assegais and knobkerries and I am frightened, but we saying mantras for Amoya then. They burning first my house and they grab some of the people and kill them. Two women they are throwing into the houses and their children too. Mr. Bannerjee telling us to run away into Awetuli, he says the Zulus will not go there. But Zetke is coming over the big bridge and making a fire in the grass and the cane is on fire, but still some of the peoples are in Awetuli by the water. But the bridge is burning down and a piece of wood is falling and killing some. Me and two others we running. Zetke is seeing us then, but we going into the cane. We seeing your lights and running on to the break, but he catching the other two."

John seemed to have fallen asleep. He moved restlessly as Aunt Lucy began to scream again.

"If he moves, call me at once, Sowa."

He shook his head in acquiescence and sat down by the window, staring at the dying fires. As I opened the door of Aunt Lucy's room, the umfaan rushed out followed by the dogs. They ran through the house into the moonlight. The clock struck four and as though in answer a rooster crowed in the yard. Aunt Lucy was quiet now, but she was not asleep. I had to bend close to hear what she was saying.

"The fire has driven them out, Helen. Listen, they're coming...."

"It's the wind in the flamboyant tree and there's still some cane untouched at the back of the house."

"They're coming. They'll crawl all over us. Puff-adders and..."

"It's the wind, I tell you. You don't want to let such a foolish idea get into your head. Come with me into John's room."

She put her foot to the floor and then withdrew it. She curled herself up at the top of the bed and glared about the room, afraid of the shadows as Amoya had been. Sweat poured from her, but she remained quiet and I found this new quietness a terrifying thing in her. I got her to swallow a sedative and while I waited for her to fall asleep, I found myself listening to the rustling of the flamboyant tree. I called one of the dogs to me for company.

I heard John and Sowa speaking and I sprang up to go, but Aunt Lucy's hands fastened like steel traps on me. We fought silently for some time before I released myself from her. I heard the rattling of John's voice, "Nicky, Nicky."

Sowa was standing in front of the window and he turned to face me as I entered. A terrible sound came from the bed. I bent over John, staring into his glazing eyeballs. Only his hand moved fecklessly up and down and presently was still. He lay on his back, staring up at the ceiling as though he viewed the inane of wide space. I pulled the sheet over his face.

"Didn't he ask for me, Sowa?"

"Twice he is asking for you, Miss Angus."

"Then why didn't you come and fetch me?"

"He is saying, 'You stinking coolie, get my daughter, tell her I wanting to see Nicky, answer me you bloody fool, I didn't kill your sister, I was waiting for the other one. Your sister ran away from me,

she falling like they say at the inquest. Now getting my daughter.'
'No, Master, she will not come, she is not liking to tell you what is
happening to Nicky. You never seeing your son, master, he is burnt
in the fire and Drew's Pride too and all the peoples living there.'"
His voice swelled with passion. "'Your son and his wife and the big
house are burnt. Looking through the window, master.' He is trying
to sit up and his face is turning blue all over. 'But Sowa's wife and
child they safe in Durban, master, my daughter she is born on the
same night you killing Amoya. . .' But he not hearing any more. He
is trying all the time to shout for Nicky, but can't doing it."

"Not only my father but you and Chanjaldi…." My hatred
flowed from me with a bitter stream of words. He had no answer for
me and went out of the room.

The day was breaking. The wind and the surf spoke her name
and beyond the sea and the hills she came towards me and passed
through me and was gone. There was no triumph in Sowa as he
moved across the fields, a part of that melancholy landscape. I looked
after him without hatred. He passed his ruined house and made his
way to the station.

The telephone was ringing. Miss Pimm gave me all the news
in a staccato burst of excitement and I had no sooner put the receiver
down than Nancy came on the line. She handed the phone to Mrs.
Lambert after a while and her voice came to me a little more breathy
but still strong.

I looked in on Aunt Lucy but she was still asleep. And then
Nicky was at the door. He spent a little time beside John and hurried
away to help with the reaping of the crop. Mr. Bannerjee had begged
a lift to the station from him and he was in the back of the car. He
made a short speech and I saw that there were gaps in his teeth and
that the diamond was gone. The car raced along the empty road and
disappeared round the bend of the hill.

The wind blew through the charred trash and the blackened
stalks of the cane. Beneath lay the roots from which the ratoons would
spring when the rains came and in a vision I saw the hills green once
more. Even now, far to the south, a miracle of movement had begun.
The cutters were in and I saw the glint of their knives as they reaped,

racing against time and the rains. With the broadening of the day I saw the first trucks start on their journey to the mill.

There was somebody on the road. Serya, her sari twisted awry, had climbed laboriously from Awetuli, where she had sheltered during the night. She waddled along, clutching the little bag that Amoya had given her. At first she glanced anxiously over her shoulder, but when she saw Chris galloping down the road from Westongate she settled down into a confident walk.

Drew's Pride from its ruined fields rose flashing to the sun.

Afterword

The Old Fires of Daphne Rooke, by R. W. Johnson

Durban, the main city of KwaZulu-Natal, is frequently celebrated as a place "where three cultures meet", for although it was built mainly by whites, within the old city limits there was a large preponderance of Indians and within the broader limits now obtaining there is a large Zulu majority. As is the case with many such public celebrations, it is also somewhat hollow, for what this rich cultural mix has actually produced is rather slender. Not many locals even know of the poets Roy Campbell and Douglas Livingstone, or the writers Alan Paton and Marguerite Poland. Yet more than fifty years ago South Africa's most important newspaper, the Johannesburg Sunday Times, opined that southern Africa was blessed in having three such wonderful young women writers as Doris Lessing, Nadine Gordimer and Daphne Rooke (née Pizzey). Of the three, it believed, the best was clearly Rooke. Today few have heard of her, because she stopped writing long ago, while the others continued. Yet to read Ratoons (published in 1953 and reissued in 1990 by Chameleon Press, Cape Town) is to understand that judgement, perhaps even to agree with it.

Ratoons, the new green leaves which sprout from sugar cane after it has been cut or burnt, are a familiar sight to anyone who knows KwaZulu-Natal, for then, as now, "sugar cane covered the low hills for mile upon mile, a green wave spilling along the South Coast northwards into Zululand". *Ratoons* is set on a sugar farm, south of Durban. It is a small world—Helen Angus, the daughter of a sugar farmer, knows only a handful of similar families, the Indian workers and their families, and those Africans from the local kraal whom her father employs. Her father, John, is a typical hard-drinking alpha male, quick to violence and imbued with a confident racial superiority towards Africans and Indians ("kaffirs" and "coolies"), though always ready for a roll in the hay with young Zulu maidens (intombis) or Indian girls ("Marys"). As the book opens, Helen's sickly mother has again fallen pregnant while Helen soon finds she is in the same condition thanks to an illicit affair with a young Afrikaner, Chris Van der Westhuizen; at which point the Anglo-Boer War breaks out. Natal is, of course, wholly English-speaking and anti-Boer, so Chris flees to join the Boer forces. Helen's mother dies in childbirth and her baby soon after, while Helen's is a strapping boy. Her father, desperate for a son and to hide Helen's disgrace, switches the babies, and Helen finds herself bringing up her child Nicky as her baby brother, never able to explain that she is really his mother. In those years in South Africa, remote farms were full of such secrets, of illicit liaisons, sexual abuse, ingrown family trees and youthful-tearaway reputations that respectable elders could not own up to.

Helen's secret is guessed by the neighbouring midwife, and the local Indians are also too shrewd and intelligent for it entirely to evade them. The Zulus—a presence held at greater distance, made up of intombis, umfaans (young boys) and the induna (foreman) Zetke—know nothing. Zetke is a powerful, elemental figure. He is honourable, cruel, straightforward; despises Indians but thinks the world of John because John shares his code of honour, a contempt for Indians and an easy recourse to violence. Natal in this period contained numerous Johns, ready to commit almost any barbarism in the name of white civilization, and loud in his preference for the (stupid, honourable) Zulu to the (crafty, scheming, and thus more competitive) Indian. Zetke, naturally, smokes dagga (marijuana) and is always keen to smoke out witches. Much to his regret, the whites won't allow too much of that, but men like John certainly learn to enjoy a joint. The midwife holds her tongue and Helen's secret disappears into the vague world of colonial scandal, a world Rooke invokes wonderfully well.

There's the cousin with a charm for snakes who is bitten three times in the back by a mamba—at least that's what the husband says, and he has a dead mamba to prove it. But when he subsequently makes love to his mother-in-law she informs the police that he'd told her he killed his wife out of lust for her. He says the mother-in-law is too fond of the bottle and gets away with it, so the truth of the matter is unclear, always widely suspected yet never quite certain. (Even in today's South Africa one comes across similar stories, sometimes about people one knows quite well, but one continues to chat to them over the barbecue, holding their meat on one's fork and trying to take into account the possibility that they might be a murderer or a child-abuser.)

As the Boers are defeated, Chris reappears and saves the infant Nicky, but is betrayed by John and shipped off to a POW camp in Ceylon. Nicky grows into the sort of can-do, outgoing son John had always wanted, but Chris, released from prison, is reincarnated as a somewhat brutal Afrikaans policeman. Helen shrinks from him and castigates him for his reputation for cruelty, but he is still the only man she can love—so she turns down the obvious marriage to a rich young neighbour. Chris reappears at intervals throughout the book, but his relationship with Helen remains complicated and Nicky never learns that Chris is his father. Helen is spoiled for other things, and like her Aunt Lucy, whom she much resembles, she recovers from her secret disgrace to become, publicly at least, a virginal spinster. Lucy and Helen are close, and Helen flees the farm from time to time to stay with her aunt in her colonial mansion overlooking the bay on the fashionable Durban Berea.

Both there and on the farm they are highly aware of the rapid upward progress of the entrepreneurial Indians, eager to leave the sugar fields and endowed with the peculiar advantage of being "able to live off the smell of an oil rag". In the countryside this is visible as they become vendors of vegetables, fruit, lucky charms—and in their steady drift to Durban, particularly the great noisy bazaar of Grey Street, every crevice of its endless arcades, alleyways and offshoots alive with commerce, the same today as Rooke described it eighty years ago. With remarkable speed the itinerant rural vegetable seller has become the silk merchant, the shop owner, the fat cat—and Aunt Lucy to her fury finds that Indians have bought the house next door and are driving her crazy with their noise and cooking smells, hoping to force her to sell her own house at a knockdown price or else buy them out at an inflated level. Organized rings and crooked lawyers abound; every angle has been covered. This, too, is just how it was. It is not often realized that a key and shameful aspect of apartheid was created not by Afrikaners but by the infuriated English-speaking bourgeoisie of the Durban Berea—the enraged Aunt Lucy and her friends, if you like—who were the first whites to face the encroachment of "inferior" races into their prime residential area, and responded with legislated segregation. This was the first, local version of the Group Areas Act, which Verwoerd later adopted and applied nationwide.

In the world of the sugar-cane farmer the worst thing that can occur is the inferno of a cane fire. While the empty husks and leaves burn easily enough, the sugar inside the cane burns at a far greater temperature—when a cane fire advances the heat is unbearable at a distance of hundreds of yards, and an avalanche of rats, snakes and other creatures of the cane comes pouring out ahead of it. So when Nicky and two little friends, one of them an Indian, Sowa, start a fire, the furious John decides to punish them by burning their hands. Immediately Sowa's mother realizes that she could cause John trouble by making a complaint to the police, and demands to be bought off; the incident is later replicated when Sowa catches the adult Nicky sleeping with his, Sowa's, sister, and covers for him—then demands to be paid. As Sowa grows to adulthood he becomes a consummate wheeler-dealer and businessman, exciting jealous comment from many whites and angry threats from Zetke when he hears that the Indians even have plans to buy property which will overlook his kraal.

Nicky grows up to be the perfect son to John—strong, outgoing and adventurous. Though under age, he joins up to fight in the First World War, and is reported missing, believed killed. John goes on a permanent bender to Durban, living in brothels, crazed by dagga and drink. Helen, distraught, trains as a nurse, breaks down, somehow soldiers on—and then hears that Nicky is alive, that he was captured by the Germans but, with his usual resourcefulness, has escaped. Helen tracks down her father in the sleaziest byways of Durban, dries him out and gets him (almost) off the dagga. Nicky returns home and marries the rich neighbour's daughter, and the little community prospers until one year the terrible floods which periodically devastate Natal arrive. Nicky, of course, rescues all he can but his friend Peter is lost, as are many of the Indian workers and their families. For a while the struggle against a common enemy binds the whites more closely to the Indians, but once the waters have subsided the whites are soon back to cursing them for "breeding like rabbits" and openly wishing that more of them had been drowned.

Quarrels with the Indians over land and money increase and a bitter row between Helen's family and Sowa's is enmeshed in, then overtaken by, a Zulu jacquerie against the Indians, quite clearly a representation of the terrible racial riots of 1949 when many hundreds of Indians were massacred in and around Durban. Zetke and his brother torch the Indians' houses; inevitably this develops into a sweeping cane fire, during which John dies. All three communities are left utterly shaken amid the ruins—but the green ratoons, the inevitable sign of fresh growth and renewal, are soon to be seen again. This is a novel that is not just a family saga but essentially the story of Natal's three racial groups over fifty years, and it achieves this in under 250 pages, such is the economy with which Rooke writes.

Typically, South African novels written by liberals and dealing with relations between the races are intrinsically preachy: the narrative will be recounted by someone who sees and protests against the monstrous bigotry or, on occasion, the action will be seen mainly through the eyes of victims, achieving the same effect of a parallel interior dialogue of protest and witness. There is none of this in Rooke, not a single judgemental or protesting adjective in the book. She writes of the Indians with an extraordinarily sharp eye and yet

with great sympathy, particularly for Indian women. Helen, the protagonist, is a woman of her time and place who accepts the racial
prejudices, abuses and stereotypes as normal, and yet Rooke displays
such insight and humane economy that the reader is made aware of
the inappropriateness and injustice of those stereotypes even when
Rooke is writing of behaviour in Indians or Africans which appears
to confirm them. Of course, too, the collision of the cultures is often
extremely funny. A sly humour runs through the book, quite the
opposite of the ponderous moralizing the South African situation
has too often elicited. It is a remarkable achievement. In the South
Africa of 1953, it was completely against the current but there is nothing shrill or assertive about it—indeed its power derives largely from
its calm understatement.

Daphne Rooke was born in 1914, to an English father and
an Afrikaans mother. Her father was killed in the First World War
and she grew up in poverty in the grim little Reef town of Boksburg,
the youngest of six children. When Daphne was twelve, her mother
noticed for the first time that she hadn't grown at all since she was six,
so she moved the whole family down to the better climate of the Natal
south coast—where Daphne did manage to grow—and acquired and
ran a little sugar farm. Having no gun with which to protect herself,
she put around stories that the farm was haunted—this was enough
to keep malefactors at bay. Mrs Pizzey was an extremely tough, independent woman, not only working the farm and rearing her children
single-handed but writing (as Mare Knevitt) The Children of the Veld.
Daphne in turn grew up to be a liberated and independent woman,
ahead of her time, and worked as a journalist—a photograph shows
her, an attractive young blonde, smoking away as she hammers at
the keys of an ancient Remington. Her most famous book, *Mittee*,
about love across the colour line, was published in many countries,
but she and her husband (who had had an Australian childhood)
were so deeply shocked by the 1949 riots in Durban that they left
for Australia. Though they tried Natal again in the 1960s, they soon
returned to Australia where, gradually, Daphne ceased to write.

She was rediscovered in the late 1980s (by the English Department at the University of Natal) when her work enjoyed enormous success with students of all races and Rooke was feted and awarded an honorary doctorate. Sadly it is now probably too "colonial" and non-PC for those who would like a straightforwardly "progressive", liberationist message, preferably recounted from an African, not a white, point of view. But *Ratoons* is too good, too much a novel of Natal, of the languid heat of Durban, of the rickshaws plying their trade and, above all, of the endless interplay between the three races, to be anything but a classic. Its time will come again.

Daphne Rooke is ninety-two now and lives near her daughter in Cambridge. "Once my husband died", she told me, "I realized there was nothing for me in Australia, so I came here. But I can't bear the grey skies. Natal is still home. I'd love to go back." She had never joined a party but she was always revolted by racism. "My main friend was Alan Paton. I went to lots of meetings with him and we were always followed by the Special Branch." What about Doris Lessing and Nadine Gordimer? "Well, I knew them of course. But they were so outside the truth. Neither of them had the first clue about what apartheid really meant. Doris wasn't South African and Nadine was from such a privileged background. They just didn't understand. So I decided to write a novel, *The Greyling*, which would really tell the truth about apartheid. And I did. Then it got banned in South Africa even before it was published. That really shocked me, not just because it meant they were spying on me and had got a copy of the manuscript from somewhere but because it showed how impossible it all was."

As we talked on, she spoke of a Natal which now hardly exists, a time when every river and lagoon harboured crocodiles and hippos. "You had to be on the lookout for wild animals all the time. Even something like a running giraffe could be dangerous. We used to walk to school and back through the cane breaks and they were just festooned with snakes, hundreds of them, and of course they kept getting in the house and were a serious nuisance. Sometimes I invited school friends to stay a weekend but they never came again. No one could cope with the snakes." And indeed, snakes are omnipresent in the book. They are the reason that Aunt Lucy will come out to the farm but rarely—and when she does it is a source of huge amusement to the Angus children to see that as soon as she sits on the verandah a puff adder sneaks out from under her chair. Anyone who has had to deal with puff adders knows that it is fairly amazing to find this funny, a sign of a degree of familiarity with deadly snakes which few indeed want to have. And when the fire starts, a black mamba shoots out from the house steps, clearly its home. The point is that snakes in this situation are like rats—rodent controllers tell us that we spend most of our lives with a rat less than five metres away.

Natal is a new place now, the newness signalled by the taking on of an older name. All the crocodiles and hippos were shot long ago, and local whites spend more time on the internet than worrying about snakes. Social attitudes have changed too, though more slowly. But in *Ratoons* the ever-present snakes run parallel with the ever-present racism, and one realizes they are much the same. If you observe certain precautions and are not squeamish then with luck you are able to live with the racism in exactly the same way that you can with the snakes. But both of them can kill you and you're a fool ever to forget that. After the 1949 riots there was much bitter accusation as to who exactly was to blame. To this day the ANC tries to lay the blame on the whites, although everyone knows that Africans dislike Indians far more than they do whites and that the feeling is thoroughly reciprocal. So how could whites be to blame?

Yet if you trace how things happen in *Ratoons* you realize that in their furious irritation at Sowa's blackmail it is the Anguses who signal to Zetke that they would hardly be sorry if something unfortunate befell Sowa and his ilk. And it is Helen Angus herself—the character the reader inevitably identifies with because it is she who tells the story, who is clearly no racist, who has dear Indian friends—who gives the final fatal signal of compliance; so that it is as if we, the readers, were culpable but only in such an indirect way that we can always deny responsibility and, indeed, may never fully realize it ourselves. That nod of complaisance is so fleeting and slight that it is only when one remembers how utterly whites were the masters of the colonial situation that one realizes the fatal power of those nods, just as it took merely an inversion of the emperor's thumb to kill a gladiator. This is managed with great subtlety, but we understand that, like those deadly snakes, this homicidal motive has been lurking in the undergrowth all the time. It only requires an unlucky circumstance, a temporary absence of mind, for the serpent's tooth to find its mark.

Daphne Rooke did not stop writing immediately she arrived in Australia, and what she wrote still had South African themes. But, cut off from her creative roots, she soon fell silent, while the publications—and reputations—of Lessing and Gordimer continued to grow. And while the world of colonial Natal may have repelled her, Australia was a sterile place by comparison, a world which she chose to leave as soon as she was forced to confront it alone. On her return to Durban to receive her honorary degree she had fallen for Natal's charms all over again, especially since now, thrillingly, she was able to have lunch with Indians and Zulus and sit and chat with them as equals—"I'd have been arrested for that before", she marvelled. That's all normal enough now, I told her, quite unnecessarily, for she needed no instruction. "Natal is paradise," she said. "I'd love to go back there but I don't suppose I will now."

About the Author

Daphne Rooke

Daphne Rook was born in Boksburg, Transvaal, of an English father and Afrikaans mother. Her grandfather was Siegfried Mare, founder of Pietersburg, and her uncle was Leon Mare, Afrikaans short story writer. Her mother was a writer and "marvellous storyteller." Her father died during the First World War and Daphne Rooke grew up in Natal, where *Ratoons* is set.

During the 1930s she worked as a journalist in South Africa. She married an Australian, Irvin Rooke, and moved to Australia with him after writing her first novel, *A Grove of Fever Trees*. In Australia Daphne Rook wrote *Mittee* (1951), her international bestseller, also available from *The* Toby Press.

After her husband died, Rooke moved to England to be near her daughter.

The fonts used in this book are from the Garamond family

Printed in Great Britain
by Amazon